The Mercy Man

THE
Mercy
Man

Rider McDowell

ST. MARTIN'S PRESS
NEW YORK

Design by Claudia DePolo

Library of Congress Cataloging-in-Publication Data

McDowell, Rider.
    The mercy man.

    I. Title.
PS3563.C3594M4   1987   813'.54   87–16000
ISBN 0–312–01022–2

First Edition

10 9 8 7 6 5 4 3 2 1

Encore for Phillida
with as much love and
marginally
less squalor

1

February, Spanish Harlem, New York City

He was a big man in a black sweater and he stood back against the crumbling brick wall watching it snow. A street lamp fifty yards into the alley carved a dim wedge of light from the darkness. The snow fell silently, angled, through the light. He coughed up some phlegm, spat it out onto the frozen pavement, and wondered where all the niggers were. This was Spanish Harlem and the niggers milled around here like ants on a cake, didn't they? Then where were they?

He thought it over. His flat face creased. Niggers wasn't Spanish. Spanish was Spanish. Spics was Spanish. Okay, then, where were the spics? He was alone. He turned and looked to confirm it. Yep, all alone.

He brushed some snow off the front of his sweater. The wind blew his cuffs up so he felt the ice on his ankles. He'd forgotten to wear socks. A car passed by behind him, its tires rolling softly over the snow. He pressed back against the brick and although he was six-five and over two hundred and fifty pounds, tried his best to look inconspicuous.

He felt nothing except boredom and, of course, hatred. Very seldom did he get nervous. It was like the nerves had been cut from him long ago and the rest of his flesh left behind to do what nerveless flesh does best: take risks. This facility had served him well in Saigon, killing gooks, but of course he didn't have the facility until he'd gotten to Saigon and his best friend had stepped on a landmine two yards ahead of him. The friend's head was lopped off and he had caught it like a football, and from then on nothing about Vietnam worried him.

He paused to think about the diary he'd found and all the bad things in it, and how tonight he was doing a good thing. Which is why he was waiting in an alley in Spanish Harlem at 11:00 at night. In the snow. This was part of that good thing. His small mind drifted: tomorrow everything would be all right. He would fix things. The idea made him proud and a tiny thrill pulsed through him; life had its good moments. The priest and the girl appeared in the alley.

The church was small and its ancient timbers creaked in a sudden strong gust of wind. The wind died and the creaking of the rafters was replaced by the soft, sifted sounds of snow landing on a slate roof.

The silence was interrupted by the sobbing of a young woman. The priest sat down beside her in the vestibule and regarded her mournfully. She had come to him again, the third time in as many nights, requesting to see the priest in private. As in the two previous times, she'd been searching for a kind word, some guidance, and if possible, a respite from her awful dilemma.

It was always the same question, and the priest knew that despite the changing social view of the act in question, his answer would always be the same. Why is life so complicated, he thought, and immediately apologized to God for his indulgence. He cleared his throat. "Maria, you must have the baby. It is God's way."

She nodded slowly like a child. "But he won't want me anymore. I know it and I love him," she said sobbing.

The priest waited until the last of the crying had passed. He took one of her hands, pausing to note how perfectly the hand was formed. The fingers were slender and aristocratic. She had a gold band on the ring finger of her right hand. "There are other men," he said simply. "You are a lovely girl, and so young. One day soon a fine young man will meet you and take you away with him, and you will make a beautiful couple and have a fine family with strong good children like the children you have now."

"But I want his children. You don't understand, I love him," she insisted. "Father Rodriguez, it hurts me inside, in my heart. Maybe I should do . . . the thing he wants." She couldn't bring herself to say the words.

The priest clasped her other hand. He pressed his large thumbs gently into the backs of her hands. She peered up anxiously. "Maria, child," he began, "what kind of a man would ask you to kill his baby? What kind of a man?"

This broke her up as it had on previous nights and she cried uncontrollably, rejecting the priest as he sought to comfort her, her ample figure trembling with rage and frustration. "But he takes such good care of me and I love him and I don't want it to end. I'd miss him so much," she moaned. "Oh Jesus, why?" She cried for ten minutes, then knelt down and genuflected and asked for God's forgiveness.

From the vestibule the priest took a carafe of watery red wine and poured her a glass. She drank it thirstily as he watched her. She was bleached blond and tall with a broad, well-proportioned frame that hid her condition well. Looking at her in her overcoat it was hard to believe she was in her fifth month of pregnancy. She drained the glass and carefully wiped a drop of wine from her perfect lips. Her thin

3

nose was faintly freckled. She dabbed at it with her hand-kerchief and dried her eyes. They left the church together to walk through the snow, across the winding alley toward her apartment.

Maria stopped on the stairs outside of the church. She looked back at the dark stone building, its pitted surface now dusted with snow. A spotlight was missing on the slate roof, but she could still make out the steeple in the blackness. "Oh, Father," she said turning, "if not for the Lord, I some-times wish I was not alive."

The priest took one of her perfect hands and wrapped it around his arm. He threw up the collar of his thick woolen overcoat. They stood for a moment side by side on the steps. The priest was a well-built man with square shoulders and a flat stomach. His moustache was clipped short over a gener-ous mouth and his neck was strong and sturdy. With his overcoat covering his priest's collar, anyone might have mis-taken them for man and wife. The snow crunched beneath their feet as they turned into the alley.

The ironic thing was that he was Catholic. The man in the alley in the black sweater was Catholic. This made it worse. He watched as they approached, their heads bowed into the snow. Unthinkingly he traced a scar on his chin with a fin-ger. His breath frosted in front of him. He hummed the theme to "The Brady Bunch."

He stepped out to greet them with his hands poised al-most sheepishly at his belt buckle. And they froze, more from the shock of seeing anyone out tonight than him in par-ticular. Neither the girl nor the priest knew him. His face was expressionless and he was squinting against the snow.

Slowly they saw just how big he was and the priest drew the girl in to his side. "Yes . . . friend?"

"Hello," the man said, staring blankly at the girl. His stare lingered, then he addressed the priest. "Hello, Father. Lousy weather, huh? It reminds me of when I was a kid."

4

"What do you want?" the priest asked.

"Not much, I was waiting here for you. I was getting cold, I don't mind telling you that. It snowed on me." He laughed at this; his laugh was boyish and friendly. The priest relaxed. He tried smiling.

"Who are you?"

"Tonight I'm the problem solver. I'm here to make things all right again."

The priest frowned. "Is there a problem, son?"

The man nodded. "A big one," he said, looking away.

"I see. Perhaps we can discuss it in the church, after I take the señorita to her home."

Snow was accumulating on the señorita and the priest and the big man who'd stepped out of the shadows. The tops of their heads were white.

"No, Father."

"Why not?"

"No, that wouldn't do no good."

"Are you a Catholic?"

"I used to be."

"Then come, wait for me in the church. It is late."

"Goodbye, Father." The man put his hand out and opened it. The priest looked at it. A line grew across his forehead. The muscles of his face strained. He took the great hand and shook it firmly.

Then the man reached forward, casually, and with his left hand drove a small paring knife into the priest's large intestine. The man jiggled it and removed it on an angle with a flourish. He stuck the priest three times, the last time carving a deep line like a question mark up the priest's belly. Hot blood splashed onto his hand. He stood back and watched it steam as it spurted from the priest's overcoat.

The big man stood at ease, his eyes never once straying from the grotesquely strained face of his victim. The priest coughed and gripped the tear in his belly where the terrible pain started. He caught a section of his intestine in one of his

5

uncalloused hands. "Oh, God," he said, and did a little cramped death dance before sinking to his knees. He stayed like that for perhaps five seconds, his face whitening, his stare pain-filled and questioning. He lost any sense of balance and toppled over onto his side.

Then he lay still. The air was silent.

The large man wiped his hands on the snow. He leaned forward and fingered the priest's open mouth.

The woman let out a long, involuntary groan. She swayed and stepped forward in her high heels, teetering in shock. The stranger peered up at her and for an instant their stares met. "He had it coming," the man said thickly and the woman seemed to draw a conclusion from his terse statement. The shocked expression left her and was replaced by one of total and utter horror. She turned and ran, away from the slaughter and the puddling blood and the crazy man with the little knife. A scream formed in her bosom but was trapped by the fear so that all she managed was a sort of choked sound from the bottom of her lungs.

The big man stood and holstered the knife without wiping it clean. "Maria, stop. Come back!"

The woman sprinted toward the far end of the alley in the direction of the church. She slipped, somersaulted onto her back on the frozen earth, and rolled over. Frantically she found her feet, pausing to rip off her high heels, discarding them to run barefoot in the snow. She ran on, crazy-legged, sobbing hysterically now.

He was coming, of course, racing toward her with powerful, long-legged strides which crunched their way across the snowy surface of the road. Within seconds he was upon her. He caught her roughly at the back of the neck and swung her around like a doll. "Why didn't you stop, goddamnit?" he asked, and slapped at her with his fingertips, a backhand that loosened two of her front teeth. He was gasping for breath and his large flat face was flushed.

"Please, God," she pleaded, not looking at him.

6

He frowned: the fucking lady was praying to God. "Fuck God," he shot back. "Where was God when we needed him?" He hoisted her up and shook her violently. "You didn't stop and I told you to," he said, as if he actually believed she would have. He gathered her long bleached hair in one hand and held her upright. Then he felt along her body, over her swollen breasts to her ribs and finally her stomach. He smoothed an enormous hand over her. His face hardened: he could feel the baby.

Her eyes were beautifully green. They glistened in the distant lamplight over her shoulder. He watched the falling snow reflect in them. "You caused all the badness," he said, and swung his right fist into the exact middle of her stomach. The punch lifted her off her feet. She gasped. He held her steady by the hair and hit her again, another crippling roundhouse. Her body leapt again and her eyes rolled back in pain as she fainted.

He let her drop and walked away. When he returned with the car, she hadn't moved. Her long brown limbs were sprawled apart. Her arms were set at impossible angles and she was covered in a light film of snow. He lifted her by the delicate bones of her neck and she sighed. "You're all right," he said. "For Christ's sake I did you a favor."

He set her in the trunk of his car and covered her with a blanket. He shook the blanket first and a small wire brush fell from it and went unnoticed in the snow. From his pocket he took a flashlight and lifted the blanket and shined it at the space where her dress was hitched up. He drew her panties aside and shined the light closer. Then he let the blanket fall and slammed the trunk shut. He collected her high heels and pocketed them.

The priest was on his knees again. Very carefully he managed to find his feet. His black shoes shimmied across the snow. He held the slashed front of his overcoat to his stomach. It was soaked with blood. There was blood everywhere,

7

on his hands, the snow, his mouth, nose, hair. He knew he would die. But he'd seen the attack on the girl, Maria, and concentrated on this above his pain. The madman had beaten her, but he hadn't killed her. He'd left and come back with a car, then he'd set her in the trunk as if he were kidnapping her. A long dark sedan. Cars had license plates. If he could read it, maybe he could alert someone and give them the plate number. The possibility kept him going.

He stayed close to the wall. His eyes were dim and un-focused. He was mumbling the Lord's Prayer. His legs weakened and he gripped the icy brick with his fingertips. His hands were numb. He cleared his eyes with tremendous effort. VJKC3. The car pulled away.

"VJKC3," he read silently. He continued praying, occa-sionally inserting the license number between verses.

Slowly he moved toward the opposite end of the alley and the street. He would look for someone, alert them, give them the license. Please, God, give me time. "VJKC3—Our Father who art in Heaven . . ."

A terrible bolt of pain ripped across him from his chest to his testicles. He flopped down hard onto his knees, blinked the sweat clear, and lay in the snow. His face was cold. VJKC3. He had an inspiration. He touched himself where his stomach used to be. The fingers came away red. He wrote the license plate number in the snow.

He still wasn't dead. The thought came to him that he mightn't die after all. Maybe the wounds weren't that se-rious. After all, he had God. "Please, God, have mercy on me and your daughter Maria and her unborn."

He felt a renewed surge of strength and kicked his legs and cried out at the pain. Eventually he was standing again. He wobbled and dragged his feet towards the street.

The blackness flickered. He passed out and came to slumped against the wall. Something had awoken him. My God—a car! Someone! Salvation! He mightn't die! His black shoes slid two dull steps over the icy ground. The wind blew his hair forward. Blood dripped on his shoes.

8

The man climbed out of the car. He walked calmly, looking concerned but at the same time annoyed. He strode over to the priest. He was very big. "I thought you were dead already, Father."

Terror blossomed in the priest as he recognized the man. He kept perfectly still and squeaked the word, "No."

The man looked past the priest at the syrupy trail of blood in the snow. From his pocket he took two bits of wood secured by a length of wire. He unraveled them and stood behind the wounded man, looped the wire beneath the chin, and put his weight on the bits of wood. His knuckles got white from the pressure. He grunted and worked the wire, the priest flailing and kicking. The man tugged and the priest's head rolled off and lay sideways at the splayed feet. The corpse flopped into the snow. A red hand was spasming.

The man knelt and nudged the head with a finger. "You dead yet, Father?"

Then he took the head by the hair and booted it down the alley, as if through its proximity to the body, it might somehow effect a reunion. He started back to his car, then paused to examine the alley. He walked back until he came to the figures "VJKC3" scrawled in the snow. These were the numbers of the car he'd driven. The priest was a tricky son of a bitch. He stood on the writing and ground it out. Then he got in the car and drove away.

2

October

Diaz woke up in a cold sweat, having dreamt about his wife. Sunshine spilled through a tear in the curtains and hurt his eyes. The whore was holding him in her sleep. An anxious moment passed before he realized where he was and that he'd spent the night here. He slipped out of her arms and she stirred. Carefully he got off the bed, found a towel, and wiped the perspiration from his body.

He dressed quickly, the lingering sweat soaking into his shirt, darkening it a shade. He laid her fee and a tip on the plate by the bed and stepped into the hall. The bathroom he knew so well was at the end of the corridor; the door was locked. A rubber mat at the foot of the door said "Come again" in sprawling yellow script. He leaned against a whitewashed wall until a woman came out wearing bikini underwear and with a towel over her shoulders covering her chest.

Her thick dyed hair was slicked back; she smiled. Diaz went in and knelt before the toilet and retched.

The hawking sounds echoed back at him off the water. He stood and washed his face and drank from the faucet, spitting the taste of vomit into the sink and rinsing it away. On the front of his shirt tail he dried his eyes. He flushed the toilet and paused before the cracked mirror: his sturdy, fine-featured face looked tired and dispirited. The flesh was drawn and the skin a little hooded: the eyes of a man ten years older. His chin needed shaving.

The whore called to him from the door to her room. Her naked hip was against the frame and she had one hand modestly covering her pubis. Her young breasts looked pendulous. "Hey, Puerto Rican, where you going?" She made it sound coarse, as if she didn't care.

"Out."

"Okay, Puerto Rican," she said and laughed mirthlessly. He left the building and crossed the street. At the corner he turned and caught her staring at him from the upstairs window. She released the curtain and stepped back out of view.

He picked up a client's pictures from the photographer on the corner for fifteen dollars. In a narrow, unlit bar on Amsterdam, he drank dark rum and smoked a cigarette. He'd pinched the filter from the cigarette with his teeth before smoking it. With a knife he slit the envelope so the pictures slid out.

A man passed by on his way to the bathroom and stared at him. Diaz waited until he'd gone, wondering why some people minded everybody's business but their own. The pictures were on contact sheets in one-inch black-and-white strips. There was a man and a woman in each frame; the sequence followed them into a hotel on Lexington Avenue and out again. Diaz laid the pictures down in a square of sunlight on the table surface. He waited until he'd finished his cigarette and put the pictures back in the envelope, folded it, and put it into his inside coat pocket.

11

Diaz knew the man, the client, who wanted the pictures would be in; in his state he would have no place to go.

He took a subway to 137th Street. The man in the third-floor apartment cracked the door and peered at Diaz across the little rope of chain. His eyes were swollen and his chin patchy with three-day-old beard. There was a knife wound across the bridge of his nose and under one eye that gave him character and made Diaz feel a little bit sorry for him; he looked bad, even if he wasn't. "I ain't home."

"Open up. It's Willy Diaz."

"Leave me alone."

His words had a doped, somewhat starchy drawl as though he hadn't spoken in days. Diaz could smell whiskey and cigarettes and the lingering sweat of pain. For some reason he didn't turn and walk away. "Open it."

The man shut the door and removed the chain. When Diaz stepped inside, the man was sitting in the darkness on a stool in the corner. He had on a tee shirt and black slacks and his big frame was bowed over, knees to elbows. He supported his chin in his hands, and one of the hands pressed a revolver sideways against his cheek. A bottle of dark liquor was on the floor.

There was a stench like spoiled meat in the air. "Jesus." Diaz opened a window.

"What did ya find out?" the man asked in the same sluggish voice. "Was she fucking him?" He raised his swollen eyes from the floorboards and shouted, "How's my wife?"

Diaz watched him, fingering the curving points of his black moustache. "What're you doing with the gun?"

"Shooting myself."

"Oh."

The man pressed the side of the revolver more deeply against his face, flatly, like a cookie cutter. "She wouldn't care," he croaked. "She wouldn't give a shit."

Diaz said, "Probably not."

The man looked at Diaz with a pained expression as

12

though the detective had struck him. He mouthed the words, "Why not?" and began crying in little suppressed whimpers. He held the revolver absently against his face and bawled openly, drunken tears beading like rain on the weapon, falling off onto a piece of paper at his feet. The writing on the paper smeared and the ink characters blossomed. Diaz wondered if he'd been composing suicide notes that no one would read. He stood over the paper and saw that the first line said "Dear Gloria" in stick figures. He realized then that he'd forgotten the client's name.

The man was down and nearly out and now it was up to Diaz to kick in the final tooth and tell him how the wife, Gloria, was screwing two different men from her office on alternate days. He thought, you poor bastard.

He was a detective and divorces were lucrative and in supply. But it rarely got this bad. Leaning over he picked the gun out of the man's hand. He broke it open and removed the three shells and closed it and set it on the painted pink mantle.

"Did ya get any pictures? Did ya prove it?" the man asked, still crying. "Tell me, I can take it."

Diaz put his hand in his pocket and fished for a cigarette. He found one, lit it. The bitter scent of sulfur cut through the stench of sweat. He transferred the cigarette to his client's lips. The man accepted it and breathed through it hungrily. "No, I never got any," Diaz said.

The large bowed head jerked. "Maybe, maybe it wasn't happening then. Maybe she wasn't cheating?" His voice held the thin, wishful note of the spurned lover. Desperate. Diaz knew it.

"I don't know."

"Look, how much do I owe you?" The man asked straightening up, shocked out of his depression into a tenuous calm. He took out the cigarette, bending it inadvertently, and cleaned the mucus from his nose with two fingers. "Come on, I know you did your job."

"Forget it this time."

"Come on. Pretty soon I'll be working again. How's one hundred sound?"

"No."

"Then two hundred?"

"You got fifty?"

"Fifty? Sure, Jesus. Fifty I got." He groped his pockets while Diaz watched. "I swear I thought I had at least one hundred."

"Then next time."

"But all the work you done for me. I don't care what you did or didn't find. Shit—you tried. Even if there wasn't proof, you tried."

"What's that bill?"

"That? A twenty."

Diaz took the single damp bill, folded it, and thanked him. The air was suffocating even with the window open. It turned his stomach. He started out. "Wait, don't go. I still owe you. Let's talk at least. Sit down, Diaz."

"It's not necessary."

The man opened his mouth and shut it like a fish. "Hey, let me ask you. Why do you do this anyway, for a living? You speak good English. You're a good-looking guy."

"I don't know," Diaz said.

"You was a cop once."

"Yes."

"Now you private detective, making a lot of money." The man smiled in a kindly hopeless way like a dog on a leash.

"Something like that. Goodbye." He paused in the dark and added, "I'm sorry."

The man thought about this, then called out, "What for? Hey!"

Diaz waited until he stepped outside to drop the three shells into the Harlem gutter. The little brass jackets disappeared head over heels into the drain grate. He dug into his coat and added the envelope with the pictures.

14

In front of an appliance store window he stopped and examined his navy blue suit. It had fit once but years of wear had taken their toll on a sixty-two dollar Mays' Columbus Day Special. The shoulders sagged some. The thin padding was defined in the material; the lapels were frayed and wouldn't lie flat. He'd lost an arm in a fight and it had been sewn back on in a darker thread like a scar. The blue was fading gradually from the creases. He'd lost the hat.

He rolled his shoulders. It came to him as he descended the subway steps that maybe he should get a job someday.

A train came after seventeen minutes—he timed it—and he rode it to Alphonse's Bar on 108th on the East Side.

3

Alphonse's Bar was the seedy type most of the world saw for only a minute when they needed cigarettes or change for a bus or had the sudden urge to urinate. The sign in front had lost a vowel since his last visit. Diaz went in and nodded at a young bartender he didn't recognize. The man followed him closely with his eyes, then slid out from behind the bar and grabbed Diaz in front of a door marked "Office" in slanted, glow-in-the-dark letters.

Diaz felt the pressure on his elbow and twisted out of it. He stared at the younger man and turned back to the door, opened it, and stepped back when the kid yanked the other elbow. "You can't go in there," the kid said in an authoritative voice.

Diaz twisted his arm free. "Don't touch what you don't know," he said. Then, "You must be new, kid. I do business with Alphonse."

"Nobody sees Alphonse without my okay. That's the rule."
The kid's face was clean-complected with a soft mouth and a
graceful forehead, curly hair. His nose was crooked and
caught the light like a lump of clay. "Alphonse got to agree
to see you. You could be anybody."

"Behave yourself, little brother," Diaz said, and this time
when the kid grabbed for him, Diaz stepped firmly on his
instep and shoved him over a stool. Diaz felt a stitch tear
under his arm. He walked into the office feeling the air rush
into the rip in his suit. He thought: shit.

The door swung shut, he threw the bolt. Alphonse looked
up from a desk full of small bills. He was doing his Las Vegas
act today, Diaz decided. Alphonse was wearing a rhinestone
and polyester jacket with a string tie. His lank black hair was
combed high into a D.A. and he had rings on his fingers.
Diaz went over and extracted fifty dollars from his pocket
and set it on the corner of the desk. Included in the money
was the wilted twenty the client had given him.

Diaz said, "Fifty. That's all I could raise."

"A slow week, hotshot?" Alphonse glanced at him for the
first time. His fat neck rolled and the pockmarks absorbed
the shadows of a desk lamp. On his pinky, set in gold, was a
large opaque stone.

"I was expecting more today. It didn't come off."

"What's the matter, hard guy, somebody stiff you?" Alphonse twisted his ring and picked up the fifty dollars and
frowned. "This money's filthy."

"It works."

"You owe me five grand. Fifty don't cover the interest."
The loanshark's small soulful eyes were pink-rimmed and
weak. Like a bookie's on a bus out of town, Diaz thought.

"I'll make up for it."

"Diaz, you keep saying that . . ." Alphonse paused. "We'll
see. Unless I get the principal, the car back there, she's
mine, *amigo*. You got three more months to make four
thousand dollars. You'd better start working for the Rocke-
fellers."

Diaz was sick of listening to him. He'd come to associate the compact office with mistakes he'd made along the way. He'd put his only possession of value, his wife's Jaguar, up against a five-thousand-dollar loan. He'd used the money to pay some bills and sent thirty-five hundred of it to his sister in San Juan for a kidney operation. His mistake was in coming to the fat man at the desk across from him. "What's with the muscle outside?" Diaz asked.

"I had some asshole smacked around on account of what he did to me money-wise. I need somebody outside with a thermometer, checking the heat. The kid's the future middleweight champ of the world, though, so don't play with him unless you can back it up. I heard your little confrontation." Alphonse caught himself and tried hard to look tolerant. Instead he looked like a middle-aged fat man who'd never really made up his mind if he was tough or not.

Diaz went out through the back screen door, across the dirt yard to the garage. He tugged open the uneven wooden door and stared at the E-Type Jaguar he'd bought for his wife. The red car shone brilliantly in the afternoon light. He snapped the electric light on, the chrome danced, and he went in and started the engine.

The sound of the motor running brought him back: Tina had always wanted a Jaguar. It was her fantasy just as his had once been to go to college and live in Connecticut. It struck him how far away that dream seemed now, all these years later. He could barely afford to dress himself, yet he'd once dreamt of living in Connecticut. Next to Paul Newman. The thought brought a forlorn smile to his lips.

After his wife had gone and he'd joined the Police Department, he'd bought a beat-up E-type from a bankrupt dealer in New Jersey. He towed it back to Manhattan, hired a neighborhood mechanic, did most of the bodywork himself on weekends. It was a grimy white; he painted it red. The same day he'd finished it, he drove to the cemetary in Queens and parked by the fence where the oak tree had

18

grown clear through the iron rails. He stood against the knotted old tree with a hand on the trunk peering in at her. He preferred to look at her from this position, rather than going into the graveyard itself. It seemed more intimate this way, somehow.

"I got it, Tina," he said to no one. "I got it for you."

He switched the engine off and put the tiny tarnished key in his shirt.

The future middleweight champ was standing by the shed door in the weeds. His movement caught Diaz's eye. "I thought I heard someone out there scratching around."

The kid's lean face tightened. "I'm here to finish what you started," he said in a constricted voice. He took a casual step forward and spat on the car. The spit ran down a curve on the elongated bonnet.

Diaz eyed the kid levelly; the detective's expression darkened. Then lightened. From his coat he removed a handkerchief and rubbed the spit off. He folded the cloth and polished the moisture in small affectionate strokes until it too disappeared.

The kid ignored a fly that was determined to get up his nose. Little dashes of perspiration clung to his shirt. His curly hair was combed back. He said provocatively, "Come on."

Diaz strolled across the garage and the younger man backed out through the open door and stopped in the weeds. His fine bony hands came up to his chest. Diaz snapped the light off. Calmly he reached for the garage door and swung it closed.

Then he faced the kid. They were within striking distance of each other—two middleweights. The kid's lips were drawn over his uneven teeth and most of the color had drained from his face.

Diaz looked deeply into his hazel eyes and thought of growing up in the South Bronx and said softly, "Go home now." He pocketed the folded handkerchief and walked away.

4

Diaz could tell the man was waiting for him from a block away. He had the somewhat haunted look of an ethnic type in the wrong part of town. Among other things, his suit gave him away. It was bright black with a funereal gray chalk stripe that could be seen from a distance. He was a little sloped in the shoulders and quite tall and his gray hair was slicked back with something wet. He had little brown shoes that peeked out from beneath his cuffs like rats.

His hand was on the railing of Diaz's building, as if he owned the place, a conscious effort to appear relaxed which only made him look more vulnerable.

Diaz crossed the street and surveyed him in a 180-degree sweep, getting a look at his side and then his back. He was narrow and the suit rode up from his shoulders over his collar.

Diaz passed him on the stoop. The man reached for him, a little desperate action. He kept the hand out and seemed to have second thoughts and withdrew it timidly. Up close he was haggard and his eyes were small and rather close together. There was a shadow in his plain face which spoke of recent pain or tragedy. It was the face of a man who once thought all the bad things happened to other people and had recently been disillusioned. Diaz recognized it.

Up close he lost much of his flash; like a stage actor without his makeup, he seemed ordinary. "Are you William Diaz?"

"Yes."

"Thank goodness. I've been waiting here in this neighborhood . . . I thought you'd never show." His suit needed pressing. It was good thick English cloth, but had lost its crease in the knees. He'd been doing too much standing or sitting or maybe praying.

Diaz appraised him. Except for the suit and the gun in his pocket he looked entirely anonymous. "How can I help you?"

"Is your office up there?" The man pointed, another quick gesture.

Diaz nodded. "You need to talk to me?"

"Yes."

"Okay then."

Diaz walked behind him up two flights of stairs watching the bob and weave of the weapon in his flannel pocket. He kept his eye on the tall figure as he unlocked the door to his office-apartment with three keys. Diaz said, "It's late. You're lucky you caught me."

The office comprised a desk, two chairs, a corduroy Castro convertible, and a small refrigerator with a television on top. Diaz sat down at the desk and unlocked the top right-hand drawer, exposing a blue .38 service revolver on an oiled cloth.

The man drew up a leather chair and slumped into it.

21

From his inside coat pocket he removed a battered silver cigarette case. He took out a cigarette and tapped it and held it nervously while he spoke. "Excuse me, I'm not used to this sort of place. In fact I'm not all that used to cities in general, anymore."

"Where do you live?"

"Me? In Maine, in Portland, outside of Portland. All my life I've been in banking and banking invariably means living in a city. But I'm retired now so I no longer have to deal with cities, and that's a godsend."

"What do you do in Portland?" Diaz asked.

"Paint pictures. It's all I've ever wanted to do really. It's the only thing I've ever been completely comfortable doing."

Diaz imagined the tall man in the suit painting pictures, comfortably, on an island somewhere. "What can I do for you?"

"I haven't introduced myself, but my name is Thomas Deluca. You know enough about me for the moment. Someone recommended you, a New York City cop who was acquainted with a friend of mine. He understood that you had quite a rapport established within the Latin community."

"I live here, I'm Latin. I like people."

"Yes." Deluca set the unlit cigarette between his lips. He opened his left hand and leaned forward and dropped a small color picture onto the desk top. Diaz took it; it was hot from the man's hand. "That's a photograph of my son's ex-girlfriend. You can't tell from the photo but she was a tall girl about five feet eight inches and she dyed her hair blond."

It was a head-and-shoulders shot of a young, olive-skinned woman with perfect features and sparkling bright green eyes. "She's very pretty."

"She's why I'm in New York. Otherwise I'd be home in Maine, painting. Her name is Maria Juarez. She lived on One hundred and twenty-first Street between Lexington and

22

Third Avenue not far from here." Deluca had been speaking around the cigarette. He took it out. "My son loved her. Although I never knew it, there's some evidence they were engaged. Maria was twenty-six and had three children from a previous marriage. Her husband died, I understand. Perhaps her children are the reason why my son, Tim, never leveled with me about his intentions with Maria. He probably thought I would disapprove."

Deluca reminisced and his eyes grew misty and vague. The cigarette rolled out of his hand and he collected himself and retrieved it.

"What's wrong with Maria?" Diaz asked.

"I don't know. She disappeared eight months ago and no one's heard from her since. There's no evidence, but it looks like kidnapping. The police don't know. They don't know very much, which is why I've come here. I want you to find her." He combed his soft gray hair back with a thin hand. When he squinted, his wrinkles showed. He had capped teeth, tobacco-stained, and a weak chin. With his hair dyed black he might have looked more like a Catskills show opener, Diaz thought.

"What makes you think I could have more luck than the police?"

"Because, Mr. Diaz, you're from the street, you live here. You must know the people. The police . . . they have 'more urgent matters to contend with.'" Deluca grinned lamely. "That's what one of them told me. Maria's been gone eight months. She's no longer immediate."

"Why do you think she was kidnapped? Maybe she just took off to live life and breathe clean air. It happens." Diaz wondered then how well thought-out the whole business was in Deluca's mind, or was he simply here to talk and weigh the enthusiasm against the despair?

"Tim convinced me. Maria was due to join him for a long weekend in Maine. I was going to be away. A gallery in Boston was exhibiting my work, so Tim and Maria would

23

have the house to themselves. Maria never showed. When Tim finally contacted her family, her younger sister had no idea where Maria was. She had simply disappeared. The sister was away. Maria's children were left unfed for two days. Maria's clothes were all there and her bed hadn't been slept in."

"Did you check the airline to see if she got on the plane?"

"Yes, and they had no record of a Maria Juarez flying anywhere that day. Tim had bought Maria's ticket for her. It was left behind at the departure desk at Newark Airport."

"That's when you called the police?"

"No," Deluca said. "Not then. Maria's sister phoned the police. Tim and I thought it best to hold off our involvement in case Maria's disappearance had been voluntary."

"Did she have a history of disappearing?"

"No, Tim didn't think so."

"Then why wait?" Diaz asked. "If your son was engaged to her, it doesn't make sense that he would wait a minute."

Deluca thought about this. He looked down at his shoes. "Tim and Maria had quarreled recently. She pressured him into the engagement, I suspect, and they'd argued about it. Then when she didn't show, well, Tim put it down to hurt feelings. Looking back, I'm not sure waiting like we did was the right thing to do. Maybe with my influence the police would have been more motivated, somehow. I don't know."

"What does the sister think?"

"Nothing. The police tell me she has no ideas."

"What does Tim think?"

"Tim thought she must have died or been murdered or kidnapped. He had no answers. He'd known her for a year, since they met in the public library near Columbia University. Maria worked there. I met her once and she seemed very nice, not the type of woman who might get involved in drugs, or things like that. I feel she's been kidnapped, or worse, which is why I need you."

Deluca stood up and dug both hands into the pockets of his coat. His eyes brightened. He withdrew his right hand and slid a stack of fifty-dollar bills across the desk. "Will that cover it?"

Diaz looked uninterestedly at the money. "What is it?"

"Cash, two thousand five hundred dollars in fifties. Is that enough?" He touched his pale face while he waited.

"That's enough."

"If you find her promptly I can promise you a bonus. I'll double what I've already given you. But you must act promptly. I don't like this city, as I've said, and I want to get back to Maine and my painting." Deluca sat down on the edge of the chair.

Diaz took a tablet of unlined paper from the desk drawer and wrote down the girl's name and a few random facts and a picture of a spaceship.

"Well, can you help me?"

Diaz said, "I can try."

"That's wonderful. You're sort of my last resort."

Diaz stared at him. "Where's Tim, Mr. Deluca?"

Deluca withdrew the silver cigarette case, opened it, and set the unlit cigarette gingerly inside. He rubbed his neck with a narrow hand as though contemplating hanging himself, and fatigue flickered in and out of his face. "My son died five months ago in a traffic accident. He had a motorcycle and I'd written to ask him not to ride it, but he did and he had an accident. I miss him terribly at times. If he'd lived he would have been such a successful man. He had that drive, you know, that stood him apart from his contemporaries. He always seemed so much older."

"I'm very sorry."

"Dying is a part of life, I suppose. It's funny how arbitrary life is, don't you think? Things, events, come at you without reason sometimes. When my wife of thirty years died, I re-

25

member how arbitrary that seemed to me," Deluca said flatly, and Diaz liked him more for the lack of self-pity in his tone. He thought of his own wife and then, incongruously, of the client in the stinking apartment uptown, sitting in it with his revolver and his false hopes.

"That's it I'm afraid."

"Don't be afraid," Diaz said. He put the wallet-sized photo of the missing Spanish girl in the corner of the leather desk blotter. Maria wasn't smiling, but something of her spirit came through the shot. She looked serene, though Diaz expected she was the kind of girl given to enthusiasm and maybe passion. She probably wouldn't put out on the first date unless she liked you.

"Where can I reach you?" Diaz asked.

"I'm staying at the Carlyle Hotel. I no longer carry business cards or I'd give you one." With a diffident gesture he smoothed the surface of his tie and stood up. The cuffs dropped onto his brown shoes. The weight of the gun hidden in the pocket sagged the coat. "I'm anxious to return to Maine and continue my normal lifestyle there if that's possible without my son. What I'm trying to say is that I'd be grateful if you could work quickly on this. I don't feel safe in New York."

Diaz recognized something of the homesick child in his expression and his tone. He looked uneasy just standing there, like an accountant in a penitentiary. They shook hands. "You know . . ." he paused and looked apprehensive, "I'm doing this for Tim, that's the real reason. He would have pursued it." Diaz nodded and put his arm around the man's narrow shoulders and held him for a moment in a sort of half-assed embrace. They continued to the hall together and Deluca proceeded on his own, a little unsure, like a captainless ship, and disappeared around the bannister.

Diaz sat on the edge of the desk and asked information for the Carlyle's number and dialed it. Did they have a Thomas Deluca staying there? They did? How long for? An

26

effeminate voice indicated that Deluca had made no plans to leave.

Diaz hung up. He unpeeled the ball of money and counted it: $2,500. He remembered something and unfolded *The New York Times* on his desk and flipped through it until he found the page. The caption of the ad was in bold black ink: MEN'S SUITS—ALL SIZES—$149.99.

He ripped the ad out.

5

Diaz sat in silence listening to the street sounds. During their impromptu embrace, he'd lifted Deluca's automatic from the taller man's coat without his knowledge. He removed it from his own pocket and released the clip, smelled the barrel: it hadn't been fired lately. The shells were real and the insides weren't too dirty by street standards. He put it away.

It was late for some things, early for others. Taking three fifties from the stack of bills, he put the rest of the money into a plastic bag, taped it shut, and tied it with a piece of string. With a penknife he opened the drain in the bathtub and tied the string to the drain cap. Then he stuffed the bag in. He set the drain cap back in place and mashed it down with the heel of his hand.

The coat to his suit had two tears under each arm: he put it on and walked the nineteen blocks to 121st Street.

28

The air was cooler at 8:30 and the autumn night held the promise of activity. The homeless would be scurrying for warmth; the lawless would be mapping their strategies. It amused Diaz as he threaded through the traffic of Third Avenue that residents of Connecticut breathed essentially the same air as this.

He passed a newsstand on the corner of 120th and Lexington. According to Deluca, this was Maria's neighborhood. Diaz bought a paper, gave the man a twenty, accepted his change, and handed back a ten spot. He held Maria's photograph to the bill with his thumb. "*Mira*. Take a look. This ring any bells with you?"

The man, half-Chinese with a long neck, took a brief, obligatory glimpse. "I don't know no one, I'm antisocial."

"Take a good look," Diaz said.

"I'm taking the best look I know how to. I never seen her."

"She's missing, she might be in trouble. She might even be dead. Her mother's worried; you know how mothers are."

"No, I haven't had one lately. How are they?"

"Okay bro'." Diaz picked up the photo.

The man said, "You're forgetting your money."

"You keep it."

"I didn't earn it."

"Neither did I," Diaz said and left. A block up the street he dropped the newspaper in a trash can.

A car went by with one headlight. Diaz heard a child crying somewhere for a tit and a womb and maybe a TV set. East 121st Street off Lexington was a strip of rowhouses mixed here and there with nests of little dead stores. Nearly all the buildings had running water. A beauty salon was in business advertising two bouffant hairdo's for ten dollars. A smiling white woman advertised brandy and cigarettes on a yellowed poster. Now there's a combination, Diaz thought: just what his people needed. He leaned against the glass of a cobbler's shop and looked at the old shoes.

29

He found the house. Only the number on the door distinguished it from the houses to either side. Its brick was black with the soot that comes from generations of despair. Maria Juarez lived on the ground floor, apartment 1A. Someone, maybe a vulture, had pried open the lid to her mailbox so it wouldn't shut. Upstairs salsa music seeped out of a radio. Diaz thought briefly of his own childhood in the South Bronx. The atmosphere was the same here, as though the life had been drained from these blocks. No one *chose* to live here and it showed.

Suddenly the door to the building opened. He hesitated. A tall young woman with black shoulder-length hair froze on the threshold. Willy said, *"Buenas noches, señorita,"* but his throat was dry and he only mumbled it.

He saw fear in the woman's hard almond eyes as they appraised him. She gradually dropped her hand from her bosom. She wore a blue dress that clung to her figure, defining it. Her hips were full though unmarred by childbearing and her ankles were slender and strong. Her legs were long. She dressed like a thirty-year-old, though, Diaz thought, she was probably in her teens.

He stared at her and saw something: a fire, intelligence, something in her eyes that was difficult to identify. Hatred? Her unblemished skin had a healthy tone in the weak light of the doorway.

"Buenas noches," she said and slid away with a little athletic shift of her shoulders. To Diaz she smelled fresh, not flowery like some women he knew. He watched her until she entered the darkness of the street and her footsteps died.

The door to her building was closing slowly on a hydraulic hinge. He stepped inside. The corridor smelled of children. A naked lightbulb was suspended from the ceiling by a frayed cord. The dim bulb threw out insufficient light that left much of the corridor in shadow. The walls needed plastering. Apartment 1A was immediately to his left. A strip of light showed beneath the door. The doorknob was turning; Diaz opened it.

A tiny boy in an undershirt stood just inside the apartment clutching the doorknob. He opened his eyes wide and tried to say hello. Then he sat down and began playing with a toy car on the floor. He made the noise of a motor with his mouth and crashed the car into a wall. He looked up, delighted.

Diaz thought: a future insurance salesman.

He stepped around him into the apartment, noting that the smell of children came from in here. A television set was blaring and he walked around a partition in the wall where an elderly Spanish couple were asleep on separate chairs, propped up before a rerun. Black-and-white light bounced off of their incontinent features. The upholstery of the chairs was threadbare. The room was neat, the furniture practical but second-hand; worse than that, third-hand. It reminded him of a priest's house he'd once visited.

The kitchen in the apartment was small; the cutlery was spread out over a towel near the sink. There was a box of *cucaracha* poison on the counter and a cartoon of a stiletto shoe squashing a roach on the box: the international symbol of extermination. He opened the fridge: empty but for a pot of rice, some milk, and a six-pack of supermarket beer. The freezer was full of TV dinners.

"Who are you?"

Diaz turned. A little girl stood in the doorway. She wore pajama bottoms rolled up at the feet. Her brown hair was braided. She sucked her thumb and clutched a pink rag to her face.

She asked, "Are you good or bad?"

"Good," he said, not expecting the question.

She looked him over. "Are you a daddy?"

"No, honey, just a friend."

"Oh." This seemed to make sense to her. She remembered something. "I want a drink."

31

In the cupboard he found a glass, the type they gave away at gas stations, and rinsed it. He filled it to the top with tap water and gave it to her. She gulped the water down greedily and looked up out of breath. "Fank you." She passed the glass back and wiped her face awkwardly on the rag. She put her thumb back in her mouth and stuck out her left hand; it was a perfectly shaped woman's hand in miniature.

Diaz felt suddenly responsible for her and wondered whether this is what it was like having children. The feeling was not altogether unpleasant. He surrendered a finger. She gripped it and led him to a bedroom at the opposite end of the apartment. The room looked fresher than the others he'd seen. The paint was newer. There were children's toys on the floor. He nearly tripped on a skate. He picked her up and laid her on the bed next to an even smaller child and tucked the covers under her tiny arms. Her large black eyes never left him. With a finger he combed the hair off of her forehead. "Night, Daddy," she said.

"Goodnight, honey, pleasant dreams."

The little boy with the toy car was asleep on the floor. Diaz boosted him up, surprised at how light he was, and laid him in bed with the other children.

He shut the door to the apartment behind him, making sure it locked.

On the stoop, the air was quiet. For the moment all radios within earshot were turned down. The cars stayed away. He thought: it's like a moment of silence for someone not yet dead. He remembered the young leggy beauty leaving the building. Why couldn't he have gotten her name?

To do what with?

He resisted the urge for a cigarette and thought of her and walked home on the street.

6

For two hundred dollars he bought a robin's-egg blue suit and a pair of brogues. They gave him back his original suit in a paper bag and encouraged him to have a nice day. Despite their encouragement he'd had anything but a nice day doing surveillance on a child-custody case in Gramercy Park. Got nowhere. He called his friend, a lieutenant at the 25th precinct, but he wasn't in. So he went home and retired the old suit in a closet with moth balls in the pockets.

By four o'clock he was back in Maria Juarez's apartment, on 121st Street, drinking high tea with her grandparents. He didn't drink tea as a rule and, he decided, these people probably didn't drink tea either but they were doing their part to befriend the man who could conceivably return their granddaughter. This moved Diaz.

They looked alike, he thought, as elderly people who've

33

lived with each other for a lifetime often do. They both had thinning white hair and deep rheumy eyes. Good bone structure had kept their faces from wrinkling too severely. They must have been a handsome couple in their day and Diaz could see the resemblance to Maria.

On the table beside the teapot was a selection of scrapbook photos of Maria taken within the last ten years. Diaz put away the photograph Deluca had given him.

"We came up from Puerto Rico when Maria disappeared," the old man said. "Her sister Carmen was having a problem caring for the children all by herself. She works as a personality. . . ." He glanced at his wife.

"Personal secretary. She works at a business on Park Avenue as the personal secretary. The man who owns it is a millionaire." The old woman smiled and genuflected with a white hand. "One day Carmen says she is going to be a millionaire too. Can you imagine it?" Her dentures clucked.

"So you hadn't seen Maria for some time?" Diaz asked.

"No, not for many, many years. We were very happy in Puerto Rico. I had a prize-winning farm," the man said.

His wife added solemnly, "He raised giant chickens, señor. Have you ever seen giant chickens?"

Diaz said he hadn't that he could remember. "How many children did she have?" He was aware of asking the question in the past tense. "Does she have?"

"Three from her husband who died two years ago." The woman genuflected again. "He fell under a pipe."

"He worked in construction," the grandfather expounded.

"Do you have any idea where Maria might have gone? Maybe she just got tired of watching after three kids alone and took some time to be on her own." He saw the shock spread across their faces. "It happens."

"Maria wasn't like that. After her husband died, all that mattered was the children. She loved them—and they were Maria's link to Pedro, her husband," the old woman said.

"Carmen told us Maria went out for a walk one evening

and never came back to the house," the man said. Diaz sipped his tea and his hosts did likewise. "This neighborhood is not so good in the dark, señor. Each week someone is killed—usually they are innocent people—but are the criminals ever brought to justice? No. The police don't care. Unless it's one of their own, they only investigate for appearances. But do you notice when it's one of theirs, they catch the man instantly."

"Popi!" The woman shushed him.

Diaz nodded. There was a certain truth to this, though not for the implied reasons. A man kills a cop: he's no longer anonymous. He's the cause of a near riot in the streets, police anarchy; cops busting everyone, everything. The blanket assault invariably "persuades" the street to cough up the killer like a tide coughing up its dead. Some laws have to be respected in any world. Even in New York.

"When a policeman's killed, they usually do find his killer," Diaz agreed.

"You would not have this in Puerto Rico," the man said.

The woman shifted a number of faded photographs chronicling Maria's youth across the table top. She sighed deeply. Her husband reached over and held her knuckly hand. She studied Diaz. "She's dead, isn't she? God tells me that she is dead and with him in heaven by his side. And my instincts are normally right, ask Popi."

Diaz wanted a cigarette. Instead he touched the points of his moustache. "We don't know. She may not be." Then, to boost them, "I'll do my best to bring her back to you." He thanked them for the tea and stood up. On the floor near his foot were two bags of groceries. "I've brought some things for the children. I know how hard it is raising a family in these times." He set the bags of vegetables and meat on the table.

"You didn't have to. We have our pension money from the government," the man said, looking self-conscious.

"You are very kind, señor. Do you have any children of your own?"

Diaz substituted his stock answer, "Not that I know of," with "No, ma'am." He withdrew a card from his pocket and presented it to the old man. "I'd like to talk to Carmen when she gets in. Would you have her call me please?" He looked around for a phone.

"Certainly."

They stopped shaking hands. The woman embraced him and told him he looked like the man in the soap opera on Channel 48. He left.

There was no sense pressing them for information they couldn't know. They'd come to this country six months before and were stuck, holed up in a three-room flat in Spanish Harlem minding their great-grandchildren. They hadn't seen their granddaughter, Maria, in years. Therefore they wouldn't know her, what her habits were, her nature, friends, lovers. Any real information would have to come from the sister, Carmen.

He stopped across the street to light the cigarette he'd thought about during their entire conversation. With two fingers he pinched the filter off and put the shredded brown end in his mouth. The woman from last night came walking up the block in his direction.

Diaz's stomach grumbled and he felt momentarily disoriented, like a kid on the playground finding romance for the first time and not knowing what to do about it. In their brief encounter on the stairs last night, he'd seen something in her face that intrigued him. What was it? Rage? Courage? Arrogance?

He decided then to ask her about the missing girl. Maria Juarez lived in her building. They would know each other. He wasn't just some nut on the make; he had a reason for talking to her. With a professional purpose, he felt better. He threw the cigarette in the gutter and rolled his shoulders into the padding of the blue cotton suit.

She moved briskly on the balls of her feet. Her fine body bounded agilely up the pavement, bosoms bouncing imperceptibly beneath the dress. He liked women with breasts you could hold on to.

The movement of a speeding car caused the cotton dress to flutter in the ensuing breeze. She'd worn that dress last night. Diaz caught a glimpse of her full thighs and a section from a garter belt.

He timed it and stepped out to greet her. "Excuse me." The woman stopped. He could see she'd been daydreaming. "I met you last night in front of your building. I'm looking for someone you know."

She frowned and the dark tips of her eyebrows joined. She seemed to be placing him in her mind's eye. "We've never met," she said flatly.

Her voice was steady but with a faint hoarse timbre, as if she'd had a late night. Her eyes were bright auburn with flecks of gold and her skin was smooth over the fine features of her face. She had, he decided, the sort of classic looks that fashion models often had that caused men to pay too much attention on the subway. In her heels she was as tall as he was.

"I saw you leaving your building last night around nine o'clock. We met at the door."

She looked at him peculiarly and he saw a flicker of recognition pass through her eyes. She stared at the new suit. "You look different. I remember you now. But we never met." She seemed to be aware she was making eye contact and looked away self-consciously.

"Maybe I just dreamt that part," he said, gaining a degree of confidence from her apparent shyness.

She said humorlessly, "I'm meeting someone and I'm already late, excuse me."

He held up the photo Deluca had given him. "I'm a detective and this woman's disappeared. She lived in your building."

She gasped. He could see her hands tightening on her purse. They were lovely hands, he thought, an artist's hands.

"You know her," he said. "Maria Juarez."

She passed the photo back hurriedly. "Someone is looking for her?"

"Yes, they're worried about her. She disappeared eight months ago and hasn't been heard from since. She lived in your building." The woman in front of him was nearly as lovely as the one in the picture. Yet something marred her natural beauty. Despite her young age there was a hardness there, an advanced cynicism. He wondered if she'd once been mistreated by a lover and now kept her emotions in reserve.

"I knew her as well as you know anyone to say hello to. She lived in my building," the girl said.

"I just said that." He put the picture away. "Did you know much about her?"

"Not very much. We never had much to say to each other, and the people in my building don't communicate."

"Have you lived there long?" Diaz asked. Having asked this he looked down the street at a blue Chevrolet station wagon cruising to a stop against the curb; the same station wagon which, minutes earlier, had sped past them up the street. No one got out although the engine died. He could see three bodies inside.

She said something. "Excuse me?" Diaz said.

"No, I haven't."

"Haven't what?"

"Lived there long," she said impatiently.

"Oh. Her full name is Maria Juarez. She has three children. You must have noticed them."

"Yes, I know them. I know the family you mean, I've just never dealt with them."

"Can you tell me anything about her? Eight months is a long time to be unaccounted for in New York when you've

38

got children," he said plainly. In his experience things usually worked in extremes, black and white, invariably clearcut, easily read if you knew the signs. Maria had been gone without the hint of an explanation for eight months, signs rarely got more obvious. He reminded himself that he'd taken the case because he genuinely hoped to find her. He *would* find her. She had to be somewhere.

The woman bit her finger without knowing she was doing it. "I'm late, I have to go now."

"Can't you tell me something, anything; what she was like as a person, what sort of reputation she had, what she did for kicks?"

"I can't tell you that."

"Nothing?"

"No, I don't know anything, Jesus!" Her handsome face flashed anger.

Diaz had an urge to comb her long black hair with his fingers. "Why do I think you can? Who was she to you?" He held her arm; she shrugged it off.

"No one, just a girl."

"Why don't I buy that?"

"She worked at the pier at the fights, I remember now."

"Fights?"

A faint blush spread across her cheeks. "The cockfights on the East Side, she worked there. I remember hearing that she worked there, okay?"

"In case you remember something. Here's my number." Diaz extended one of his cards, she took it. "What's your name?" he said.

"Sally."

"You don't look like a Sally."

She studied him. "No? Well you don't look like much of a detective."

He laughed at that, and for a second a smile tugged at the corners of her mouth. She walked off, her broad back and shoulders swaying girlishly.

His heart was pounding. He repeated her name: Sally. Sally knew something. He knew from the way she'd reacted to the photo. She had his number, if she thought of something she could call him. She might. If not he'd come back and knock on doors until he found her.

He recalled seeing her last night in the same clothes leaving the apartment. That was ten o'clock. Now it was afternoon and she was just coming home. Her clothes were still pressed; therefore she hadn't worn them all the time. So what? So why wouldn't she wear her clothes all the time? She'd been doing things with her clothes off.

There was only one explanation. She wore no wedding ring, so she must have a lover. From the looks of it a rich one. The thought was demoralizing.

"Call me," he said, but she was gone.

He walked two blocks, far enough away so he could still see the blue Chevrolet without being seen. It hadn't moved. He made two deductions: if they were thieves casing apartments, they wouldn't be casing Maria's apartment because there was nothing of value in it. On the other hand, they might be casing Sally's apartment.

He walked to a pay phone and dialed his friend, a lieutenant from the 25th precinct, and made a dinner date. The friend, Leary, asked what the matter was and Diaz responded by asking him what Maria Juarez meant to the Missing Persons' Bureau. He gave Leary the particulars.

He walked around the block casually and came back to her street from east to west. The Chevrolet was gone.

At the newsstand on 120th Street the half-Chinese man was leaning on the counter doing the *Times* crossword. He stared at Diaz uncuriously. "You again, back to lay another ten-spot on me for the hell of it?" This time he grinned slightly.

Diaz bought a pack of Kools with exact change. He opened the pack, speared a cigarette to his lips, snipped off the filter with his teeth and spat it out. "I've come into some money, I'm looking to invest it for a quick return. I heard they still have the cockfights at night."

The half-Chinese man said, "Play a number, it's easier."

"I like the sport."

"Congratulations, I hope you pick a winner."

"Where would I pick it?"

The man stared at Diaz and began to get the message. "You want to play, but you don't know how?"

"Something like that."

"And you figure I owe you," the man said.

Diaz said, "Nope."

The man looked down at the crossword puzzle. He put the eraser end of his pencil against his bottom lip and leaned on it. "Give me a three-letter word for a physician's moniker."

Diaz said, "Doc."

The newspaper man looked up, surprised. "There you go, you ain't as dumb as you look." Diaz stood there. The man said, "Over on One hundred and twenty-eighth Street on the pier. On the dock. Nine o'clock most nights and you didn't hear it from me."

41

7

The blue Chevrolet wagon, registered to a vacant lot in Newark, pulled off the access route to the Major Deegan Expressway and coasted to a stop on the corner of 138th Street in the Bronx. Two men got out while a third stayed behind.

The two men were of the same build, short and broad-backed with tight-fitting clothes to show off physiques formed by pumping iron twice a week. One was light-skinned and one dark. Their lineage was hard to place: they might have been Hispanic, yet they could have passed for two Sicilians back from a week in Lauderdale.

A group of junkies loitered around a steel garbage can hunched over the scraps of burning wood—chattering, waiting for the monkey to seduce them into robbery or worse and send them back into the streets.

The two men from the Chevrolet met Joey Irish in a park beside some railroad tracks. He was wearing a pigskin cap and an old tweed coat with a knife and a blackjack in the pockets.

The three men nodded to one another. There was a cautious look in the bloodshot eyes of the Irishman. "So you two seen him. He met her there?" Joey Irish asked. He was less sure of himself with knives than blackjacks, so he kept his hand in the coat on the leather handle of the blackjack just in case. His fingers were sweating.

"Yeah, he was there just like you said he'd be." The two from the Chevrolet were Puerto Rican but spoke English like the blacks, with elongated vowels and accents on the last syllables.

"You're sure it was him? He fits the description?" Joey Irish had an Irish brogue.

"Yeah, no question we were looking right at him and at her."

"He didn't see you? You know what I said about him walking up on you with your dick in your hand. Then the deal's off and I don't pay nobody!" Joey Irish could talk to them this way because he'd been feeding them dope on and off for seven years.

"Six bucks an hour," the darker of the two said. "That's what Cat told me, six bucks clear."

The light-skinned man, Cat, agreed.

"Did you see anybody else? The big guy with the combat boots?"

They shrugged, "Nope."

Joey Irish trusted these two as much as any dealer trusted his regular customers. They'd go to the ends of the earth for him if dope was involved. But something was different; they seemed somehow more independent. He hadn't dealt smack to them in six months; they'd been in a Methadone House or jail or some fucking place, and it took Joey Irish a while to get his confidence back. "You want cash?" he asked.

43

Cat said, "You know what we want."

Irish thought: I still own them. He nearly smiled. From his knife pocket he removed a plastic film container. "How many hours was it?"

"We worked eight hours," Cat said, lying by half.

"And there are three of you."

"Today there were four," he lied again. "Usually there are just three."

"I only want three," Irish said. "You can't be any more conspicuous than you are."

Cat shrugged. His partner, Mario, nodded. Their eyes were on the magic little plastic container. Mario's moist upper lip twitched.

The October air was cool and Joey Irish tossed them the container and jerked down his cap. "This place is like standing in a fucking graveyard." He never chose the same place twice for dealing purposes and made a mental note never to come within ten miles of here again.

Cat caught the container and held it with the reverence of a wounded veteran holding morphine.

"That more than covers it," Irish said to them. "From now on you know what to do for your six bucks an hour. I want you on this twelve hours a day every day until I tell you different. Be sure to keep notes like I told you to. And if the big guy shows up with the short hair and the combat boots, call the number you got and leave a message."

"Sure."

"Yeah sure," Mario said, perspiring visibly now.

The Irishman paused and smiled coyly and asked Cat, "You still carry that knife like the old days?" He shifted the weight on his brown shoes from side to side.

Cat looked at Mario then removed a compact iridescent handle from his jeans. He squeezed it and six inches of thin sparkling knife leapt out. Cat flipped it and caught it evenly by its mother-of-pearl handle. "I'd never lose this. It's my personality," he said.

Joey Irish was itching to show the man his latest purchase. He said, "Wait," and withdrew his own version of a stilletto purchased from a Times Square pawn shop. The knife edged out in a dull sluggish motion. The blade was fully as long as Cat's, though wider. Joey Irish smiled.

Cat put his knife away, took Joey Irish's, and calmly snapped the blade in half between his strong fingers. He said, "You have to check the hardening number. With this piece of shit you'd be better off stickin' 'em with your finger."

Irish took the knife back and dropped the pieces. He'd paid twenty-three dollars for it. He forced a grin. "Goodbye then, lads," he said, and walked away across a lawn of dead leaves.

8

They met at an Italian bistro on 96th Street frequented by cops and small-time gangsters looking to make friends. They sat in a booth in the front corner of the room near the door. Accordion music issued out of two speakers suspended by wire from the ceiling. Diaz munched on a breadstick and drank Chianti from an oversized wine glass.

Leary glanced up from his third plate of linguini. He wet a napkin and blotted it against a fresh stain on his tie. He said with his mouth full, "Shit."

He was a big-boned man, forty pounds overweight, with thinning red hair and large arms. He wasn't overly strong, his muscles were the kind maintained by raising a beer mug and climbing out of bed and occasionally from doing it missionary style with his wife of fourteen years. He sucked in another spoonful of pasta and looked at his watch. "You ain't eating?"

46

"I gave it up recently."

"Where'd the suit come from? You finally start selling co-caine to pay the rent?"

"I've considered it," Diaz said.

"I'll bet you have." Leary dropped his fork and poured an empty water glass to the top with Chianti. He downed it and wiped the wine off his chin with a red-checked napkin. "Ever think about coming back on the force? Now that I'm lieutenant I could make sure you got some office work. You'd be on my staff."

"I'll think it over."

"You've been thinking it over for three years, ever since . . ." Leary stopped and looked down at his hands on the table. They were short, square hands covered in a red down.

"Look at that." Diaz put the photo of Maria to one side of his plate. "That's the missing girl I asked you about. Anything on her?"

Leary blotted the sweat off his forehead with the red-checked napkin and managed to spread tomato sauce on his brow. He took a bite out of a piece of garlic bread and crushed out his cigarette. "Lotta flies in this dump, did you notice?" He addressed the picture. "That's her, huh? Not bad at all." He drew a folded sheet of lined paper from his pants and opened it carefully on a space on the table. "Maria Juarez. Address: One hundred sixty-seven East One hundred and twenty-first Street. Nationality: Puerto Rican. Born: San Juan, nineteen-fifty-nine. Three children, widowed, lives with sister Carmen. Worked part-time at the public library on One hundred fourteenth off Amsterdam. Reported missing February twentieth by sister Carmen. Right so far?"

Diaz nodded.

"According to the sister she disappeared on the evening of the nineteenth of February. Carmen, the sister, was away for that night. When she got back the house was a mess, the kids were hungry, Maria was gone. Maria's clothes were there, the sister got nervous and called the cops. They took the information, put out bulletins. It was snowing that night, there were no witnesses. We managed to find out that the missing woman had a boyfriend, a young guy, rich; as far as we can tell he was clean out of town when it happened. Then the kid gets himself killed in a motorcycle accident. End of story."

Diaz took a breadstick from his plate and rolled it between his fingers. "I could have given you that much."

Leary smiled. "I lied, there's more. According to the sister, Carmen, Maria was close to the parish priest over on One hundred sixteenth Street—Our Lady of Mercy, Catholics. She remembered noticing that her sister, for whatever reason, had been spending time recently at this church with this priest, so bam, we check the files. Father Josef Rodriguez from the same church is found minus his head in an alley on the morning of the twentieth. They did a thorough job whoever it was. They stabbed him first, then came back later and cut the head off with some sort of wire. According to the coroner, he was still alive."

"How come that story never made the papers?"

"It did. A priest was killed in an alley, front page *El Diario,* February twenty-first. The *Post* and the *News* had their hands full with a mass murder and stuffed the priest in up front near the WINGO's. What the media never got was the way he was killed. The church agreed with the police that we should hold onto that information in case we caught the guy."

"Did you?"

"If we had, you bet your ass the media would've run with it. Right now the detectives involved are 'exploring new evidence,' which as you know means they don't have a clue."

Diaz said, "A young mother of three who regularly attends the same church as the butchered priest is reported missing. According to the sister and my client, she disappeared on or around the same night that Father Rodriguez is found with his head cut off in an alley in the snow."

48

"There's more than one angle here, Diaz. The woman had a penchant for making friends at bars and staying overnight. That's what the sister told the two-three detectives."

"And on that basis nobody bothers to note the coincidence between the priest and the missing girl. Beautiful police work."

"Look, it wasn't my case, it wasn't my precinct. They've got their men on it. You're not the only genius in New York. I'm sure they've figured out this angle and it led nowhere. So maybe it *was* a coincidence. I don't know."

"A lunatic kills a priest at night in Spanish Harlem and no one sees anything. Did the guy leave any clues, sometimes lunatics get sloppy," Diaz said.

"Sometimes, but not all the time. This guy was professional, from the car he drove right down to his size fifteen boots. The car's tires were so bald, they couldn't lift the tread out of the snow."

"He was big?"

"Two hundred fifty, maybe three hundred pounds. He makes me look like an altar boy and next to him you weren't even born; you were still a seed in Ponce. The priest's neck was sawn clean through, not torn. It takes muscle to do that with wire. It takes weight."

"Is that all?" Diaz asked, imagining the night in the alley in the snow, picturing the killing, the snow flecked with blood, Maria.

"No, this is all." Leary reached into his hung-up jacket, fished around, and pulled out a black wire brush with a cardboard tag dangling from its handle. "He dropped this. We think it fell out of the car."

Diaz had seen its type before. Short and square with half-inch wire bristles, it was the type of brush used for grooming dogs. "He a dog lover?"

"Yep, Doberman Pinschers. Saint Nicholas Avenue Pekinese. The wire was full of Doberman hairs when they found it. No prints, just hairs, so they did a rundown of the kennels within the city limits. No one knew anyone matching the big guy's MO who raised dobermans or dogs or had a thing for priests or Spanish women. No one knew much of anything except that the priest was well-liked in the neighborhood. If there's a homo connection or if this Father Rodriguez was dicking Maria, no one knew it."

"How was it left?" Diaz asked. "Is this another case of a victim bound for anonymity?"

"Could be. Could be." Leary took a long sip of wine and sighed. "In the event that the girl was in the alley with the priest and wasn't just a runaway, then it would look like she was kidnapped and the priest got in the way."

"Brilliant."

"Okay, wise guy, what's your solution? Are you the one with all the answers? If so, don't waste my time and get out there and do your number."

Diaz said, "I heard that Maria slept around. Did they do a rundown of past partners or Tim Deluca when he was alive?"

"There's only so much anyone can do in a case where there are no suspects and no witnesses and the immediate family is in the dark about what their dead relation was really up to. Shit, Diaz, you should know that. You were a cop. Quit this playing cute shit. It don't suit you." Leary stared at Diaz while he lit another cigarette. "How you doing these days, anybody serious in the picture to wash your underwear?"

"No, no one. How's Nilsa?"

Leary withdrew his wallet and pulled a billfold from inside it. He extended a plastic-coated color photograph of a rather heavy-set Hispanic woman with curly hair and an astonishingly pretty smile. "Forty years old last August and she's still turning heads."

"She's still pretty. How are the kids?"

"They're fine, only Nilsa's moaning that she wants another one. Can you imagine it, as if five ain't enough already. What's wrong with your people, Diaz, what's this obsession with screaming babies and changing diapers?"

50

"Haven't you heard? It's a plot to take over New York."

Both men smiled and Leary said, "Spics," under his breath. "Who gave you the suit? I don't recognize you without that navy blue thing you used to wear. You look like you should be running a whorehouse somewhere, which I guess is an improvement."

Diaz remembered the young woman who lived in Maria's building, trying without success to picture her. He got the raven hair and full cheeks and most of the dark eyes and chin, but the face as a whole eluded him. He remembered her anger.

Sally had mentioned the cockfights. So far Leary hadn't. "What do you know about the cockfights, they still doing that?"

"You asking me, you're the Puerto Rican, remember? I'm just the humble Irish hard-on who tries to keep junk off the playground and his dick in a warm place." Leary drumrolled his squat fingers. "Why cockfights?"

"I don't know, I wouldn't mind seeing one, that's all. I'd like to make more of an effort to understand my culture." He smiled.

"I got that from the suit."

9

He walked home from dinner via Lexington Avenue, past the house where the women worked at selling affection by the half hour. One of the girls was downstairs on the stoop in front of her building dressed in leather shorts and a tee shirt. She recognized him and smiled. "Hey there, dude. Maybe you like some Dominican love today?" She jerked the tee shirt up so he could glimpse her breasts. The nipples were long and brown.

"No thank you," Diaz said, his words flat and unswayable. The girl bummed a cigarette off him and went back inside. He looked up at the house. There were nine rooms on three different floors in the tenement and he knew them all. The madam had a fetish for trying to "type" you and sending you to the same room and the same girl again and again, making it easier for her to know who was screwing whom and where.

52

Diaz didn't like this. He visited infrequently and wanted no routine; having a routine meant he needed it.

For a moment he lost himself and was transported back to the apartment in the Bronx. Tina, whom he'd been determined to marry, was coming home from her job at the laundry. She was devoutly Catholic, and more to please her than for any other reason Diaz had become nearly as devout. Each night in bed, the lust coursing through them, they would lie awake in each other's arms, professing their love, reiterating their belief in a God who forbade them sex before marriage. And each night as they lay tightly entwined, impassioned as only the truly frustrated are impassioned, his erect penis against her flat stomach, she would say a prayer to help her in her quest for chastity.

She'd come home from the laundry and he was studying the material from the Police Academy in the tiny half-room that served as a kitchen. She'd come up behind him, throwing her arms around him suddenly. He leapt up away from her. (The particular manual he was studying dealt with cop killings.) "Goddamnit, don't do that!" he snapped.

She felt embarrassed and yelled back how he was always studying.

Diaz replied that if he didn't study they'd never get out of this dump.

"This dump" happened to be her mother's apartment. She called him insensitive and said that studying for the Police Department was more important to him than her; and very seriously he'd answered, "Yes, it is."

"You admit it!" She fled the room in tears.

He found her in their bedroom under the sheets pretending to be asleep. He undressed and got in beside her and she turned immediately to hold him. They apologized. He said that nothing meant more to him than her. She said he was not "insensitive," just ambitious which was a good thing. They kissed. Her nightgown was pulled low so one of her breasts showed. He kissed it and she let him. Before he

53

knew it he was inside her and all the passion they'd felt for so long but never yielded to, overwhelmed them. They made love all night and when the morning came, they greeted it like any other morning only now they were truly a couple, and nothing could ever come between them and their love would never wane.

And until she was shot to death in a Shopwell three years later, it never did.

A gust of cool air scattered leaves across the street. A can rolled up the gutter making a hollow sound, urban music. The autumn wind made his ears cool. He thought of the dark-haired girl, Sally. An odd mixture of longing and guilt moved through him, and suddenly the need to go into the tenement wasn't so great.

10

In his apartment Diaz dressed in a dark corduroy coat, faded jeans, and a pair of cowboy boots, which he pulled on while lying on the floor. In his pocket were five hundred forty dollars from his stash beneath the bathtub drain. Five hundred was for Alphonse toward the Jaguar. Forty was for the cockfights: he felt lucky tonight.

He stepped into the smoke of Alphonse's Bar. An old man in a hat slapped a domino on the bar and cackled. The middleweight champ picked his teeth with a toothpick and stared at Diaz. The kid looked lean and young tonight and Diaz had the sudden notion that maybe he'd been too rough on him. "What's the matter, you don't serve Puerto Ricans in here?" Diaz asked.

The Spanish men along the bar looked at him. The domino player said something unintelligible and moved a domino around on the bar top. The kid watched Diaz from the register. "What?"

"A beer."

When it came Diaz thanked him. "Alphonse in?"

"You see his car outside?" the kid asked.

Diaz hadn't. "Nope, where is he?"

"I ain't his old lady."

Diaz watched him polish a polished glass and wondered: can I trust this prick with five hundred dollars for the fat man? Alternatively he could bring the money to the fights: risky. He appraised the kid: riskier.

Diaz sipped deeply from the beer. He sighed. "Life treating you any better, Pancho, since I last saw you? You still preoccupied watching Alphonse's ass for him?"

The kid looked at him suddenly as if he might charge.

"Look, I'm not saying that's a bad thing. In fact, that's my line of work, watching over others," Diaz said.

"Hey, save it. I don't get paid to listen to every bullshitter that walks in here, that ain't my job."

"Still riled about our altercation. Life is full of altercations, man, get used to it." Diaz finished the beer in one long sustained swig. He wiped his mouth and cleared the suds off of his moustache. "Maybe you were only doing your job and I jumped the gun. I'm a very jumpy guy, sometimes."

Diaz peeled a ten from his stack of mostly fifties and put it under the glass. "Tell him you saw me, will you?"

"I'm leaving early tonight," the kid said, and Diaz shrugged.

He found the dock on 138th Street and the Harlem River. A vacated warehouse stood at the end of the pier propped up on a stretch of old pilings. The pilings were slanted and uneven and colored black with creosote. At first he saw no activity from the warehouse and he wondered if it was happening tonight. Then came the faint impassioned shouting of a crowd of gamblers. Soft light trickled through a space in the door. The door swung open or shut, Diaz couldn't tell which. A blanket was pulled to one side. Two silhouetted figures hurried past it.

Diaz opened the dilapidated plank door and brushed past the moth-eaten blanket. He smelt beer and beyond this the coppery smell of animal blood. The cavernous room was filled with wooden bleachers and strung with spotlights aimed at what he thought must have been a fight pit. It was obscured by the bleachers. People were hollering and jumping up and down waving fistfuls of colored paper.

Then the noise subsided dramatically followed by a sort of jointly uttered sigh. Most of the spectators sat down, tearing their colored betting slips to pieces and throwing them into the air. Some of the luckier ones remained on their feet, cheering.

"You got anything to declare?" a gruff voice asked. Someone touched him. Diaz turned toward a squat bearded man in a Greek fisherman's cap. On his chest was a little yellow button that said, "Staff."

"No," Diaz said.

"You're a new face. I got to check you anyway."

The squat man wasn't Spanish. Diaz thought he was probably Greek or Arab. His face had been beaten before and one of his cheeks was flat. Brusquely, he ran his hands over the detective's body. "You're all right. Give your donation and move on."

Diaz asked, "Donation for what?" Two patrons moved in line behind him.

"The church, wise guy, and all the starving orphans and Tony-the-Muscle who owns the operation and pays the 'man' off. We ain't been busted in three years which is like a record in the business. You go back there, you'll find two cops and a sergeant. Pay the donation or get out. I don't care what you do, but do something."

Willy produced a stray five-dollar bill. "That'll do," the man said, and plucked it. He handed the note to an even

57

squatter man in a houndstooth jacket, smoking a cigar in a holder. "Next."

The smoke and sawdust swirled ethereally toward the rafters, growing cloudy in the heat of the spotlights. Diaz sat down in the bleachers beside three brothers dressed in identical green leisure suits. Below, in the pit formed by the four sides of the bleachers, was the arena. It was squared with sheets of plywood, and the wood was spattered with blood and feathers like a tapestry of the macabre. The sawdust in the pit was lumpy with congealed animal blood and bits of torn feathers and flesh. The intense heat of the spotlights served to cook the insides of the pit, emitting a sour metallic smell, which reminded Diaz vaguely of his three professional fights.

A boy in a white coat came up to him and from a cigar box sold him ten slips of red paper. "Good choice man," the boy said. "Him's the favorite." Each slip had "Zoro" penned across it next to the signature of the bird's owner.

Two men appeared on either side of the arena. The cock birds they carried were large and full breasted, their feathers puffed up in fear. Spurs secured to their obscenely thick ankles glimmered like quicksilver under the lights.

A trumpeter belted two discordant notes. The birds flew into the ring after an encouraging shove from their handlers. Bits of feathers and sawdust billowed up as the animals circled, their magnificent clipped wings spread for balance. After a minute of this, Diaz's bird, "Zoro," the favorite, saw an opening and made a valiant lunge at the smaller bird. The smaller bird dodged adroitly like a boxer, then sprang, catching "Zoro" with a short kick to his neck. The wounded bird stumbled and made a human sound, silencing for an instant the roar of the spectators.

For a few long seconds the hurt bird sauntered around the ring, considering its options, looking distracted, blood soaking the bright downy breast. The smaller bird struck again, ripping into "Zoro" and kicking ferociously at the wound in its neck. The larger bird sank to its knees under the barrage. Spurs gleamed like tiny knives. And then it was over.

Diaz watched the fight with a squeamish expression. The "favorite" had just lost him ten dollars. The birds were separated. A rake was drawn over the sawdust in the pit blotting the carnage. Two more handlers with two more birds appeared near the arena. The handlers were arguing with each other. The crowd of regulars seemed to enjoy this and it reminded Diaz of the bantering between the managers in professional wrestling. The comparison was not far off.

He sat through three fights, enough to blow thirty dollars. By then the morbid fascination of the sport had worn off and he simply felt repulsed. The bleachers were packed by now. When he stood up, his space was immediately filled by the mass of spectators.

He'd noticed a woman in a wooden booth selling beer. He waited in line to talk to her. The trumpet sounded and the line dispersed as the next fight commenced. Diaz ordered a beer. She served him one in a paper quart container; it tasted flat. "Señorita," he said above the noise, "I'm looking for a friend who worked here at nights. She's disappeared and her family's very worried because she's sick. I want to know if you've seen her."

"Are you a cop?"

"Yes."

She looked him over and opened her eyes wide to stretch the wrinkles. Her lipstick was smeared. "You ain't no cop, handsome, and if you are you got no business here so kiss my patoot."

He slid Maria's photo along the counter. "Her name was Maria Juarez. She had long bleached hair. She's been missing for eight months."

"Is that so." The woman flicked the photo back at him. "Nope, never seen her. Somebody must have bullshit you. No girl like that was ever here, and I been here forever."

She raised a quart cup of beer and inhaled from it. "You lonely tonight?"

Diaz pocketed the picture. He believed her. The more he saw of the scene, the less probable it seemed that Maria would ever work here. She could have sold beer or taken in bets or worked the door, but that didn't seem likely given what Deluca had told him.

He did a circuit of the filthy hall, and thought of Sally's tip. Hesitating in the midst of the cavernous room he thought: *she bluffed you*, and he walked out.

The air had a wet chill and the night was black. There were lights on the bank, but none on the pier, and for the length of his walk on the dock he'd be traveling in total darkness. He lowered his neck. Four men walked by him into the warehouse.

Twenty yards toward the land a man moved into his path on the dock. After a second Diaz recognized the outline of the Greek who'd searched him at the door. The man's hands were in an unnaturally stiff position at his sides. "You didn't come to see no fights, *amigo*, am I right?"

Diaz continued toward him. "I'm looking for a woman, she wasn't there."

"That's just like a woman," the Greek said, sidestepping so he rested more squarely before the detective.

"Is it?" Diaz moved slowly, feeling the air.

"Who are you?"

The Harlem River lapped against the pilings below. Diaz heard a creek of timber. The muffled roars of the crowd inside covered the sound. He turned to see two men approaching with their hands out. In the darkness he didn't think he saw a weapon. He'd taken his eyes off the Greek; this was his mistake.

Immediately he felt a sickening bolt of pain in his gut. The air rushed out of his lungs as the Greek's head buried into his solar plexus. Diaz buckled under the sudden force. He did a quick two-step to keep from falling on his back, then rocked forward onto his knees. He hit hard and felt a sharp pain up his spine.

"You shouldn't interfere, tough guy," the Greek said. "Now we have to teach you a lesson." The two men joined the Greek and took up places to either side, cutting off Diaz's exit from the pier. They were large men and powerful. The Greek whipped a length of chain from his belt. He wrapped it once around his hand, stepped, and swung. The chain whistled. Diaz leapt forward, cutting off the distance, and took the chain on his extended arm, felt it wrap and catch, cutting off the circulation. Instantly he tugged on it, using his weight. The Greek lost his balance and had no alternative but to go with the momentum. Diaz struck him as hard as he could on the mouth; blood spurted across his knuckles. The man staggered; Diaz tripped him and put a boot in his testicles. The Greek screamed. The chain went flying.

Diaz turned toward the gap in the human blockade. They'd closed in on him. One of the men kicked at him and his left knee throbbed with pain. He stood still and got hit on the jaw. Light flashed in his eyes.

He came to in a fetal position with his ribs on fire. They were kicking him and instinctively he had balled up. The Greek was back. He took his turn and swung his short leg. Diaz grabbed the foot and twisted it savagely, something snapped and the Greek fell backward into the arms of his companions. Diaz pushed off against the splintery dock.

The chain hit him in the base of the throat and he slipped and suddenly all three of them were holding him, forcing him to his feet. His boots scraped the boardwalk. Someone was pulling his hair. They stood him up and Diaz waited for them to force him to the edge and into the cold black river.

The Greek's mouth was bleeding and his eyes were wet. He caught his breath, taking great gulpfuls of air through his broken mouth. "You cocksucker . . . now you're getting yours."

61

Diaz struggled fiercely for a second. The Greek took a breath and swung solidly into the detective's belly. "Oof!" Diaz crumpled. The chain was on the dock behind them. Suddenly Diaz noticed the middleweight champ from Alphonse's Bar standing casually along the pier watching it all. He figured he was hallucinating, then wondered if the kid was behind the attack.

One of the others said, "Let me take a whack."

"Shut up your mouth, he's mine." The Greek jerked Diaz's head up by the hair. He punched him on the temple; his head snapped but he stayed conscious. He squinted and saw the kid, still back there, watching it like a spectator. "Okay, pretty boy, you had to interfere." The Greek sucked air through his loose teeth. "Now we're going to fix it so you ain't pretty no more. Then next time when I see you, you'll know better than to fuck with anybody who has anything to do with this establishment."

He probed Diaz's pockets and removed the cash without counting it and stuffed it into his coat. "You probably won that money off me anyway."

Then the bartender from Alphonse's lifted the discarded chain from the dock and hit the Greek with it in the back of the head. The tough Greek whinnied and fell bonelessly.

The kid threw the chain into the water. "Okay, it's fair now."

The men dropped Diaz and went for the younger man, their hard faces furious. Diaz staggered and spread his legs for balance. The pier loomed up at him in the blackness.

The kid threw two quick left-right combinations and the men were on their asses on the pier. After a moment the tallest man stood back up slowly, shaking his head. He raised his hands like a boxer. One of his eyes was swelling. The kid tipped forward calmly and, when the man got near enough, jumped, landing a terrific blow to the body beneath the ribs. The victim dropped and immediately began to vomit.

The kid took Diaz by the forearm and steadied him.

62

"What took you so long?"

"You were doing okay," the kid said. "We should throw them over."

"No," said Diaz hoarsely, holding his ribs. "Don't."

After a pause, the kid said, "It's your gig."

Diaz took a deep breath and stooped over the Greek. He located his five hundred dollars and pried it loose from the pocket. It came out with an additional hundred. This he put back. He nearly fell over when he stood and again the kid had to steady him.

"You know," Diaz said, hesitating to get his breath. "I thought tonight I was going to be lucky. I really believed that." He heard himself speak. The words were distant and muted, as if he were speaking underwater.

"You were," the kid said. "I was here."

On Second Avenue they stopped under a streetlight. Diaz watched for a cab. He looked at the kid. The younger man's hands were in his pockets and his forehead was sweaty. "I got to go," the kid said.

"Where?" Diaz wondered then why he'd asked it. Maybe the kid looked lonely.

"The dock. I got some money to win back from last week."

"What about your friends?"

"They ain't my friends," he said looking at the street, avoiding eye contact. "I'll risk it."

Diaz took his money out and separated two hundred dollars from the pile. "Alphonse tells me you've got ambition. You want to be a fighter."

"Not want to be, I am. I got my license Tuesday."

"Here." Diaz handed him the two hundred. "Consider that your first pro fight back there. I'm glad I was around to see it."

The kid pushed the money away so Diaz stuffed it into the kid's baggy trousers. "Goodnight." He stepped forward to hail a taxi. He didn't turn, but after a minute he heard the little cleated walk of the kid's boots on the pavement. Then a cab stopped.

11

A doctor at St. Luke's whom Diaz knew from his police days put two stitches in a gash on his brow. The ribs weren't broken, just badly bruised, as was his collarbone where he'd been hit with the chain. He walked home full of aspirin, limping.

He had the Doberman lead and ran with it, spending the morning on the telephone, calling every dog kennel outside of the city within a fifteen-mile radius. According to Leary, the police had checked the inner-city establishments and come up empty. Diaz's line went like this: "Hello, this is Mr. Winston of *Field and Stream* magazine. I've got a problem and I thought I would ask the advice of an expert." (Quickly but calmly.) "To whom do I have the pleasure of speaking?"

"Tom, Tom Fowler."

"Tom, I know this might sound unusual, but we're doing a piece in the magazine on some of the well-known Doberman Pinscher breeders in the area."

"Which magazine?"

"Field and Stream."

"Really?"

"Yeah, and there's this one Doberman owner I've been trying to track down."

"Well, who is it? I been in the business twenty-five years, maybe I know him?" Tom asked, caught up in the enthusiasm.

"I'm sure you would, Tom, but the crazy thing is I can't remember his name. A big fellow, huge. Tall and about two hundred fifty to three hundred pounds."

"Christ, if I'd seen him I'd remember. It doesn't sound like anyone in this area. Did you try Hawke breeders? They're pretty well-connected."

Diaz made fifty-eight calls and got nothing, no leads. The world was full of small people who bought Dobermans to compensate for their lack of stature. He changed tactics, altering his pitch slightly, and called those businesses that sold, trained, and supplied attack dogs. One lead: there was a big guy who owned a kennel in Rye, New York. Diaz called him. He was big all right, his wife said, but he'd been dead for two years and frankly, she thought the world was a better place without him and if this was about a debt he could jolly well . . .

It was ten to three when he finished. He'd been on the case for almost two days. Deluca had promised to double the money if Diaz found the girl within the week. The prospect of a fast find was growing less likely.

He lit a filterless cigarette and set his legs on the desk, using the pain he knew this maneuver would generate as a stimulus to clear his mind. The sister would have to know something, he decided. Christ they lived together. The fact that the cops weren't able to get anything out of her didn't

65

mean much. Unless Maria's disappearance was a random act by a madman, there had to be a connection somewhere. He thought: three-quarters of all kidnap victims know their abductors.

Unless it was the work of a madman, in which case nothing he could do would turn up a body that was rolled up in a rug and stuck in an abandoned car, or buried in the Pine Barrens of New Jersey, or sunk in a lake.

According to the cops the killer had stabbed the priest first, then gone back ten minutes later to cut the head off. What kind of a lunatic has the patience or nerve to take ten minutes to kill anyone? Murders are swift, impetuous acts, rarely thought out. Leary had given him some figures: the killer was huge, wore size fifteen shoes.

The phone rang and he jumped. He let it ring while he gathered his composure. Why were phones so fucking loud? He grabbed it. "Yes. Diaz."

"I'm calling you about yesterday," the female voice said. It took him an instant to place it. It was the same voice, but strained.

"Go on," he said smoothly.

"I lied to you. I had no idea who you were."

"This is Sally," Diaz said, remembering.

"That's not my name." She paused. There followed a space of fifteen seconds when he thought maybe she'd hung up. "I want to meet with you. You know where I live."

"I can be there in twenty minutes," Diaz said. "Or whenever suits you." His heart was pounding in his throat beneath the sore collarbone.

"Twenty minutes is fine. Don't come in, I'll meet you outside."

For three days he'd been wearing the same white shirt. He showered, put on a fresh one, and changed into a brown tie with a stripe in it.

She was standing by the stoop to her building. Her black hair was pinned back with a slight fringe falling on her per-

66

fect forehead. A blue cotton skirt fell to her knees. The ankles were slender and the calves firm and her skin was a shade darker than he'd remembered it. He offered his hand as an excuse to touch her. She seemed to realize this and instead of shaking it, simply stared at it.

Diaz said, "You're not Sally, of course you're not. There is no Sally. You're Carmen and Maria was your sister and you're worried about her. You lied to me because you didn't know what side I was on."

"Which side are you on?"

"There only is one side, the side that wants Maria found."

This made sense to her and she nodded. "You brought food for the children. My grandparents said you were kind. That's partly why I called."

Her look was that of a penned-up animal, calm, but not altogether trusting. He wondered if she ever smiled. "Should we go inside?" Diaz asked.

"No." She looked at him. "You got those cuts last night at the cockfights." When he didn't answer she said, "I have a cousin who works there and he told me there was a fight outside. Someone was asking questions who they thought was a gangster from the West Side. Three men were badly beaten on the pier and one is in the hospital. You must've won."

"I had help."

"Well, I'm sorry." She wrapped her thin arms defensively around her chest and her bosom looked bigger. "I shouldn't have sent you there," she said more to herself than out loud.

"Why did you? Did Maria go to the fights?"

"My sister didn't know what the fights were. I don't know why, it just came into my head. You were determined that I tell you something, so I did to get rid of you. It was crazy."

Diaz laughed. She looked at him, bemused. "Come on." They walked two blocks and stood at a water fountain near the subway. The fountain was broken and the copper had

67

been sawed off long ago and sold by the pound to finance a dope habit.

Carmen said, "I've thought about this for months, although I could never really make sense of it. It still seems unreal to me that Maria is missing. You hear about all the terrible things that can happen to people in this world, but you never think it could happen to you. Maria was a good person, as a mother she was incredibly caring, especially after she lost her husband."

Diaz nodded and wondered how old Carmen was.

"Maria never lost hope. That's the thing I admire most about her; she was so strong and had such faith."

She had flawless teeth. He wondered if she'd ever had braces. "Faith in what?" he asked. "In God?"

"Yes, in God too, but mostly she had faith in mankind."

"Was Maria close to a priest named Rodriguez from Our Lady of Mercy?"

She nodded solemnly.

"He's dead, you know?"

"Yes."

"Had Maria been seeing him more recently than at other times?"

"I don't think . . ." She stopped. "Yes. It was hard for her to make Mass everyday with the children. But lately, before she disappeared, she'd been going regularly, at least once a day and twice on the weekends."

"Did that seem odd to you?"

"No. I loved Maria but we had different characters. We were close but distant if you can understand that. If she needed me, however, I was there for her and I hope she felt the same way about me. I think she did."

"What about men, did she date anyone in particular that you knew?"

"She dated, but she never brought the men home. Home and her children were sacred to Maria."

"They miss their daddy," Diaz said, thinking out loud, remembering the little girl.

"They were all very small when the accident happened. I think it's more a question of them seeing other children with their fathers. Children are very observant people and very little escapes them. They see the other fathers and they want one. They need a man's influence—especially the boys."

"Did she ever mention her relationship with Tim Deluca, the young man who was killed on the motorcycle? There's some evidence she was thinking of marrying him." Diaz realized how little information he had on his client's son. A photo of the boy would have helped.

"Maria never mentioned wanting to marry anyone. I only heard about him through the police and he never came to the house ever, none of them did. She normally liked older men, though. She always had. Pedro, her husband, was fifteen years older than Maria." A police car sped down the avenue with its lights flashing. It swerved to avoid hitting a boy on a bicycle.

"The day Maria disappeared, she was planning to visit Tim Deluca in Maine for the weekend."

"She never mentioned it."

"Does that sound like Maria, to take a holiday and leave her kids behind?"

Carmen frowned. "She loved her children, but she had her own life too. Two or three times she took a brief vacation from the city and I looked after them. She would never leave them alone for long though, never. It went against her character." She checked her watch.

"When the police investigated, you told them all you knew. You'd been away for the night and when you got home Maria wasn't there and the kids were alone."

"Look, I've got an appointment, and I've been through this before."

Diaz took her by the wrist. Her skin was warm and he could feel her heart beating. "Why did you call me, Carmen?"

"Don't touch me." He let go. "Thank you."

She cleared her throat and looked at the spot on her arm

where he'd held her. "Because I remembered something and talking to you now I can't see that it's of any importance." She looked at him questioningly. She wanted support.

"It can't hurt. We both want to find your sister."

His words seemed to relax her and her expression softened. "Maria was having an affair. It wasn't her first and I'm not sure it was with only one man. You've probably gathered that much anyway. Maria liked men and saw nothing wrong with this. It was just her makeup, she needed them more than most women. Maria was also a dreamer and the men she knew represented an escape, from this." Carmen indicated the neighborhood with a negligent jerk of her head.

"One night I answered the phone. Maria and I sound alike and whomever it was must've thought I was my sister. He said to meet him at the regular 'watering hole.' He used those words. I said, 'Where?' and he said, 'Silly, the Madison Pub.' Then Maria picked up. I don't think he realized he had even spoken to me."

"Why does that stick out?"

"Maria had given up drinking. For her to meet a date at a bar meant it was a very special man, someone she genuinely cared for."

Diaz made a mental note of this and the name of the bar. "You never told the police?"

"No, I only just thought of it. Should I?"

"No, let me run with it first."

"Who hired you?"

"Tim Deluca's father. Losing his son took a lot out of him and I think he feels this is one way to show his love for the boy."

She hesitated, "I wouldn't have expected you to say something like that."

"It's never easy when you lose something special that you care about."

"No."

He changed subjects. "You didn't look like a Sally."

"Oh no?"

"No. You look more like a Rita or a Nina."

"Are you an authority on names or something?"

"Yes," he said earnestly. "As a matter of fact I am."

"How does Carmen rate?"

"Carmen's all right."

"Why thank you, sir."

Diaz realized suddenly that they were flirting. She didn't seem to mind. It had been years, he thought, since he'd been on a proper date and he wondered whether he was up to it or whether he should make the first move, and if he made a move whether he would make an ass out of himself. She moved and he said simply, "Can I see you sometime for a drink?"

She said, "Why?"

Why? Why the hell do you think? He looked at her and said honestly, "Because I think you could use a friend. And I know I could."

She seemed a little startled by his response and as he awaited an almost certain rejection, her eyes widened and some of the coldness left them. "Yes, I'd like that," she said.

Diaz thanked her and smiled nervously and walked away. He went a block before he found himself thinking: now what did I thank her for?

12

Cat and Mario were in the Chevrolet with the third man, Hector, a thin man with a bad complexion and small boyish features. They'd gone to see Joey Irish that morning for an advance: he'd given them just enough, and they'd shot it up and were parked illegally watching the girl's apartment. Cat had put it to Joey Irish that the dope he'd been feeding them was so stepped on that they barely got high from it. Irish said he would look into it and to placate Cat had promised him a job, later on, running cigarettes up from Georgia. Cat had to hand it to Irish, he sure had his fingers in a lot of pies.

The girl came out at 3:40 and waited on the sidewalk in front of her building. Cat entered the "development" onto the back of a magazine he used for taking notes. Sure enough the detective showed up shortly afterward; he recorded this on the magazine.

When the two of them went strolling, the blue Chevrolet started up and cruised a safe two blocks behind them. Diaz and the lady split and Cat followed her taxi to the building where he supposed she worked on 89th Street and Park Avenue. He parked the Chevy and decided, quite impulsively, that for a high-school dropout, he had an okay life. All he had to do was watch this cunt and look out for Diaz and a man in combat boots, and in return Joey Irish would keep him in junk plus slip him the odd fifty dollars for food. Joey Irish was an all right kind of guy. Cat wondered if all people from Ireland were as "regular" as Joey Irish was. . . . It could be. He made up his mind to go there someday. He might even join the IRA, whatever that was.

Diaz opened the Chevrolet's door on Mario's side of the car. He flashed a badge and put a .45 automatic across Mario's lap. He wedged in. "Start driving." Cat looked at him and blanched. He thought of Joey Irish and the supply of junk and what was at stake. He thought: fuck.

They drove to the waterfront on the West Side, downtown, and parked the car against a prostrated phone pole facing the Hudson.

Diaz asked for ID; they had none. He searched them in turn, keeping Deluca's confiscated automatic against Mario's throat. Mario, like Cat, was muscular and long-armed and rangy, but there was fear in his eyes. Diaz pegged him for the weak link and kept the automatic flush to his esophagus while he patted the others down as best he could. The third man, Hector, smiled at him.

"You ain't a cop," Cat protested.

"Shut up."

Diaz removed two switchblades and a pair of brass knuckles. As an afterthought he took the car keys and pocketed them. He got out of the Chevy and threw the weapons in the Hudson. Diaz got back in carefully; his search had been superficial: they may have had more.

Something in their faces prompted him to roll up Mario's

sleeves past the wrist. His hands were swollen at the joints. His dark skin was cratered and scarred.

He asked, "What would three junkies want with a secretary from Spanish Harlem?"

No one spoke so Diaz cocked the hammer on the automatic. Still no one said anything. He stepped out again, leaving the door open, and used the butt of the gun to break the rear window. Then he lowered the station wagon's tailgate and pulled back the tarp inside and stared at a selection of stolen video equipment. The merchandise was still in its boxes. In a blanket were some heavy shears, two crowbars, and a ball-peen hammer. Tools of the trade. An old gas receipt was crumpled in the space of the tailgate. He took it.

This could have explained it, Diaz mused. They were junkies and nothing meant more than their next fix. Their minds and ambitions were limited by this fact. But why would they be following her to work? Unless they planned to rob her office, or unless they were determining a pattern when she would be away from home. Intuitively he didn't buy it.

Diaz got back in the car and tried to bluff them again and got nowhere. There was no sense roughing them up. They were high. They could endure more than he could deliver; besides they hadn't actually done anything yet. Among other things he could be arrested for assault.

He took the registration and insurance card from the glove compartment. These would be forged.

He remembered something. He addressed the driver. "How'd you know I'm not a cop?"

Cat looked at him contemptuously. "You're too much of a prick even to be a cop. Cops got laws."

"That's a pretty naive statement coming from a pincushion like you," Diaz said.

"And that ain't a badge," Cat added.

This quieted Diaz. In reality the badge designated him as a member of the Parks Department. He wondered. Maybe

74

the guy was an authority on cop badges—it could be. Career criminals were experts on the most bizarre things. They had all that free time in prison thinking things out.

"I've seen you," Diaz said in parting. "Anything goes down with the lady in her apartment, at work, I'll spot you out of a mug book before you can pull your pants up."

They nodded back from their own drug-induced world.

Diaz opened the Chevrolet's hood and put five bullets in the engine block and carburetor. He leaned back inside the car. "Here." He tossed the keys in, then walked to Tenth Avenue and caught a bus.

13

At the apartment on Park Avenue, Carmen fixed herself a drink and folded her blazer over the arm of the couch. Before sitting down she snapped the light on over a ship painting above the mantle. She'd always had an interest in art and David had encouraged this. The walls of his apartment were adorned with paintings and sketches from the nineteenth and twentieth centuries. David owned a Thomas Hart Benton and a small Klee that hung, of all places, in the bathroom. His attitude toward art confused her. He professed to enjoy it, but when he spoke of his own collection, he invariably talked in terms of investments.

David came in as he always did, in a dinner jacket, carrying a book. It was as if he hadn't expected her. He smiled and leaned down and kissed her cheek. "You like that drink, don't you?"

76

"It has a good effect on me," she said matter of factly. "I don't get hung over." He'd taught her to drink dry martinis.

He put his book down. She saw the cover. He seemed to have been reading that same novel, a spy story, since they'd met. It was part of the charade, she decided: their evening together wasn't premeditated; she'd just dropped in out of the blue as she did every now and then.

"Did you have a good day?" David asked, fixing a brandy.

"Nothing unusual happened. I got some chores done and did a little reading. I wrote to a friend." She'd known him for four months and this was the depth and extent of their talks. She told him nothing and he accepted it.

"That sounds pleasant enough. Did you see the weather reports? It's snowing in Vermont already."

"No, I missed that," she said.

David nodded and finished his brandy. Always one drink, no more. He stopped to admire the painting over his fireplace. "I heard from a dealer Jacobsons are now bringing five figures," he said.

He might have been good-looking once. From the pictures she'd seen, she thought so. He was a large man, a little heavy in the hips. His legs were too short to make him well proportioned. His face was lean and his expression thoughtful but remote. He'd had acne as a young man and had some scars on one cheek.

"Shall we rest?" he asked.

Always that word.

Carmen felt a sensation like heat running through her. "Yes."

He lay on the bed in a robe. The bed was vast and covered with a satin duvet. Propping himself up against the large quilted headboard, he lit a joint.

Carmen removed her blouse and hung it up. She stepped out of her skirt and added this to the hanger. Then she went over, this was how he liked her, and stood beside him at the bed. He probed the spot beneath her cotton panties with

77

strong fingers. "You're very wet tonight." She took the joint from him and hit on it, then crushed it dead in the ashtray.

His fingers slid in to the hilt into the warmth and she shuddered. Kneeling on the bed she reached behind and unfastened her brassiere. Her breasts were heavy and pert, the nipples fully erect and red with blood. She lifted his head and drew it closer. He suckled her while he worked the slippery flesh beneath the panties. Her mouth opened and her lips snapped back. "Oh God."

She clasped her flat belly with two open hands and closed her eyes while the fever built. It was happening tonight, she thought, she would come. She opened her dark eyes and reached for him. The robe fell away. His penis was monstrous. She gripped it and felt its heat and strength and burning desire. Her body was drained of everything but the hunger for his cock inside her.

She stooped and sucked him, smelling him. He groaned. She could barely get her lips around it, his girth was so enormous. Then she sat up and shimmied around and put her vagina before his face and he rubbed his prickly chin against her full thighs and placed his hands on her round buttocks and worked the muscle. He ate her right through the panties and she cried, "Harder," and he yanked the panties aside with his teeth and plunged his long tongue inside her, probing, licking wildly, sucking her insides into his mouth. She came violently.

While she lay in a pleasurable exhausted delirium on the bed, he moved her around and positioned himself on top of her. With his hand he directed his huge penis to the mouth of her vagina. It slid in easily, all but an inch sinking inside her. He grabbed her breasts and kissed her deeply. She tasted herself. He began stroking slowly. Carmen felt the fire come alive again and responded, meeting each thrust, raising her pelvis, matching his energy with hers. Their movements grew more furious. She grabbed his testicles and squeezed and felt him begin to buck and then the violent jerking of his loins, and finally the heat of his come. She cried out reflexively and he gripped her. "Carmen," he gasped. And for a brief fading moment she was in love with him.

David was curled up, asleep, beside her. She smoked a joint and stared at the molding along the ceiling and mused over the animal satisfaction and delights of sex. Eventually these thoughts departed and she was left with herself in bed with David, and she tried vainly to keep the picture of Willy Diaz from her mind. For some reason he kept coming back until she thought about her date with him. The idea of it made her uncomfortable so she fixed another martini, drank it, and got back in bed.

In the morning they repeated their performance, David choosing to mount her from behind. Afterward she dressed and put Kleenex beneath her panties to blot his seed.

He met her in the kitchen. She kissed him lightly on the chin. They ate a desultory breakfast of toast and eggs and drank orange juice with champagne in it, a "Buck's Fizz," David called it.

"I've got a full day ahead of me," David said. "Will I see you tonight?"

"No," she said, though she wasn't sure why she'd said it.

"Really, very well. Why don't you call me when you're next free. All right?"

They paused in the drawing room. Her empty martini glass was there from last night. Looking at it and the painting and the room, depressed her. Maybe she was outgrowing this, she thought . . . but the money.

"Here you are, darling." David extended a short white envelope. His initials were engraved on the back side. "I hope these expenses will suffice. It's been lovely as usual."

Carmen nodded—the rules of their charade decreed that she never thank him. They embraced. He kissed her black shiny head of hair. She felt his kiss linger for longer than usual. Then he stepped back. "I'll miss you."

79

"Yes, David," she said, and left.

She waited until she reached her bank uptown to open the envelope. She stood in line with her bankbook out, tore the envelope, and peered inside. She gasped. The check was for two thousand dollars. He'd never given that much money before. Quickly she calculated the two thousand against her savings. She now had eight thousand five hundred dollars; another twelve thousand and she could put the down payment on the house in New Jersey, for Maria's children. Guilt assailed her. They were her children now. Her turn came up in line: she deposited the check and withdrew one hundred fifty dollars in cash for household expenses.

The air was milder than last night, though still cool. As she walked into the church on 96th Street, she wondered if rain was imminent. She liked the rain.

The priest came in after ten minutes and sat on the opposite side of the confessional and blessed her. She began in a controlled fashion, then burst into floods of tears. It was worse than normal and she wondered why. She looked at her hands and saw she was trembling.

The priest moved—a dim silhouette behind the screen. "Come now child, God will never ostracize you from His kingdom as long as you don't deny him. Take your time. Begin again." The priest's words were gentle and sympathetic.

She breathed deeply and held her hands tightly to her chest. She nodded once, a short tight movement, and shut her eyes. It took a great deal of strength and she was exhausted, but she managed. "Forgive me, Father, for I have sinned . . ."

14

Diaz went to the Madison Pub and drank whiskeys and water. The small bar was situated below street level; you could gaze up and see the sidewalk and the passersby peering in at the privileged. Occasionally a little dog pissed on the window. The room smelt of pipe tobacco and had the clubby ambience that reminded Diaz of churches and of Ivy League colleges he'd never seen. He'd almost gone to City College.

A man in a tweed coat got up and fed some money into the jukebox and got a dollar's worth of Sinatra. He looked at Diaz as the detective lit a filterless cigarette.

It was mildly crowded for a Thursday night, nice crowd, Upper East Side, youngish; charge cards and trust funds and weekends in the country in houses with Portuguese maids. He knew this world from books.

After forty-five minutes he figured he'd been there long enough and drunk enough bourbons for the bartender to feel relaxed with him. The barman passed by and Diaz said, "You know, I'm looking for a friend who used to come here. She's disappeared and her family's worried. I thought maybe you'd recognize her." He added, "The police are on it."

The bartender looked at him disdainfully. "You're the police?"

Diaz said, "No."

"Can't help you, friend." The bartender sauntered back to talk to a pair of businessmen at the far end of the bar. He was vintage New York: crew cut and wise-guy demeanor with shirts tailored to show off his shoulders and arms. A tattoo on one of them said "Louise." Diaz knew the type: an asshole. New York bars were renowned for them.

Taking the picture from his coat, he laid it face up on the bar. The bartender couldn't help looking over. "You're Mickey," Diaz said in his direction.

Mickey lifted his bulk slowly off of his elbows. He strode over. "Yeah, that's me, but who are you?"

"I telephoned earlier. I'm looking for this woman, Maria, who used to drink here. There's a chance she's been abducted. Kidnapped."

"I know what abducted means, friend."

Diaz thought cynically: he's educated. Mickey took an obligatory glance at Maria. The loose skin around his eyes tightened and he waited a beat. "Never met her."

"She came here regularly with a date up until six or seven months ago."

"You're guessing, friend," Mickey said without much interest. "Because she never came here. I'd know her if she did. I know everybody regular."

"No, I think maybe you just forgot. I know she came here. I have witnesses who'll swear it."

Mickey picked a piece of ice from a bowl and sucked on it. He said out of the side of his mouth, "You looking for an

82

argument, friend? She never came here and you got no witnesses." He spat the ice over Diaz's shoulder. "Look around,
this is a white establishment, lots of gringos here. Very few
bean eaters. We don't get lots of your kind dancing in giving
the place atmosphere."

Diaz felt his throat tighten. "I've had a long day," he said
wearily. "Is that necessary?"

Mickey laughed and crossed his thick arms. Louise's tattoo
undulated. "You're beautiful, you are." He spread a hand flat
on the bar. The knuckles were scarred and mangled. He
made sure Diaz saw them.

Diaz had Deluca's automatic in his coat.

Mickey pressed forward against the bar and leaned to
within six inches of Diaz. He lowered his voice to a whisper
and Diaz could smell his breath. "You've had a long day,
amigo? Haven't we all, haven't we fucking all. I don't know
what you meant by that, but listen pancho, you don't know
shit so you're fishing. You got no evidence that bitch was
here before, but someone tells you she was so you believed
them and you come in here to shake it out of me. I told you
one thing and you don't want to listen."

"I'll listen when you say something."

"Get out you piece a shit."

Diaz stirred his drink with a finger. He tasted it and put it
down and stared at Mickey. A waiter slipped behind the bar
and set six beer mugs on a tray. Sinatra came on singing
about the summer wind. The waiter, a black, walked
by Diaz, frowning. Diaz kept one finger pinned to the picture of Maria. "What are you afraid of, man?" Diaz said.
"You'd think a guy your size would have some balls . . .
somewhere."

Mickey toyed with his scarred fingers. He picked up
Diaz's drink and threw it in his face. Diaz reached instinctively into his pocket. Mickey flushed a piece of pipe from
under the bar and raised it. "Get the fuck out of here spic-
boy before I smack you. And if you find Charo, tell her she's

keeping the wrong kind of company if she's got a faggot like you on her ass."

Then Diaz smiled, faintly, and Mickey raised the pipe an inch. For a moment Willy expected him to swing it and he prepared to duck. The moment dragged on and he said, "Thanks, Mickey. And I'll see you again."

The bartender said something Diaz couldn't hear over the hammering of his heart. He stood outside on the curb, feeling weak with the fear.

Mickey had called her "Charo," Diaz thought. Wasn't Charo the name of a middle-aged Spanish singer who featured big breasts and skimpy sequined outfits and blond hair? Bleached blond hair like Maria's? Diaz remembered that Deluca had said she had bleached blond hair. He withdrew the photograph and looked at the fine handsome features of the girl and her luminous eyes and the paisley scarf about her head completely covering her hair. Now why would he call *her* Charo? he wondered.

He went home and tried not to think about the priest in the alley or Mickey and drank two quarts of beer with the lights off.

15

Diaz waited until a secretary in a miniskirt came out to the reception area and smiled at him. "Mr. Ramone will see you now." He stood up and smoothed down the crease in his pants and followed her. The corridors of the building owned by Channel 5 were dark and somewhat cheap looking, not at all what he'd expected from one of the major local television stations in the country. A woman he recognized as the "Miss Manner's" hostess came skipping through a side door carrying a valise. Two gay men dressed as clowns complained about the temperature of the coffeemaker.

Diaz was ushered into a large office consisting of a Persian carpet and a large ornate wooden desk more appropriate for a Knight of the Realm than for a news producer for Channel 5.

Luis Ramone, a tall, spindly man with a hair transplant,

came up to him. They shook hands. "Good to see you, Willy, it's been years hasn't it? What do I owe this visit to?" Luis took a comb from his flannel blazer and ran it gingerly through his transplanted hair. He thanked the secretary; she left, shutting the door.

"I've got a story for you that could improve your ratings," Diaz began. He had known Luis Ramone for twenty years, since they'd hung around the same poolroom in the South Bronx. They weren't friends then: he'd always associated Luis with the type of Puerto Rican who regretted his Hispanic birthright and did what he had to do to please the white man and get ahead. Standing toe-to-toe with his old acquaintance, Diaz wondered if the latter trait was such a bad thing. Look where it had gotten the man.

Ramone's ears pricked up at the mention of ratings. He was a segment news producer and the battle for ratings in the New York market kept him constantly alert for possible stories. As a former cop, Diaz knew this. "Let's hear your story."

They assumed seats on either side of the Knight of the Realm desk. Ramone picked up a pipe and lit it. Diaz noticed that Ramone's hair was lightly frosted at the edges. "I'm representing a man who is looking for Maria Juarez, the woman who disappeared eight months ago from Spanish Harlem. She'd been out visiting Father Josef Rodriguez at his church on a Hundred 'n' sixteenth Street. It was snowing that night. The following morning Rodriguez is found with his head cut off. Maria's still missing."

Ramone squinted. The sweet smell of tobacco spread across the desk into the room. "I heard about the priest. The rest is fact?"

"Off the record, yes. There's no hard evidence to put Maria with Rodriguez at the precise time of the murder, but circumstantially it fits." There was only so much Diaz could divulge. Much of what Leary had told him was confidential. Therefore he would have to confine himself to relating infor-

86

mation he personally had uncovered. "I know she was dating a man in Manhattan. Whether he was from the city or not, I don't know, but I've traced them both to a bar on Madison Avenue where they met secretly, more than once."

"Which bar?"

"The Madison Pub."

"Oh yes, I know it. Great spot," Ramone said, and when he spoke, a little knife wound on his chin stretched against the bone. He'd had balls, Diaz remembered. He was just overly eager to please.

"She went there with this man, whoever he was. The evidence suggests that this guy is responsible for her disappearance." Diaz exaggerated the unknown man's involvement to get his point across.

"Does it really?" Ramone asked. The pipe had gone out; he lit it again.

Diaz could see he'd won his interest. Now he would gamble and speak honestly. "Of course I have no proof that they were at the bar together outside of the girl's sister hearing Maria mention it in conversation. I went to the bar and showed the bartender Maria's picture. He recognized her, but for some reason I think he lied."

"Why would he lie?"

"I don't know. Maybe he doesn't want to get involved or doesn't want the publicity. He serves an Upper East Side crowd and Maria doesn't fit that bill. That was clear."

Ramone nodded. There were some things you picked up in a youth spent on the street and through nodding Ramone had acknowledged this. He hadn't yet lost the instincts acquired during those years. He would assume Diaz hadn't either. Liars, especially liars under pressure, were like faggots in men's rooms; you couldn't miss them.

Diaz said, "Airing a piece on the bar might get the bartender talking. Someone else might have seen Maria there and make the connection from your program."

"It interests me, Willy. Could you supply me with a picture of the missing woman?"

Diaz could.

The intercom buzzed on his desk. Ramone stood up with his pipe in his teeth. Talking around it, he said, "I have to go. They're thinking of canceling 'Russett's Garden Workshop' for an all-weather program." He took the pipe out. "I could do the segment from the angle of whatever happened to Maria Juarez." The intercom buzzed again and more persistently.

They shook hands and Diaz thanked him. Ramone made Diaz promise to join him for lunch sometime soon. For a moment Diaz thought he might enjoy lunch with Ramone. Back out on the street the feeling faded.

16

The library was on the north side of the street between Broadway and Amsterdam on the edge of the Columbia University campus. It didn't look like much. The entire inside consisted of one cramped room, bisected by rows of aging books. There were two reading tables and a checkout counter. At the reading tables was a collection of elderly people looking as if they had nowhere else to go, their heads bowed into magazines and today's editions of the papers. One man read with the aid of a magnifying glass. He peered up and regarded Diaz with a giant watery eye.

Diaz stepped up to the counter. "You don't seem very busy today."

A short bosomy woman in a dress ten pounds too small for her glanced at him over her bifocals. "What?"

"It seems empty in here," Diaz offered again.

"Not really. We don't do much more business than this. The neighborhood consists mainly of students and they use the university facilities."

On the counter there was a stack of sex education manuals. The librarian caught Diaz staring at them and shoved them firmly aside. "Can I help you further?"

He said yes and took Maria's snapshot out of his pocket and set it squarely on the counter. "The police are investigating the abduction of Maria Juarez. I'd like some information if I may."

"Maria." The woman said and touched the photograph with a pink nail. "You're a policeman?"

"I'm a detective."

"I see." She fixed her bifocals on her broad nose. There was about an inch of cleavage showing above her dress. "I don't know what I can add. I told the policemen everything I knew the last time. Maria just didn't show up one day. As I never heard from her, I just assumed she'd chosen another job . . . until the police came by."

Diaz spiced it up. "I'm investigating the likelihood that she's been murdered by a boyfriend. During the time she worked here, did she have any regular male visitors or phone calls maybe? Was there anyone she talked about whose name stood out?"

The librarian massaged her lips with ink-stained fingers. She looked thoughtful for a moment. Her eyes wandered to the stack of sex manuals. They leapt back to Maria's picture. "No," she said quickly. "Not one."

"Does the name Tim Deluca mean anything to you? Maria was planning a weekend in Maine with his family when she disappeared. He was young, in his mid-twenties. Supposedly he lived in this neighborhood." He realized yet again that his own knowledge of the boy was inadequate and made a note to ask Deluca for more on him.

"Maria did make the occasional phone call, but we discourage that here. It's too upsetting for the patrons. As for her private life, Maria kept that to herself. Oh, occasionally some of the men would flirt with her, but these are mostly older people who don't mean anything by it."

Diaz looked around the room at the would-be flirters. If he ran this place, he thought, he'd have a doctor on hand full-time in case someone had a heart attack. "Was there anything bothering Maria? Did she mention if anyone ever threatened her or her children?"

"No, never. She did become preoccupied, like when she dreamt of what careers she would like. She liked to read. One of her ambitions was to become a nurse so she could care for children when hers grew up and moved away. She loved children." The woman smoothed her dress over sturdy thighs.

"Did you ever meet any of her children?" Diaz asked.

The woman put some thought into this. An almost maternal glow spread across her severe face. "Yes, I did. They were a delight. So well-behaved. Sometimes Maria felt guilty for neglecting them and brought them here to the library. They never so much as made a peep. Not even the baby."

"Do you like children, miss?"

"Why yes, very much. They represent the hope of tomorrow."

He thanked her. Before leaving he thumbed through a copy of *Road & Track* magazine on a stack by the door— looking for photos of red Jaguars. When he turned around, the librarian was behind him extending two small hardcover books. Each book was covered in the ubiquitous library plastic. There was a picture of a dog on one and a nurse on the other. "This may be something. Maria left these behind with some other things. The police took those. For some reason I never got around to putting these back on the shelf." She looked suddenly more thoughtful. "I suppose I wanted to believe she would come back for them one day." She stared into Diaz's eyes. "We were friends."

The first book was about joining the nursing field as a prenatal-care specialist. The second was entitled *Know Your Doberman*. Diaz asked, "Did Maria have a dog?"

"No, not that I knew of. She always said her apartment was too small for pets."

"Didn't it seem funny then that she would be reading a book on Doberman Pinschers?"

"No. Yes. But it wasn't my affair. Maria is . . . was a very curious woman. I think part of the reason she enjoyed her job with us so, was because of the opportunity it gave her to look at so many different books."

"And she never mentioned a friend of hers who owned a Doberman, or anything about the breed?" Two people had gotten in line at the checkout counter. The librarian looked over at them. "No . . ." Diaz could see she was anxious to return to work. He thanked her and passed back the nursing book. "Would you mind if I kept the dog book for a day or two? It might be important and I'm sure the police would be interested in seeing it."

"Aren't you the police?"

"I'm a private detective working for a friend of Maria's family."

"Oh." She glanced at the dog book, then over her shoulder at the growing line of people waiting to check books out. "I suppose it's okay. For a couple of days."

Diaz thanked her again and gave her his card, which she stared at as if accepting it meant they were engaged. He left her with three impatient senior citizens.

He bought a sixteen-ounce Miller and sat on the terrace at Morningside Drive and 116th Street. Over the stone wall below was Morningside Park and beyond this the colored lights of the East Side where Spanish Harlem fused with black Harlem: the War Zone.

The sky was a peculiar blue color today. There were no clouds and the air was cooler so you could cross the street or hustle for a bus without breaking into a sweat. He was sweating now, however, and held the cold beer can to his forehead and loosened his tie. His head hurt from the sudden intense cold of the can.

The sun made his back warm. He took his coat off, smoked two cigarettes, and lit a third. A car went down the hill, its horn blaring. His nerves were up and he wondered if his date tonight would lead to anything. Could he thaw her? He doubted it.

The beer was tasteless but he finished it.

He knew why he felt the way he did. At dinner Leary had mentioned the Doberman brush in the alley. Diaz pictured the priest crumpled up and headless, shoes bloodied, blood everywhere, and the footprint in the snow and the almost inhuman strength required to sever a man's head that way . . . wire pulled through the bone. Jesus Christ.

He took the book out and tapped it against his knee. Before, it was speculation that put Maria in the alley on the night of the killing. The dog book she'd left behind in the library changed that and dropped her in the fire in earnest. She was there on that wintry night in February.

He thought of it in personal terms: Carmen's sister was there.

The incident with the junkies kept coming back to haunt him. Something about it didn't ring true. If they were casing Carmen's Park Avenue office with the intent to rob it, why follow her? Why stake out her apartment building? What point would that serve?

On the subway to the Bronx Diaz unfurled the service station receipt. Someone had paid for eighteen dollars' worth of gas on August 3rd. That proved two things. As the car was registered in New Jersey, it either wasn't stolen, or it had been stolen before August 3rd. Nor was it a rental car. Rental cars are cleaned out before being leased again. Whoever drove it had occasion to be in the South Bronx on the date on the receipt. The junkies could have stolen it from the Bronx, this was possible. But the paint job was old and unless they were particularly stupid junkies, they wouldn't keep driving it in its original condition in its old neighborhood, with stolen goods in it, and while casing apartments.

Diaz found the gas station at an intersection of Tremont and Webster Avenues. The station manager, an ugly man with a German Shepherd, didn't remember the Chevrolet, knew no junkies, stayed on the straight and narrow, and paid his taxes. Diaz patted the dog; it growled at him.

He untucked his shirt and put his collar up, took off his tie, and started asking questions in front of a liquor store. An old white man with rings under his eyes hit him up for a dollar, then directed him to a shooting gallery three blocks over near the subway.

The building was old and decaying. Traffic in and out of it looked brisk. For appearances' sake the junkies stood directly across the street with their cups of water. Diaz was familiar with the ritual from his days on the street. The heroin went in the water. The mixture was distilled in parts, usually in a spoon. The impurities rose and were burned off; the rest was base junk, poured into a syringe and injected. Occasionally too much sediment was left in the dope after distillation, in which case the shooter would get violently sick, sometimes freeze up and go into convulsions. Heart attacks among junkies were common.

As he often did, he wondered what it was in a person that compelled him to shoot dope. Hard drugs were not simply a phenomenon of the ghetto, as portrayed in movies and cop shows on television. It was more prevalent here though, and Diaz supposed it was because drugs were a haven for the hopeless and the sick. And in the ghetto the sick suffered openly without the benefit of institutions or hospitals.

Diaz once knew a doctor, a cancer specialist, who swallowed an entire phial of morphine in a suicide attempt, only the doctor had forgotten that stomach acid can digest morphine, so the doctor got high, not dead, and was forced to jump five stories onto a meat truck to finish it.

Diaz recalled a quote from a neighborhood church news-letter: we are most hopeless who had once most hope.

He picked his man, a young black hustler who needed a fix and was shaking down the others for pocket change to get his afternoon dope. Those he approached ignored him, but sympathetically, and in a familiar way: he was a local down on his luck. Diaz gave the man five dollars and walked with him around the corner.

"Bro', I need some assistance. Three brothers of mine are looking for me for personal reasons and I need to find them." Diaz gave the man his cigarettes.

The man was shivering, but he had five dollars and a fix was imminent. "What they look like?"

"Like I said they're brothers, Ricans. They're into the dope kind of heavy now." Diaz paused.

"Ain't nothing wrong with that," the black man said, wiping his nose. "Gots to have something to live for in this world."

"I hear you. They drive a blue station wagon, kind of old model." He thought it unlikely that the man would recognize the various makes of cars. "They's about my size, maybe shorter. Two lift weights as a hobby. Sometimes they're forced into a little crime, you know how it is."

"Shit yeah." The man gummed a cigarette and lit it looking over Diaz's shoulder. "They's around. Couple times a week. I know the dudes you mean. They run with the Irish."

"The what?"

"White guy who gives them their smack. They don't be hustling like everybody else. I thought you said you know them?"

"I do."

"Yeah, well the Irish is part of a big crime syndicate, Mafia and all the rest. I think the Puerto Ricans rob for him."

It made sense. Irish was probably their fence and he paid for stolen merchandise in heroin.

"I think one of them dates a sister in the neighborhood," the man added.

Diaz asked, "Have you seen them lately?"

The man screwed up his young face and thought about it. "No, I ain't, but thems who you want all right."

Diaz let him go. He tucked his shirt back in and walked around the neighborhood in a five-block radius of the shooting gallery. He asked a few other people and got tired of smart-ass answers and rode the subway home.

17

The big man was in his rented room in Tribeca watching the television and eating Chinese food left over from the day before. The set was tuned to Channel 5, one of the few local channels he got without a cable or an aerial. An obese reporter was in front of a bar on Madison Avenue. The reporter looked like a fat guy he'd known in Nam who shat himself every time the sirens sounded. The fat reporter was talking seriously the way they did when they wanted to act cute to the TV audience and keep their attention.

The big man was attentive for another reason.

He edged forward and turned the volume full up. The reporter was investigating the disappearance of Maria Juarez, and the bar on Madison Avenue figured as a possible meeting place between the girl and her "alleged abductor." Reporters talked such bullshit, he thought.

Someone pounded on the wall for him to cut the noise out. The walls in the doss house were of cheap plasterboard and the sound carried. Leaning to one side, the big man pounded back. The wall shook and plaster dust sprinkled down through a crack onto his cot. He turned the sound down.

His mind remembered things. As a boy he'd always been able to remember the names of sports heroes, movie stars, dates, and faces. By ascribing one salient characteristic to something, anything, he found he could retain it. This faculty, manifested at such an early age, led some of his teachers to wrongly predict an extraordinary academic future for the boy. Indeed, he'd done exceptionally well through the fourth grade. Then with the advent of more complex problems than sheer memorization could handle, the boy faltered. His failing in the face of original thought was his academic downfall. From then on he was known as a stupid boy who remembered things.

Though he'd read the diary only once, the Madison Pub had been mentioned in it three times. Now here it was, smack dab in front of him on the TV screen. And the reporter was talking about Maria Juarez. He felt somewhat nauseous, the way he used to feel in school when he'd neglected to do his homework because he hadn't understood it.

He watched some more as a barrel-chested man, the bartender, was being interviewed by the reporter. The bartender flatly denied any knowledge of the missing girl. He didn't say he didn't remember, he came out and made a denial. The big man sat forward on his cot and squinted: the bartender had the face of a liar. The cameras cut to the alley near 116th Street and a picture of a priest and the big man felt uneasy and switched the set off.

He knew what he had to do. Changing clothes, he put his combat boots back on, ignoring the smell of the leather, and

98

combed his hair using water from the sink. Then he lay on the bed, peering out the window with the crack in it, waiting for evening. He had a friend from Vietnam who, if he was still in business, could sell him a gun. A gun would make it simpler.

18

At the Madison Pub Mickey polished the bar one last time. He wiped his graceless hands on his apron and transferred a dozen clean glasses from the sink to the shelf. It was 9:30 and most of the dinner crowd had left and the late-night crowd had yet to stagger in. He enjoyed the interval, particularly tonight as he was leaving any minute to catch a boxing match at the Garden. Mickey's brother Otis was now due to relieve him.

Mickey took a bottle from the mirrored shelf and poured a glass halfway to the top with Triple Sec. He squirted some soda water into the drink and added three ice cubes. He swigged the liquor and wiped a drop from the hard blue line of his jaw.

Otis was late and the bar was empty and the quiet gave Mickey a moment for reflection. It had been a good week;

he'd made just short of two hundred dollars in tips and another three hundred in salary. Plus he'd drunk four bottles of Triple Sec and pilfered two hundred dollars from the receipts and another thirty from the jukebox. He set down his glass and handed a draft beer to a waiter. The waiter thanked him. He grunted and looked at the clock nailed to the dark mahogany wall. Where the fuck was Otis? Another half an hour and he'd miss the first fight. And it was a good one: an Irish bantamweight was matched against a Ugandan. The Ugandan had a record of eleven and oh with nine KO's. The Irishman had a less sterling history, but he'd killed a guy in the ring and this was his first fight since coming out of retirement two months ago. *Come on Otis.*

Mickey looked at the clock again: 9:47. This was when the man used to come in with the blond Puerto Rican. He remembered, she was a spic and her hair was dyed, but boy she had some tits on her . . . and her eyes. Mickey had never seen such eyes. They were clear and narrow and green and sparkled in the dark.

His thoughts jumped to the reporters who'd come around to hassle him, insisting that the missing girl came to the bar, and Mickey insisting that they were full of it. Fuck them. The last thing he wanted was to be at the center of a Puerto Rican's kidnapping trial. He wondered if the Puerto Rican who'd been in earlier asking about the girl had sicked the media on him? Screw that guy too!

Mickey had no loyalties to anyone but himself, and therefore no reason to protect the girl or her boyfriend from the outsiders. He simply lacked the interest to get involved. What's more, he didn't know anything anyway. He'd only seen her a half a dozen times, always with the same guy, an executive type. Mickey thought nothing of it, a rich white man and a foxy Puerto Rican. *Let people alone.* That should be his motto, he decided. Besides, he sort of liked the guy she was dating. He was polite and good for at least a ten-dollar tip no matter what he was having. Mickey knew the

101

man was rich from the cars he drove and the clothes he wore; everything about him spelled class. Usually he arrived at the bar in a limousine. Mickey looked out from the sunken picture window of the pub. Neither the girl nor the guy had been in for over six months anyway. He thought: screw it, it's history.

He fixed another drink, polished some glasses, and put on his leather overcoat.

Otis banged through the door at 9:55. Like his older brother he was coarse-faced and thick, but three inches shorter. "Hello Mick, sorry I'm late." They had identical jaws, a promontory of bone and muscle. Their straight black hair was parted on the same side.

Mickey belted the leather overcoat and threw the soiled apron at his brother, hitting him in the chest. "Remind me not to call you next time I need a favor."

"But Mick, it's only nine-thirty," Otis said.

"Bullshit. It's five-to-fuckin'-ten. Just do me a favor and remind me not to call you. At this rate I'll be lucky to get there before the knockout punch." Mickey barged past his brother and sulked up the short flight of stairs to ground level and the street. He walked into the sharp air, yanked the leather belt tighter, and pointed his thick jaw toward Madison Square Garden.

Relief swept through Otis as his brother trudged out the door. In fact his brother's presence always made him uneasy. Otis was big and beefy, a smaller version of Mickey. But where Mickey was loud and brash and genuinely tough, Otis was mild-mannered and on the sensitive side and had once thought of joining a local jazz dance theater. He used the imposing frame nature had dealt him to shield himself from the unpleasantries of life; he looked as if he could handle himself even if he couldn't and consequently very few people gave him a hard time.

Otis took off his windbreaker and folded it neatly on the seat behind the bar. The staff came over and he chatted with them for a few minutes. They smiled and went about their business. He changed a dollar at the cash register and slipped four quarters into the jukebox. While Tony Bennett warbled about San Francisco, he lit a cigar and thought about jazz dancing.

The big man in the combat boots left the rooming house at 10:30. After leaving a cash deposit he drove his rental car uptown and took the 59th Street bridge into Long Island City to see Eddie Traub, whom he'd known in Vietnam.

Eddie wasn't home. A woman came out of the battered apartment door with curlers in her hair. She had on a flowered print robe and she had large sagging bosoms. "What d'ya want?"

"Eddie."

"Christ, it's eleven o'clock at night. Ain't you got no manners? What kind of big bum are you?" The woman watched as the man fingered his pathetic fringe of a moustache. Remorse for the stranger lightened her weary features. "What're you a friend of Eddie's or something?"

"We was in Nam together, now I'm a client. Where's he at?"

The stranger was staring at the swell of her bosom in the robe. She wrapped herself more tightly in the cloth. Her fingers felt for the pistol in the terrycloth pocket. "Well, he ain't here."

"Then where?"

"You wanna make a purchase?" The man nodded. "He's on the street like every Friday, back in New York by the Park. Do you know his car?"

"No, I didn't know Eddie had a car."

"What're you crazy?" She made a face. "It's a green Cadillac. Go to One hundred and seventh and the park on the West Side." The woman touched her eyelashes with the back of a finger. She checked for smudging. The man hadn't budged. "What d'ya want, an affidavit? Beat it."

103

He was staring at her calves. They were sinewy and boney like nuns' legs, he thought. "Where?" He found he couldn't concentrate on anything but the woman's figure. In the face she looked like an older version of the girl from "Gilligan's Island." The tall one.

"The high-rent district, One hundred and seventh and Central Park West. Now get outta here." She showed him the butt of the pistol by pulling her pocket down. He thanked her and walked away.

The car was on 109th, not 107th. The silhouette told him there was only one man inside. He got out of his rental car as the Cadillac was pulling away and caught up to it. He leaned his large head in the window. "Eddie."

Eddie braked. The car wheezed; Eddie lowered the polished German Luger and holstered it under his arm. Brittle nervous fingers touched the .45 in his crotch. Then Eddie slid down his shades: his eyes were red, as though they'd been dipped in blood. "It's you, you big faggot, you scared the ham out of me."

The big man looked into Eddie's eyes. "Long time, Eddie. How's the war?"

"The pacifists are ruining me. Glad to see you. What can I do for you, stud? Don't tell me a big prick like you needs heat."

"I need a sawed-off shotgun," the man said, just now deciding upon it.

From that point on, Eddie was all business. "Get in your car and follow." Eddie tapped the shades back in place. Easing the Cadillac away from the curb, he did a U-turn. They drove in a convoy of two for twenty blocks and parked before a storage warehouse. The big man got in the car with him; the Cadillac sagged. "Shit, I forgot how big you really was," Eddie smiled. He toyed with the gold chain around his neck. His velour shirt was open. The chest hairs were black. Eddie dyed them. "This place is okay because the niggers keep the cops away. This territory is occupied." He flicked off the radio with a quick finger and got serious. "Whatever you need, bro', you tell Eddie. I'm here to serve. Anything whatsoever."

"I'm in a hurry," the man said. "And I need a shotgun." He stared at the phone under the dash, and for one uneasy moment thought Eddie had become a cop.

"You're in a hurry, you make your order, we exchange values, kaboom. Wait here."

Eddie got out of the car, opened the trunk, removed something, and got back in. He handed the big man a compact, solid object wrapped in butchers' paper. The man traced the contours of the gun, judging the weight and noting the length. Eddie reached under the seat and produced a box of shells.

Eddie said, "I filed the serial numbers off last week. The trigger and the barrel are taped and won't take prints. The saw job is neat and clean, beveled." Eddie touched the package. "A bill and a half since you're a friend."

The man picked an imitation rawhide wallet from his shirt and drew out three fifty-dollar bills. He laid them individually on the dashboard. They nodded to each other. Eddie smiled a three-Quaalude smile. The man took his purchase and drove to 79th and Madison.

At the head of the stairs Otis held the door for the last two customers. "Good night." They thanked him. Back at the bar he logged his hours for the night and slipped into his windbreaker. Outside he shut the door and locked it with two different keys. The bar's lights went off automatically. He slid the keys through the mail slot. The morning shift had their own set.

It was early still and Otis considered heading uptown to the Rat Pack to go drinking. He pulled a flannel cap out of his windbreaker and adjusted it on his thick head of hair. It was a cool autumn night and the cap made him look more like Gerry Cooney, the boxer.

"I guess you're closed."

A man appeared from the blackness. He'd been standing in the threshold of the art gallery next door and Otis hadn't seen him. At first Otis thought he saw a shadow, for the shape was huge, exaggerated as shadows often are. Then the shadow advanced and came into the weak light of the pub window. Its features were pulled into three dimensions. The man was dressed in a black coat with green khaki trousers and combat boots. Otis realized that the man was fully as large as his brother Mickey, bigger even, and he was carrying a package. His eyes looked wild and Otis thought: I'm being mugged. In his nastiest voice Otis shot back "Yeah, we're closed, what does it look like?"

"It looks like you are," the man said pleasantly. "It took you friggin' long enough." The huge man stepped nearer.

The movement scared Otis and instead of carrying on as he planned to, he stood quite still. The man apparently mistook this for a challenge of some sort and started smacking Otis back into the tight alcove of the bar. Otis's hat flew off. The big man kicked him. Suddenly they were out of view in between the buildings.

Otis recovered from his first instincts to crumble. He'd been literally backed up against a wall; his weakness transformed into a brief desperate energy, he surged forward, arms flailing like a woman's.

The big man retreated one step, then brought the same foot sweeping forward with terrific force into Otis's testicles. There was a crunch. Otis hawked, tumbling backwards; the pain swept up into his stomach and his lungs seemed to close. The breath rattled out of him.

The man waited, then pulled Otis to his feet. He wobbled and stood leaning against the wall. Otis's senses returned.

"Be good, man," the stranger said.

Cowardice had yielded to rage and now, terrified by the first violence he'd experienced in years and with the promise of more to come, something snapped in Otis. Something like

106

courage flickered inside him. His mind was clear enough to recall the pocketknife he carried for just such emergencies. With palsied hands he pushed out at the stranger, stepped away, and got the knife out; his fingernail broke, he opened it. "Stay away or I'll cut you . . ." Saliva dribbled out of his mouth.

The big man hadn't moved. Perhaps, thought Otis, the knife had worked. "If you're good, I won't hurt you," the stranger said suddenly.

"What do you want?" Otis said, his voice quaking. He realized his lip was cut. The knife was slipping in his hand and he wondered if he could hold onto it if he actually had to stab the stranger.

Then the large man showed his hand and Otis caved in. The stranger tore the butcher's paper from his package and slipped two shells from his pocket into the breech of the tiny shotgun. The man's flat face was grim and expressionless. Perhaps if he'd shown some human element Otis would have appealed to it. Instead Otis let out a low, involuntary squeak. "I'll be good." He dropped the knife on the pavement. It clattered and landed with the picture of the Statue of Liberty face up.

Holding a wire hanger the man stepped up to Otis. It took him a minute to twist the wire around the bartender's throat. Next, he secured it to the barrel of the gun. The wooden stock of the weapon disappeared in a tear in his coat sleeve. It would be hard for an outsider to see he was carrying a weapon. "This is only insurance," the man said, and Otis agreed readily although he hadn't understood.

In the initial smacking assault Otis had pissed himself and now the powerful stench infected the alcove. The man smelled it and in a calming voice told Otis not to be scared. He shifted the wire around Otis's neck so that he and the gun were behind him. "Let's go for a walk. I'm going to take you to the park near the river and ask you questions. If you panic I'll have to use this." He tugged the gun.

"Yes, sir." Otis had been reduced to a slobbering idiot. He would now do anything the stranger asked. Above all he would be good. All his life he'd been good; there was no reason why he couldn't be now.

Keeping very close together, they marched into the street, Otis never more than an arm's span from the stranger. In this fashion they made it to the small park overlooking the East River and Roosevelt Island. Otis had begun to mumble aloud, soothing, hopeless things, like the comments of a priest at a deathbed.

Minutes later they stood at the stone balustrade overlooking the river. Its corrugated surface rode roughly over an uneven river basin. The swells crested and broke randomly, picking brief patches of light out of the moonlit sky.

At a break in the railing they descended a metal parapet along the concrete bank leading down to the river. Otis continued to step in a highly spirited manner like a soldier, a good soldier. The stranger had given Otis his word and Otis had clung to it like a life preserver. If Otis was good, the man would not hurt him.

They stopped as the platform leveled off along the water. A second series of steps, these made of stone, had been built in the event of a drought, and led directly into the river along the wall. A small steel hurdle separated the two sides. "Go over that." Otis leapt over the hurdle with all the grace of the jazz dancer he'd never become.

At last they stood on the final stone step before the water. The river was calmer than it had looked from above, and dirtier. There was very little wind, a fact that made conversation possible. The air had grown cooler.

"You would have opened up a whole can of worms," the man said.

Otis turned and looked at the stranger. His expression was calm; they might have done this every night. He nodded dumbly. "Why did you . . ." But the thought was never articulated as an entire lobe of Otis's brain exploded, spattering the stone wall. The big man jumped back, releasing the gun. Otis spilled into the water, his arms twitching, doggy paddling downstream to a better life.

In the recoil the shotgun became dislodged from the wire hanger around Otis's neck. It lay now on the stone steps under water. The big man fished it out and heaved it into the river. Then he did something he'd never done before. He stood at the railing leaning over the water and threw up.

A sentiment resembling conscience tugged at his soul. The bartender hadn't seemed like such a bad guy. He seemed tougher on TV than he had in real life, the big man thought. And he'd had balls in a way; he hadn't given in immediately as most would have.

Tears welled in his tiny witless eyes. It was over now, he thought. For ten long minutes he watched the foam-flecked waters, thinking about the dead man and about what he'd just done.

He staggered back across the cold streets as far as the rental car. At the rooming house he collected his things and wiped the fixtures and what little furniture there was with a tee shirt. He thought of all those times in Vietnam when everybody was dying and the only thing that really concerned him was when he was going home. During the last two months of his tour he'd adopted a cat that he fed and talked to and paid a native woman to care for when he was at the front. It was a pretty cat with stripes and an orange coat, and of course it wasn't very old because cats were considered chow in Vietnam and the wild ones were generally caught before too long and cooked and devoured.

He'd called his cat Pinky for no particular reason and for the two months he'd had her they'd been inseparable. Every free moment he had back at base camp, he'd devote to Pinky: grooming her, preparing her food, discussing the things that concerned him, talking about home. Somehow Pinky had survived the two months without getting run over or eaten or shot. He'd once known two Americans from Alabama who'd taped a small plastic explosive to a cat's hind-quarters, and the idea of that happening to Pinky after he left terrified the big man. And he didn't trust the gook lady he was paying not to make Pinky into a fucking stew when he was gone.

The alternative was a crude sort of euthanasia using a straight razor and chloroform, only they were out of chloroform at the hospital, or said they were. So he'd had to use the razor without the sedative.

The memory of Pinky's trusting face disturbed him and brought back the war in a series of horrible, vivid pictures. The shrill deadly whistle of a mortar pierced his ears and nearly caused him to drive off the highway. Sweat broke out on his face and under his armpits and ran down along his ribs and stomach. Somehow he made it home.

19

Diaz met Carmen at a fish place in midtown on Second Avenue. She was there as promised, looking lean and lovely in a blue dress with a velvet jacket. Her shoulders were wide. Her full breasts might have looked too big on a smaller frame. The dress with a white lace ruffle around the collar reminded Diaz of something an actress might wear on her night off.

He'd gotten there early and drunk three rum and tonics and made friends with a blond school teacher from Hightstown. When Carmen arrived, Diaz noticed how she glanced at the bony school teacher. Had he detected a flash of jealousy? The prospect excited something in him. They shook hands and she apologized for being late, which she wasn't, and Diaz kissed her hand (the behavioral product of three rums drunk at six-minute intervals).

111

They sat down at a table under a suspended shark jaw. "I'm glad you showed. I wasn't sure you would," he said.

"I said I would."

"Yep." He reached automatically for his cigarettes. "Do you smoke?"

She eyed him cooly. "No, not since high school."

"Do you mind if I do?" She shrugged. Her face was wider than he remembered. Her nose was just a sliver and her eyes were large and bright. He looked at his cigarettes, lit one, and asked, "Do you usually have this effect on men?"

"What effect is that?" Her tone was matter-of-fact. She studied him.

"Do you make them feel fifteen years old again?"

"I've never heard it put that way," she said stiffly.

"No, I suppose not, but why don't we bottle it and sell it as the fountain of youth. You could make your million."

She smiled cooly. "Are you always this flattering?"

"Only the first date. It goes downhill quickly as I get bored."

"And you always get bored?"

"Usually," he said. "To be perfectly honest I'm pretty bored now."

She laughed. "You are? Well, then maybe I did make a mistake in coming here."

Diaz reached over and instead of taking her hand, set his own hand down beside hers. "You could never bore me. That's just my way, leave 'em before they leave you." He sat back. "I had a friend who used to say, 'Willy, you're at that stage in your relationship when you should be either ignoring them or being mean to them.'"

"And you believed him?" Carmen asked, leaning forward.

The waiter came by and set their drinks down. Carmen had ordered an orange juice and Diaz another rum. He paused until the waiter had left. "No, I used to wonder though. Women confuse me." He saw he'd gotten her attention and went on. "I can never really determine what they're after."

"Maybe they're not after anything. Maybe they like you for you. That happens."

"Maybe they're lonely."

"Maybe." She reached and took his rum and exchanged it for her orange juice. "Maybe they're just after your rum."

They ate scallops and French fried potatoes, garlic bread and a salad. Between them they polished off two bottles of California Chablis. Carmen had cheesecake for dessert and Diaz, coffee.

Dinner had gone better than he'd hoped. After their initial sounding out, Carmen had relaxed visibly. She'd entered the conversation with genuine interest, expressing her opinions, pressing him for details about his life. He'd put it succinctly and without comment. He was thirty-six, spoke Spanish but couldn't read it, had grown up in Queens and the Bronx and for a year in Staten Island. He had family in P.R. He'd fought professionally, three fights, been a cop. Had married, but his wife had died.

He'd tried turning the tables on her but she shrugged off any inquiries and he'd let it rest. Her life was her business. And for the rest of the dinner he found himself thinking: I want her but she's having an affair. And he wanted her that much more.

Carmen listened intently. He fascinated her. She'd heard of similar stories of the down-and-out Puerto Rican who'd battled back against the odds and won. But she'd never quite met anyone like him. He was strong yet vulnerable, awkward yet confident. She sensed in him a loneliness and when she listened to him speak, the soft tones of his voice made her wonder if he'd ever been hurt before emotionally. Perhaps by some woman. Maybe recently, but maybe not. Then when he'd mentioned his wife's death—a terse, unembellished remark—it made sense. He had been hurt, and, however long ago, the scars remained. But what impressed her the most was his ability to keep his spirit and good humor. He could be relating a story about pain or death, and

113

change the mood with a smile or a purposefully silly remark. It was as if, she thought, he was immune to pain because it had always been there for him and probably always would be. Carmen's father had been like this, until the bad times caught up to him and his business failed and he'd come home and taken a target pistol . . .

. . . But you're not like that, Carmen thought as she watched Diaz. You're stronger. On an impulse she touched his hand. He wrapped his fingers around hers and she felt a pounding in her heart beneath her own sadness. She remembered herself and broke the hold. He was staring curiously at her now and she felt angry for her behavior.

"I'm sorry, I was thinking about something else," she said tersely, wondering if she should explain. But explain what? That she liked him and that he reminded her of her father, but at the same time didn't remind her of her father; was stronger than her father, and handsomer, younger, entirely different. She felt confused. She'd drunk too much, she thought, and suddenly felt like leaving.

"Don't say anything," Diaz said.

"Thanks."

They walked as far as Rockefeller Center and watched the men laying the foundation for the ice rink. It was autumn and within a month the terrace below would be filled with skaters. Diaz pictured them skating together, him holding her, her hair billowing in the cold wind. Leaning over the brass railing he could see her splendid profile and the planes of her face in the terrace light. She turned abruptly and caught him looking. They smiled at each other.

"You don't seem so angry anymore," he said. "I had this notion you would be angry and independent." She looked a little confused so Diaz added, "Not that those two go hand in hand. I mean you still seem independent. I think that's what intrigues me."

"I'm glad I intrigue you," she said, also looking out over

the imaginary skaters, watching the two fat men in overalls shoveling sand between the pipes.

"Can we do this again?" he asked, and she nodded. He wanted to touch her hair. It was the thickest, blackest, and straightest hair he'd ever seen. "May I touch your hair?"

"You don't have to ask permission," she said, still not looking at him.

He stroked it with the backs of his fingers. She shut her eyes. "I don't think I've ever seen hair this pretty outside of a wig."

"Diaz!"

He grinned. "I meant that in a nice way." Their eyes met and he felt a comforting feeling spread through him. He leaned forward and kissed her lightly on the lips. She let the kiss happen, then swiftly turned away and resumed watching the ice rink.

"I'm sorry," Diaz said. They stood perfectly still. The cool air had made his ears and nose cold. He could still feel her kiss on his lips.

"I've got to go now," Carmen said suddenly. "I forgot what time it was."

"I'm sorry if I got too forward."

"It's not that," she said. "I made plans for later."

What kind of a woman makes two dates in one night, he wondered. "I want to see you again, soon. I haven't had this good a time in a long time."

She turned toward him and put her arms on his shoulders. "You're very special to say that." She kissed his forehead.

"Are you busy this weekend?" he asked.

"I have your card. I'll call you." When she saw she'd disappointed him, she added, "There's something I have to straighten out before I start seeing you . . ." They kissed again. "You're very handsome," she said and backed off and started toward Fifth Avenue with Diaz watching her.

20

Joey Irish had watched them go into the fish restaurant and stood near a mailbox while he recorded the name, address, and time on a tablet of lined paper he'd taken from his shirt. He wore a tweed coat and a pigskin cap pulled low on his brow. His cheeks were flushed and his long pointy nose was veined. He stood stoop-shouldered in the night, watching the door to the restaurant for any sign of the girl or the detective.

While he was waiting, he took a pint bottle of whiskey from his shirt and sipped it. He let the liquor seep into his tongue and the sensitive area around his gums. He cleaned his teeth with it then swallowed and felt the dull line it made going down. The girl, Carmen, was on his mind.

"What are you waiting for?"

Irish spun around in his pigskin cap. He fumbled the bottle and caught it and spilled whiskey on the knee of his baggy pants. He murmured the word "shit," then relaxed. The intruder was nothing more than a bum: he wore a long camel's hair overcoat with stains on it and carried a bag of empty soda cans.

"Give us a cigarette, mister."

Irish put the whiskey bottle under his arm and drew a package of cigarettes from his pants. He tapped one out and the bum took it.

The bum said, "Light it for me will ya, I ain't so steady."

"Jesus, do you want me to smoke it for you too?" Irish said, cupping a lit match in his hands. The bum breathed the flame through the point of the cigarette. Irish dropped the match and cardboard folder into the gutter.

"You're Irish ain't ya?" the bum asked. He directed an unsteady hand to his lips and smoked. He held the breath and said, exhaling, "I got some Irish family in Long Beach Island. They're rich people. Long Beach Island is for the rich."

The Irishman suddenly felt irate. Here he was trying to monitor the restaurant door, inconspicuously, and now he had a bum for company. "Look you, piss off. I got things to do and I don't need a friend."

"You are Irish, ain't ya?" the bum said ignoring him, impressed with his deduction. "What you waiting on, paddy?" The bum chuckled.

Joey Irish thought of what was at stake. He was to follow the girl and Diaz, take notes, watch out for the big man. . . . The ledger! He felt for the tablet in his shirt and finding it there, wondered if he wasn't getting a little high on the whiskey. He held up the pint bottle. Three fingers of whiskey remained.

"Hey, can I have that?" the bum asked.

Irish turned on his heels, swiftly. "Look you, get the fuck outta here. I got business to do."

The bum interrupted. "You can't make me. This is public

117

property and there ain't no curfews no more, so shut your gob, paddy, or I'm calling me a cop."

Joey Irish made a frustrated whimper. He glanced at the restaurant, then at the street in each direction. From his pocket he withdrew his blackjack and struck the bum savagely on the temple just once. There was a snap. The bum sagged and dropped his cans, they clattered and rolled out of the bag.

Irish grabbed his overcoat and dragged him off of the avenue. He dropped his whiskey bottle and winced at the sound of glass breaking. Using all of his strength he propped the bum up against a stoop. A pair of debutantes strolled by. Irish embraced the bum and grinned at them.

When he got back on the avenue, two taxis were pulling away from the restaurant. A crowd of diners had just exited and were halfway down the block in both directions. He thought he recognized Carmen getting into a cab but he couldn't be sure. Maybe they'd left? He cursed softly and the cool dank air frosted his breath. His heart was no longer in it tonight.

He went back and woke up the bum. "How are you, pop?"

The bum stirred. He blinked his eyes open slowly. His eyes were glassy and pink rimmed. "My head hurts. I thought I got mugged. Did ya see who did it?"

He felt angry at the bum's stupidity. He crouched forward. "Yeah, you dumb fuck, I did it," he said mildly and drew a crumpled five-dollar bill from a battered wallet and stuffed it into the bum's hand. "Happy Birthday." Five minutes later he got on a bus on Madison Avenue, whistling absently as he read the ledger.

21

Diaz dismissed a stray urge to follow her. They'd spent two hours together in their entire lifetime and now she was gone for two minutes and he missed her. He'd rarely felt like that, not since Tina.

He went to Alphonse's Bar and pushed through a crowd of Mexicans doing a hat dance in the entrance. Alphonse was half Mexican and let his people drink for half price on Fridays. Diaz recalled this as he stepped inside. Tonight was Mexican night. Someone, one of the Mexicans, had thrown up in the room; the sweetly repugnant smell lingered. The bar was filled to capacity tonight, and Diaz did a quick figure of the money in the register.

He nodded at a man he didn't recognize tending bar and ordered a beer. Someone's cigarette was languishing in a tin saucer. A thin thread of smoke reached for the ceiling. Diaz crushed the cigarette dead.

This time there was no one guarding Alphonse's door. The kid apparently had the night off and the present barman, a middle-aged man, didn't seem to care. Diaz forgot about the beer he'd ordered and made his way to the office door and shouldered it, looking behind him.

"Hold it."

Diaz stiffened, holding the door open with his shoulder, his hands down. Alphonse was behind his desk. The lamp was on pointing away from him in the otherwise dark room. His fat frame was jammed down in a leather chair, his lank black hair was disheveled, and from where he stood Diaz could see the sweat shine in his pockmarks.

Alphonse looked at him levelly in a tired squint. He counted to three out loud and lowered the revolver in his right hand. His body sagged noticeably. He rebounded enough to grab a glass of dark liquid on the desk blotter and drink it. "Diaz, shut the fucking door," he said hoarsely. "And lock it."

Diaz swung the door shut and slid the bolt. The noise from the bar died. He stood at the foot of the desk wondering what he was doing here, voluntarily, at the fat man's at this hour. All of a sudden he felt strangely depressed.

Alphonse's weak red eyes turned up to him. His voice was sluggish and drained. "I ain't playing with you today. Just say why you're here and get out." He was still clutching the revolver as he wiped the sweat from the sockets of his eyes. The room smelled. Diaz watched the fat man's hands trembling. The anguish was palpable on his rubbery Latin face. Upside down in a wastebasket were two empty Scotch bottles. He looked like a man who's been given three months to live if he gives up drinking, and one if he doesn't.

"You ought to get out more," Diaz said and withdrew two hundred dollars in twenties from his pocket. "You need some color in those cheeks."

"Fuck you."

Diaz dropped the money on the desk. The bills fanned

120

out. Alphonse nudged them with the revolver tip. "For the car," Diaz said.

"Two hundred dollars. You're moving up in the world, Puerto Rican. That, I got to give you credit for." Alphonse spread the bills out negligently. "What happen, you mug some old faggot, or did the governor bribe you to stop banging his wife. Which is it?"

The voice was warbly. Alphonse wasn't making sense. Diaz just listened. Something had happened to scare the hell out of the fat man. Alphonse's skin was pale and his eyes red-yellow: the pigment of drugs and alcohol. The room was uncomfortably hot. Diaz found the radiator and turned the heat down. He stood up to leave. "See you later."

"Wait, hold it Diaz." Diaz held. Alphonse said, "Aren't you even curious, I mean why I'm in here shittin' myself on a Friday night?"

"It's not my affair."

Alphonse wiped his tired face again with his hands. He breathed sharply through his mouth and turned toward the door. "Some wop owes me some money, some wop right off the boat from Sicily for Christ's sake. And when he gets here he don't even go to his own. They'd a seen him ten large any fucking day of the week. No, this dumb wop comes to me and we did business. I spot him a grand."

"So."

"So then somebody sees the son of a bitch ditching his hotel room heading for the docks carrying a suitcase. Turns out he don't like New York, wants to try Chicago without telling no one with my grand in his guinea pocket picking up lint from his balls. He was trying to play the ditch on Alphonse." He gazed forlornly at Diaz and repeated his own name with a reverence usually reserved for John F. Kennedy or Christ.

"You're half Italian," Diaz said. "Maybe he figured you for his Godfather. Next time, he owes you."

"Don't be funny." Alphonse sucked the stub of a dead

121

cigar. His fugitive eyes glanced quickly at the door as his mind wandered through the mist of two bottles of Scotch. He took the cigar and set it on the desk lip as if it were lit. "So I caught him and to teach him a lesson in American ethics, I sent an acquaintance from the Bronx, but like a cunt this guy, my guy, nearly kicks the wop's little head in. That I didn't want. The cops pull up, old ladies are screaming, some vigilante tries to get into the act.

"Anyway, the wop's got family and they find out how I humiliated their guy, and that's where it stands. I been waiting for them to make a move and tonight I got word. The bastard's sent some slobs to see me and hand me my bones in a bag. Which is exactly why I got this." He waved the gun weakly, like a flag at a surrender. It dropped and thudded on the desk top. "I'm ready for them."

Diaz knew he could have stood there all night and Alphonse would have told him the story a hundred times, each time with a new angle. But this was the loanshark game and Alphonse was a loanshark and sharks by nature are not the most stable of beasts; they move in packs in a tenuous peace, poised for an opportunity to turn. Diaz knew the business; he'd been a cop. Peering down he thought, good luck fat man. "Those who live by the sword . . . good luck."

Alphonse stood up unsteadily. He picked the gun back up in his fat olive fingers. His body was soaked through with perspiration and he was breathing hard. "Fuck your luck, it'll blow over. I just got to worry about the immediate." He itched himself with the muzzle of the gun. "Get the hell outta here."

scratched

Diaz had a reason to leave, to go home to his apartment straight away and sleep it off, whatever feeling it was that brought him here. Then Alphonse said, "You want to see the car?" Diaz stopped. "Here." Alphonse threw a set of keys at him, overhand, the way a girl throws dice. The keys hit him and dropped on the floor. He bent over and picked them up by the key ring.

Alphonse said, "I got the big lock on tonight."

Diaz shrugged and stared at the little blunt pieces of shaped metal. "I'm not sure I want to see it tonight."

"Bullshit. I know how sentimental you Ricans can be. You didn't come here at midnight to pay me off." Diaz started. Alphonse came back hoarsely. "The kid's off tonight. While you're out there have a look around, will ya?"

Outside Diaz freed the padlocks and dropped the heavy chain and opened the unpainted doors to the garage. Its dry hinges screamed at him.

For a moment he couldn't think of what to say. He stretched his neck and looked away fidgeting, then snapped the light on. The red car gleamed.

"Hello, Tina." He stepped forward boyishly, his hands crossed before him. "I had a date tonight, my first since you, baby. I didn't look for her, she was the sister of the girl I'm looking for, so . . . anyway it just happened. I didn't look for it like I said and she's very nice." With his fingers he combed his hair down. "I think if you were here or if you two could meet sometime, you'd like her. She's like you, in fact she reminds me of you, and that's why I like her. She likes kids like you did and has three of them. They're not hers really, they're her sister's, but I remember how much you liked kids. We would've had them. Remember that?" His voice expired. The room was silent and he had to wait some minutes before he could continue.

"You'll always be here with me, Tina, you know that and you know you'll always be the only one. Anyone I meet has got to accept that. I'll tell this one about us and what we had and what we still have. I promise. I'll tell her it can't be any other way."

He unbuttoned his coat. "I haven't spent that much time with her, only tonight, but I think it's something . . . un-usual. I haven't liked anyone since we, since you were here." He swallowed and his tears made the car glisten and sparkle. "Remember how happy we were going to be, just us

123

and nobody else because we could depend on each other."
He remembered her and unconsciously made fists of his
hands.

He sat down behind the steering wheel missing his wife,
distantly thinking of the last time he'd seen her and then the
first time and the thrill he'd felt. It was not unlike the feeling
he'd gotten when he'd first seen Carmen.

In his office Alphonse was sitting at the desk, sweatier,
alert, gun drawn. Diaz lobbed him the keys, the gun came
down so that only its tip rested on the cheap formica desk-
top. "I didn't see anything out there," Diaz said. "But don't
count on that."

"I got three grams of coke," Alphonse said ignoring him,
crouching over his cocaine. "It's gotta last me." His eyes
were narrowed to fine points.

Diaz watched while he snorted a fat line's worth. He left
the bar and walked home. His sweat made him cool.

22

Diaz was halfway to the third floor of his building when he smelled the cigarette. At first he thought he was smelling Alphonse's bar in his clothes. He moved slowly until finally he saw the red tip of a cigarette and a tall figure standing in the corridor to his office. He recognized Deluca and slid his client's appropriated automatic back into his coat.

"I thought it was safer to wait in here," Deluca said. He stooped and put out his cigarette on the floor but held onto the butt.

"Safer than what?" Diaz unlocked his door and threw on the lights.

Deluca followed him into the room and went directly to the chair and sat down. Diaz stopped at his desk to remove the notepad from a drawer. He subtracted the two hundred he'd given Alphonse from his thirty-four hundred dollar debt.

"I'm sorry for being here so late, but I don't believe in phones," Deluca said.

Diaz put the ledger back. "What's to believe, they're not a theory anymore. They work."

"I hate the impersonal touch to anything, and we had to talk."

Diaz opened a window to let the cool air in. He was thinking of Alphonse again and what the mob would do to him if they were out to prove a point.

"It's been four days, Mr. Diaz," Deluca began suddenly.

Diaz understood now and looked at his watch. It was an hour after midnight. "Five days."

"Well, and where are we? What has my money bought me? I paid you twenty-five hundred dollars and am obliged to know what results there've been so far."

"So far none."

"What?" For a moment Deluca looked distraught, like a vegetarian at a slaughterhouse. The look turned to one of indignation. "Can you . . . explain that?" The extinguished cigarette was lodged between his bony fingers like a punctuation point.

"Don't talk so loudly. There are other apartments in this building," Diaz said. "It's late. This could have waited."

"Oh, is that it, it's late. So what if it's late. You're awake aren't you?"

There was an energy in his client's eyes Diaz hadn't seen before: his hair was mussed and his tie was loose and the top button of his shirt unbuttoned. Diaz said, "I'm tired, I've had a long day working for you. From now on if you want me for any reason, use the phone. Call collect. I have other clients, and if they all came in after hours . . ." He realized he was making it sound like a lecture. "It's not an emergency, is it?"

Deluca nodded ambiguously. His eyelids drooped, then blinked open, and he looked confused.

"No," Diaz said, "I didn't think so. You're just anxious and

126

you've had too many drinks so you thought you'd visit me to see what's become of Maria and your two thousand five hundred dollars."

"I'm not drunk. I've been drinking, but I'm certainly not drunk. At my age . . . I've got to watch alcohol . . ." His voice faded into a mumble. He stared at the cold cigarette in his fingers. "I'm not sure that I like you, Diaz. I give you the benefit of the doubt and my money and when I ask for an update, what do I get, abuse. I've had my share of abuse from this world, I was a banker, remember? I don't need it from you and I won't get it." His small chin sagged onto his chest. His eyes closed and opened.

"I wasn't aware I was abusing you."

"Oh screw you, man."

"You are drunk," Diaz said.

"I dunno."

"You should drink more often, Deluca. It suits you."

"Look—" Deluca removed a second cigarette from the battered silver case and replaced it with the extinguished butt and put the case away. "I came to this godforsaken city for a reason, to find Maria. Can you find her or can't you? I tried calling here, all day long I tried calling, but there was no answer. I thought maybe you'd taken me, or were ripping me off. I don't know what I thought so I came over and here I am." Deluca dropped the unlit cigarette and watched it roll across the wooden floor. "Shit, I wanted that."

Diaz said, "I spoke to Maria's family on Tuesday and from what they could tell me, which wasn't much, Maria was very religious and liked men. Now those two things don't always go together, but sometimes they do. They do more than you think. Maria lived with her sister Carmen and her kids, and after she disappeared her sister took over the house and brought her grandparents up from Puerto Rico. They hadn't seen either of their grandchildren in ten years; they barely knew Maria. The two sisters weren't close and consequently they didn't share much.

127

"Carmen did remember overhearing a phone conversation between her sister and a lover and the Madison Pub, which is a bar on Madison Avenue, was mentioned. Apparently it was a regular meeting spot for Maria and this man whose name I don't know. I'm confident it was not your son, however." Diaz waited but got no reaction. "I visited the bar and no one there knew or remembered Maria. I'm not convinced. I don't know why I'm not, but I'm not. When I learn a little more I'm going back to talk to the bartender. He might simply be scared of getting involved, I don't know." Diaz thought: I can't see that big bastard being scared of anything.

"I went to the library where Maria worked. The librarian who worked beside her knew Maria and liked her. No one knew your son, though, and the librarian didn't remember Maria having any other visitors. Besides this bit of information, Maria left behind a library book which the librarian hadn't put back on the shelf." Diaz stood up and picked a beer out of the tiny refrigerator and drained it. It gave him a mild rush that moistened his eyes. The rush quickly faded and the feeling of fatigue returned.

"Would you like a beer?"

"No, I don't . . . I rarely drink beer." Deluca sat a little straighter in the chair. His long legs were sloppy and his feet sideways on the floor. "It seems you should have found out more in five days or however long it's been." He bent and stooped and retrieved the unlit cigarette. His gray hair stood out in tufts. It was long in front and hung down into his bloodshot eyes.

Diaz felt for Deluca's automatic in the pocket of his coat. "You don't strike me as the impatient type. But then you do," he said. "It's your naive quality; things take time but you can't understand that. It means nothing to you that the police have been working on the same case for seven months and have found out nothing." He paused and kept his temper. "A priest was murdered eight months ago on the same night that Maria disappeared. The priest was from Our Lady of Mercy on One hundred and sixteenth Street. I had lunch with a cop who told me the police thought the two events were connected. That sounded like a fair statement and I remembered it when I found Maria's book at the library. It was a book on Doberman Pinschers, which may not seem like much unto itself, but it so happens that the man, or whatever it was that killed the priest, accidentally dropped a brush full of Doberman hairs in the alley. Then to cement it, I find out Maria knew the priest intimately and visited him often, sometimes at night."

"You're sure of this?" Deluca asked, setting his feet flat.

"As sure of that as most things."

The older man sat forward. "Christ, if you know all that, tell the police. Have them locate the killers!"

"The police have tried to locate the 'killers' for seven months. All I've done is establish Maria's connection to the dead priest."

"Then you're saying she's dead," Deluca said with a note of desperation. "You're thinking that since the priest is dead, Maria must be dead. Admit it, Diaz, don't mince words with me. I employ you!" *(implore?)*

Diaz ignored that. "I don't know."

"It's been five days for Christ's sake."

"There you go again."

Deluca stood up and stepped sideways and balanced a hand on the chair. "Listen you . . . I heard good things about you which is why I came to you in the first place. I came to you in good faith. That was nearly a week ago. Now if you can't help me, I'm, I am tempted to look beyond your . . . race. After all if one Hispanic can't find another . . ." He stopped and looked at the floor. The room throbbed with a sudden drunken silence. "Maybe I'll just say the hell with it and go home and forget I was ever involved." His lean face was perspiring and the natural timidity was creeping back into his eyes.

"That's your option; it always has been. I've been busting hump on this for five days. I've annoyed my contacts. I've been beaten, insulted, taken things from people I otherwise wouldn't have said shit to, and I did this for a woman I've never met and maybe will never meet, and possibly wouldn't even care to meet if I had the chance. But you paid me. I sold my life to you by the hour; it was my decision to do that. Five days is forty hours. You gave me two thousand five hundred dollars. I'm willing to take five hundred and return the rest to you now, and then you can dance out of here and I won't have to be bothered again by your moods or your surprise midnight visits or have my ribs kicked in or my face scarred; it's got enough scars for this life. I don't think my ego could take many more. So you decide, pop, take your money and blow or let me handle it."

Deluca said, "Jesus."

"Or let Jesus handle it."

"I'm just saying that it's taking more time than I budgeted." The older man's voice had lost some of its crackle. "I need results. . . . I can't take the waiting."

"We're talking about a life, and not just Maria's. Your son's mistress had three kids at home when she stepped out, and they're still there, wondering why this is happening to them and when the hell their mother's coming back. I think maybe you should take your budget and your money and get back on the bus to Maine."

Deluca shifted and sat back down on the edge of the chair. His eyes were black and small like wet stones gouged from the surface of a deserted road. He spoke in the whispering tones of humility. "I can't do that. You're my last resort, really." He reached into his suit and withdrew a checkbook. He produced a pen and scribbled something, tore the check out and laid it on the desk. "There. I'm authorizing you to pass these monies on to Maria's family. See if you can that the children are the beneficiaries and not the sister or the grandparents. I am not a callous man, Diaz, though lately

I've been acting callously. When you're as determined as I am, I think you lose perspective. In fact I've always thought of myself as something of a humanitarian . . . Do you find that ironic?"

"I don't know."

Deluca stood. He wavered. "Say, you haven't seen a gun, my gun? I bought one for protection."

"What did it look like?"

"It was brown. I think it was small for a gun."

"No, I haven't."

"Oh well . . . Do whatever you can, please. I have to at least think we're making progress. New York is a strange place and I don't like it." He tasted something and sagged a little against the chair. His black eyes rolled up into his head like the eyes in a doll. For the first time all night he actually looked as if he might pass out. "I been drinking martinis, they don't agree with me." He focused on Diaz. "And honestly, I am sorry for those children."

The blue-suited man shuffled from the room and Diaz listened to his slow ungraceful descent of the stairs. "I'm sorry too," Diaz said aloud. "But for you, Deluca."

The check was for five hundred dollars. He pinched it up and folded it and dropped it into a desk drawer. He hung his suit over the desk chair and slept with his shirt on. He could hear the rain.

At 2:00 A.M. he awoke and dialed the number of the Carlyle Hotel. The receptionist put him on to Deluca. When the voice sounded, it was gruff like a smoker's voice and dazed. "Mr. Deluca, it's Diaz. One more thing, where did Tim die?"

There was a brief hesitation as Deluca found his bearings. "Does that matter?"

"No, but tell me."

"In New York. Why?"

"No reason, goodnight."

131

23

Carmen lay back on the bed feeling David's seed seep between her legs onto the covers. David sighed loudly in his sleep and stretched an arm over her and held her. The room as she studied it was more beautiful than any room she'd ever seen. The furnishings were antique, tastefully chosen and in excellent condition. The far wall was occupied by a nineteenth-century "high boy" with scrolled teak-wood legs—the sort of piece she'd seen before in museums. The wallpaper, the curtains, and the sheets all were of the same paisley pattern. The rug was thick and felt good beneath the feet. Two framed Oriental prints and a watercolor of a duck hung on the walls. This was class, she thought, bringing the covers up between her legs to blot the stickiness. She'd studied interior design and decorating at NYU for a year some time ago; David's bedroom would have fallen under the category "Classic Colonial" or maybe "Queen Anne." There was nothing eclectic about it. Yet she pondered, lying there in the semi-darkness with a man she didn't love, that there was a lived-in quality missing from the room. It lacked the vital human element that might have induced her to live in it and be happy.

David stirred and lowered his hand on her pubis. He slid a finger inside her reflexively and kissed her shoulder and started to snore.

Carmen edged away from him. She wondered if her sudden view of the room and its apparent coldness was a product of something else. Maybe, she thought, it's a general reflection of the state of things. It hadn't felt right tonight. It was never perfect, she conceded, but she usually enjoyed their lovemaking and had genuinely come to care for David. Tonight it felt cheap. When he sucked her down there, she felt only a tingley, sensitive sensation and when he finally mounted her, she felt little pleasure. Her breasts were sore as he squeezed them. David's moaning sounded ridiculous, and after it was over, she felt dirty.

She'd never thought of herself as dirty or cheap. Although she viewed all prostitutes as obscene, she'd never felt bad about herself or in the least way morally compromised. David was paying her, but it was more than that: they were friends. Sometimes she was convinced he loved her. They'd met in the park at an exhibition of local artists, and after that first dinner and the promise of "compensation," she'd had no qualms about their relationship. She was attracted to him and she went with him because he represented everything the world should offer: success, happiness, freedom. And she hadn't actually expected him to pay for her company.

But when he had, she took it. Life was hard. Here was someone she would be sleeping with anyway, most likely, and he could make life that much easier for her and her newly adopted family. She'd seen nothing wrong with this. Weren't most housewives simply kept women after all?

She'd been sleeping with David for five months and everything had worked out fine, until now.

Tonight when he'd held her, she'd closed her eyes and
thought of Diaz; she missed him. She sat up and wondered
where Diaz was and if he was alone or with another woman
or whether he was thinking of her.

"You're awake." David sat up next to her. He stroked her
hair and cupped a breast and licked the nipple. It perked up
into a fine red point. Then he pulled the covers back exposing himself. "I'm getting hard."

She tried to keep the sudden panic from her voice. "Can
we wait, please?"

He frowned, then smiled. "Certainly. You're worth waiting for, darling." He found a joint in the ashtray by the bed
and lit it. Holding the hit in his lungs, he gasped, "You're
exquisite to look at. That's why I love you." He exhaled a
lungful of resinous smoke. He touched her face. "You're so
unspoiled."

She said, "Thank you."

"I had no idea I'd ever feel quite like this, Carmen. Quite
so . . ." He searched for the word. "Attached. You're growing on me."

"We hadn't planned on that, David," she said. "We promised to remain friends."

"But we are friends. We're just becoming closer friends."

"Maybe," she conceded.

"This week I'm doubling your . . . the check will be
larger. I want you to buy yourself something nice."

She turned to him suddenly. This defined it. No matter
what the evolution of their relationship, it came down to
this. For a second she wanted to scream. He put his arms
around her waist. His touch was cold. She felt uncomfortable
and wanted to leave. He began massaging her vagina with
his fingers and with his other hand he started to masturbate.
His erection grew and he took her hand and placed it there.
She gripped the shaft; she did it because it was expected and

because she lacked the energy to explain what she was feeling and why she wanted to leave and why it was that Diaz had suddenly occupied her thoughts and not David. But had David ever occupied her thoughts, she wondered? Carmen looked into his lustful thin eyes and couldn't deny the crude animal pleasures he sometimes engendered in her. His fingers felt good, and though she hated to admit the lust, it rose in her.

She checked to see that he was truly asleep, then eased off of the bed and tiptoed across the room to her clothes. She dressed quickly. The room was warm and she felt vaguely guilty, but she had to leave. The prospect of facing him again in the morning sickened her.

Carmen left the apartment and pulled the heavy door closed behind her. Outside on Park Avenue the guilt left her and was replaced with a lighthearted feeling of freedom. She felt free and happy and not remotely angry or discontented. She walked proudly and began to think of Diaz and what their future might hold and it rallied her. It was raining but the rain seemed fresh, like country rain, and carried a cleansing sensation as she opened her arms and stood in it, laughing nervously. And the night belonged to her.

24

The air smelled stale and fishy and probably, Diaz thought, the East River had something to do with this. He walked along the edge of the bulkhead toward the police cars and the ambulance. Last night's rain had dwindled to a faint drizzle which kept the ground damp and spotted the surface of the river like trout rising. Diaz stepped around a series of puddles to where they were dragging the dead woman ashore. Then he realized what the smell was.

At first it had smelled like old fish because old fish was something you'd expect to find stinking up the East River. But as he approached, the stink got musky and livery and he remembered the time as a cop when he'd found a five-day-old kid in a four-day-old canvas sack under a porch.

Lieutenant Leary was standing by the broken and decaying pier near where the kids had found the body. It had sunk upstream and drifted half-submerged until it hit the pilings. A loose coil of wire snagged it. The fermentation process produced the gas that ballooned the stomach. The corpse was caught on the wire at the knee when they found it, but had then surfaced with its head just breaking water, its torso draped hopelessly against the pilings doing a death dance with the tides.

Leary said, "A suicide or maybe a homicide made to look like a suicide. Her wrists were slashed lengthways and there's pennies jammed in the pockets of the coat to make her sink. Probably a lover's quarrel although nobody's reported her missing yet."

Leary's last sentence started a cold sensation deep in the pit of Diaz's stomach. Automatically he turned and regarded the dead woman stretched loosely on the wet earth. Maria had bleached blond hair; the woman on the embankment was a brunette with kinky hair and bone white skin. According to Leary the body had been roped under the arms and then, in a sort of mismatched tug of war, hoisted off the pilings by two policemen. She was pale and swollen and the rabbit skin coat she'd died in was taut around her shoulders and stomach. The coat, its pockets laden with pennies—the death ballast—was open in front and the woman's breasts poked through a tear in the pink shirt underneath. Her face was rubbery and anonymous and her eyes black circles.

A physician supervised the final touches as two men in white hauled the corpse along the gravel and stuffed it into a nylon body bag. Eventually only the sneakers remained outside the bag; they were swollen and gray from the water. Someone jammed them in with the rest of it and tied the cord and Diaz thought of a birth in reverse.

It had taken him half the morning to find Leary. They shook hands belatedly and walked along the rough wet ground away from the ambulance. "You think you get used to it, working this far north with the animals. But just when

137

you think it can no longer shock you, something like this happens and you give up lunch for two days."

"That's partly why I got out," Diaz said. "I like lunch."

They walked until the smell of death was behind them and the chatter of the growing crowd had subsided. "Sometimes I think about getting out, taking my sixteen years and saying ''shove you' and finding a nice quiet job like being a watchman in Mau Mau land." He looked at Diaz. "In Africa," and then, "A joke."

Diaz nodded.

"Give me a cigarette."

Diaz gave him one.

Leary took it, a toothpick in his freckled hand, and stoked it with a match. He set the cigarette between his lips and put his hands in the pockets of his raincoat. "Diaz, you know you pricked the department with that news stunt. If that was my precinct I wouldn't love you so much any more. The Police Commissioner's raising hell about the priest and the girl and what's happening. The NAACP thinks we're dragging our heels on account of them being spics which may or may not be true."

"I needed a break. I thought the news could cough up a witness."

"You gave them everything, even what I told you in secret."

"No, I didn't. I gave them the bar where they drank. The rest they already had. I kept our talk out of it."

Leary stared at him. "You got the ethics of a lawyer."

"Maybe."

"You're here for a reason, *amigo*. Let me guess, the news people didn't come through and now you're out of leads?"

"Almost."

"When you're *almost* out of anything you ain't out of it yet. Ask any junkie. You were a cop, shit."

"That's not it entirely."

"Uh, oh. Favor time." Leary squatted down on ham-sized

haunches and touched the point of his cigarette to a rain puddle. It hissed. "I'm trying to quit." He left it floating in the stagnant water. He turned toward the ambulance and the cop cars. "I wish they'd turn off those fucking lights once they've stopped moving. It draws too much attention. There ought to be a law against it."

"There probably is," Diaz said. "I've thought of a move on the priest's killing."

"Have you now?" Leary asked, bored.

"Maria was a Doberman lover. I talked to her coworker at the library. She gave me a book Maria'd been reading called *Know Your Doberman*. There were Doberman hairs on the brush in the alley. It fits, whoever killed the priest took Maria."

"Good gosh!"

"You didn't have that."

Leary said, "We'd guessed it, but so what. It ties things together, but when you tie shit together it's still shit."

"And people who eat meat are meat-eaters."

"You know maybe you missed your calling, did you ever think of that, Diaz? You're really very poetic in a pathetic sort of way."

"People who read books about Dobermans usually own them; at the very least they spend time with them. Maria had no pets, but I think her boyfriend did."

"And I know a cop who eats meat and raises Dobermans. Damn, I've solved it."

"Have your department feed the media a story, an update about the priest and Maria. Give them the Doberman link. The topic's hot, they'd run with it."

"So?" Leary spat into the puddle next to the cigarette.

"Whoever did it will want to get rid of his dogs in a hurry and there are only so many ways to do this. He probably wouldn't kill his dog, a dog lover wouldn't do that. He'd probably give it away, maybe to the ASPCA, or he could abandon it."

139

"What do we do?" Leary asked.

"We check with the ASPCA and the vets and the dog pounds, anyone who takes in abandoned animals. We check the dumps and the dog wardens."

"He could kill it and bury it somewhere."

Diaz acknowledged the option. "And he could not even own one and we could be dancing before we hear the music."

"So?"

"So where are we now?"

Neither man spoke until they reached the squad cars. Diaz walked along two paces behind his friend wondering if the dogs were the key. His shoes were mud-covered on the toes. He caught up to Leary and the smell of decay and tried not to look at the human shape in the bag.

Leary stared out across the shifting water, his pale face pensive. Diaz noted a growing bald spot in the patch of red hair. "Maybe you have something," Leary said. "You probably don't, but maybe. I'll think about it." He spat over the bulkhead into the water. "Beats shit out of me how fish can live in that gasoline and toilet juice."

"But they manage."

"Yeah, they do. They've been managing for centuries which is why they're still fish and haven't evolved."

Diaz hesitated in the rain outside of the Madison Pub. The drizzle had picked up into a steady cold blanket of water. Rain channeled down a gutter into a cement flower pot. It overflowed and splashed knee high on the cold pavement. Since he was a boy, rain had made him feverish and had a way of causing his bowels to cramp.

He waited a moment longer wondering why he was back. He knew why, but he didn't know quite why at that particular moment, without having prepared himself or thought it through, why he was back. But how did you prepare yourself for this? It was his instincts against another man's resolve

140

to stay silent. The probing questions of the news teams had failed to solicit any information from Mickey the bartender. How, then, was Diaz supposed to? And maybe the guy didn't know anything anyway. Maybe Mickey had been telling the truth and Maria didn't come here and it was another lover who lured her into that alley on a freezing night in February. The bartender had had a pipe last time. Maybe this time it would be a gun and maybe Diaz would have to take it away from him and maybe Diaz wasn't tough enough. He smoked two quick cigarettes until the rain started to seep down his neck.

But the bartender wasn't there, just some sloppy redhead who worked when "Mickey's little brother couldn't make it." Mickey worked nights, she said. Mickey and nobody else except his little brother Otis. The same Otis who couldn't make it today.

He asked her if she recognized Maria's picture and she didn't. They chatted. She looked uncomfortably lonely the way buxom women can when they're over the hill and all they've got left is the charm. She said he reminded her of an actor. At the first pause he left, his head tucked between his broad shoulders.

Outside he could feel the wind on his sweat. The smell of dead flesh was still with him, so he walked eleven blocks and caught a bus on 90th Street.

25

It took Diaz six phone calls to locate the cemetery where Tim Deluca was buried. According to the Coroner's staff the young man had hit a truck on Tenth Avenue on a March night in the rain. Witnesses had confirmed statements by the truck driver that the motorcycle had crossed lanes suddenly on a trajectory toward the truck. Either the kid had rammed the truck deliberately, or he'd misjudged his acceleration in making a daring right turn. The conditions being what they were, cold and slick, and New York traffic being what it is, no conclusions were drawn outside of the obvious ones.

Diaz rented a Ford Escort and drove to Great Hill Road in Princeton, New Jersey, where Deluca was buried in a field near a day school.

The private cemetery was enclosed within a waist-high

wrought iron fence. There were perhaps one hundred graves lined up within its one acre of land with another half acre reserved for the still living. Large trees marked the four corners of the fence. Two of the elms were dying. Somewhere someone was mowing a lawn and the scent of newly cut grass mingled with the brisk ochre scent of fall. The air was cool and peaceful and Diaz thought how nice it would be to have Tina here. Among the relatively few graves she might not seem as anonymous.

A young father in a cloth cap with two small children stood before one grave. The little girls were dressed up for the occasion and took their turns throwing roses at the gravestone. Twenty graves to their right was a tall man in a Burberry coat belted at the waist. His arms were crossed and he was poised before a grave, his head down, studying the site before him as though he planned to build on it. Diaz went over and Deluca turned toward him, startled. His eyes were shiny and the cigarette in his hand was unlit.

"Diaz," he said and stared back down at the remains of his son. "So you followed me." For several seconds he said nothing. His voice when it came was dispirited and self-conscious, like a recording. "It's beautiful here in the country where life seems so uncomplicated. I went to school here, class of nineteen-forty-five. I associate Princeton with some of the only peace I've ever had."

"Is that why he's buried here?" Diaz asked.

"It is. I always thought someday I'd return and retire here. Maybe I will. Maybe this is where I belong." His stare remained on the neatly carved headstone and the flat stretch of lawn before it.

Behind the grave a groundhog had dug a hole in the soil. The opening of the hole was lined with brown shale and Diaz wondered what the groundhog had found at the end of his trail. He looked at Deluca and felt a sudden intense guilt at intruding on the man at such a moment. "I don't know really why I came. It could have waited."

"I wouldn't know."

"Yes, it could. I needed to talk to you today. When I checked with your hotel, they told me you'd gone to Princeton for the day. When I found out where your son was buried, I made the connection and rented a car and came out."

Deluca looked beyond him into the distant forests. "It doesn't make sense. My son was in the prime of his youth and had everything to look forward to. The twenties are the most difficult years for any young person and he had his ups and downs, but that's life. That's what makes it challenging. If only he could have endured his twenties. I almost didn't make it out of mine."

Diaz felt he owed an explanation. "I had some free time and it dawned on me how little about Tim I really knew. I suppose I thought I could learn something about your boy by coming here. I'd like a picture of Tim if you have one."

Deluca looked at his unlit cigarette. He withdrew it and dropped it in his overcoat pocket. "Timmy was a wonderful young man; honest, dependable, hard-working. He respected others and they revered him. He was one of those rare people with leadership qualities which we spotted in the beginning and which would have made him a truly great man." He turned toward Diaz. "I loved him enormously. I think he's all I ever loved, totally." The grass was springy and wet beneath their feet. Deluca shifted toward the headstone as if addressing it. "Didn't I, Timmy?" he whispered. "Weren't we the best of friends?" He stood straight.

Then Deluca began to shake, quietly.

Diaz stood, "God takes those he can't do without." He recited the Hail Mary under his breath and Deluca joined him. Both men crossed themselves.

"Amen."

"Amén."

Diaz waited for him at the rental car. Deluca appeared ten minutes later, his eyes red. "You know it's been five months since I lost him, but in some ways it seems forever, and in others it seems like just yesterday. Isn't life strange that way, the way it plays tricks with time?"

Diaz understood and considered how far away Tina seemed at that moment. She'd been gone seven years. Could it actually have been seven years?

Deluca buttoned the top button of his overcoat and said, "I've given this matter a lot of thought, and I've decided to give you the bonus I promised in spite of what's transpired; unless you genuinely feel you're getting somewhere, then by all means continue. I don't know that Tim would want me to beat this to death. He would want me to go on living."

"She might be alive," Diaz said. "All I need is a break and I'll find her."

"As long as the hope remains, she remains a link to my son. Somehow I don't feel that's so likely anymore, but that's why I wanted to find her, the link." Deluca seemed to be staring directly through him.

Diaz glanced at his shoes, then at the graveyard. "I'm not giving up."

Deluca said, "It's up to you now, but thank you," and shook his hand firmly. "You know I always wished I'd painted Tim. That remains one of my chief regrets. Then I'd have something to remember him by."

"I'd like to see your paintings sometime," Diaz said. "I've always liked art. I have a Diego Rivera print in my office."

"Have you? Yes, he's very good." Deluca rolled his slender shoulders. The bones pressed against the material of the coat. "If you're interested, my work is being exhibited at a gallery on West Broadway in Soho."

"Maybe one day when I have time," Diaz said.

"Maybe."

It occurred to Diaz as he looked around that Deluca didn't have a car. "Can I drive you somewhere?"

"No, thank you. I'm getting a ride. But I think I'll take a stroll before they get here." The tall man hesitated. "About last night. I apologize if I was out of bounds arriving there

145

like I did, talking that way. But you see . . . yesterday was Timmy's birthday. He'd have been thirty."

Diaz passed Deluca in the car, a tall solitary figure picking its way down the country road with grief in its heart, consumed by the memories of a dead son. He drove back to Manhattan with the radio off wondering what point his trip to the country had served.

He walked up West Broadway until he found Deluca's gallery on the corner of Prince Street. His client's work was interesting if somewhat unappealing; Diaz had long since decided that the only good art was the art you liked looking at. Deluca's paintings were bleak and realistically barren landscapes of a gray Maine shoreline. Diaz read the titles; each work depicted a different view of a beach in Portland. The scenes depressed him; he left.

26

The two men sat on a bench near the croquet lawn adjacent to Sheep's Meadow in Central Park. The sun was drifting among the clouds but one of the men had dark glasses on. The other, Joey Irish, wore a pigskin cap. "I've got to pay them what they want. You know how the likes of these are. They ain't like you and me, governor, they've been figurin' all the angles since they got off the bloody boat."

"I'm compromising myself," the man with the dark glasses said. "Do you appreciate that?"

"Sure I do, governor, bloody hell, I know the feeling. And don't think for one minute I don't appreciate the predicament you're in, so sir-ree." He rubbed his damp palms up and down on his trousers. "Bloody hell, guv'."

The sunglassed man let him finish. He said, "Good, that's why I'm paying you more. My predicament forces me to.

147

Don't think a group of Puerto Rican juveniles is going to intimidate me."

"Sure, guv'."

The man took a packet from his coat and passed it in a folded newspaper to the Irishman. "Here it is, and I want no excuses this time. I know how these things work. First it's one hundred, then it's five hundred." The man faltered and leaned forward and the dark glasses drooped across his prominent nose. He thumbed them back anxiously. "Since they demanded more money, I anticipated you would too. I've got an extra thousand dollars for you which I'll give you when I see the completed ledger."

For a minute Joey Irish was stunned; good fortune was such a rarity with him that he had to assimilate it in stages. "Thanks," he said with a dry throat.

"That's all there is. I don't expect to pay one dime more."

"Of course, mate. I ain't a shylock."

"We both know that."

"Thank you, guv'."

Joey Irish had contracted with the man on the bench to follow the movements of two New Yorkers, Willy Diaz and Carmen Juarez, and a third man, a veteran in combat boots, if he showed up. An ex-Congo mercenary, Irish had advertised his services in the "trade" magazines: *Soldier of Fortune, True Detective*, to monitor whomever, whatever, wherever at competitive rates. The client had contacted him with the assignment to watch the couple and to look for the "veteran." A fee was agreed upon and paid for by certified check. Irish was to follow Diaz and Carmen and record their movements, make lists of what they did, where they went, whom they saw. If he spotted the third man, the "veteran," Irish was to trail him back to his residence and contact the client immediately through a classified ad in *The New York Times*. Under no circumstances were any of the people to know they were being monitored.

All this had been fine and dandy and went reasonably well

until the client got a message over the paging system at Newark International Airport, where he'd arranged to meet Joey Irish for the second and last time. Irish couldn't make it and was on the phone apologizing. He'd explained that hiring Puerto Rican sentries, as he had with the client's okay, had precipitated unforeseen complications. The PR's wanted more money before parting with their surveillance notes—scrawlings in pencil on the inside cover of a *Hustler* magazine.

"We agreed on a price. I don't like to be taken," the client said from the phone in the People's Express terminal.

"We're both being taken, guv'. It's those PR's, they got no business ethics."

"They're your work force. Can't you control them?" the man snapped.

"I thought I could. I was wrong. They got to have more money, it's that simple."

"How much more?"

"One thousand total, split three ways."

"Then I get my notes?"

"Certainly."

In the park a bank of clouds loomed up before what little sun remained in the afternoon sky. The air darkened perceptibly. "I want you to contact those men immediately and give them the money and get my ledger. When you've done that, come back here. I'll be here in two hours. That should be sufficient time."

"What if they're not around?"

"That's not good enough. Find them," the man said crossly.

"Okay, I will." Irish reacted to the man's anger and held up his hands in a conciliatory gesture. He stood, tugging his cap down low and regarded the stranger with interest. "Say, mate, you ain't from around here are you? What're you, some kind of European?"

"I'm from Poland originally," the man said, preoccupied.

"Poland, that's a pisser. What are the birds like in Poland, governor? Are there lots of single girls? I heard there were lots of single girls in Europe."

"You're Irish, you tell me."

"I don't consider Ireland Europe," Joey Irish said proudly.

"Why don't you get on with it."

"Certainly, governor."

The Irishman walked off in a short, sloped stride. He went fifty yards into the trees of the park, turned around, advanced thirty yards and stood behind an oak tree. He removed a camera from his tweed coat and snapped twelve shots of the man with the sunglasses. Lady luck was with him today. First the money—now this: the man was actually removing his sunglasses and standing up, the silly bastard; nine more quick snaps of the shutter. He closed the camera and fled.

He went to a dinge bar off 41st Street and Seventh Avenue where members of the Provisional IRA got their mail delivered and where he had a safety deposit box in back. He found his box, opened it, extracted the ledger, and added the envelope with the money. He sat down in a booth facing the door and sipped Irish whiskey from a half-pint glass.

There was no beef with the Puerto Ricans, of course; that was merely him exercising his "angle." You had to have an angle to get over in this world, he had no doubt about that.

He'd known Cat and his friend Mario for seven years, since he'd first started dealing smack out of a laundromat on 116th Street. Hector, the third wheel, was a new addition, no different from his friends. They were junkies with life sentences in society with no real ambition outside of poking that vein and taking it easy. Providing Joey Irish never crossed them and fed them their dope when and where promised, they were in his pocket. He had them on a veritable feeding schedule.

150

Thinking of them reminded Irish of their meeting at the West End Café on Broadway and 114th Street later that night. He planned to give them their due plus a three-hundred-dollar bonus to ensure that they stayed high for the amount of time it took him to leave town for a holiday in Nassau. By the time he returned, they would be someone else's liability or in jail again.

He gulped his whiskey and lit a cigarette, then left the bar and walked five blocks to a strip joint to kill time. There were so many ways to do what he was about to do. He spent some time debating his approach and decided the best way would be the simplest way. He would say simply: "Governor, you're looking at a man before you in need of funds." No, too verbose. "Guv', my ass is out, my bills are overwhelming me and my . . ." No, too roundabout. Jesus. He cleared his mind with a quick mouthful of Scotch on the rocks and watched a bony blonde with a shaved pussy eat a banana. Somebody threw a rose onto the stage. —The blonde sat on it.

Suddenly he had the approach. No bullshit. No unnecessary words: "Governor, I've got all this information copied in my own book at home and I'm blackmailing you for another ten grand for me to destroy it." Good. "I don't know what it is or why you want it, but if I don't get the money in two days, I'm sending everything I know to the geezers I been following, including pictures of you. I know this ain't ethical, but I'm singing my swan song; an old soldier is hanging up his guns."

He decided to omit the last sentence.

Irish liked the forwardness of the approach. The client would buy it as genuine and not think he was bluffing. The client seemed like the nervous type, and God knows he had money to spare. Irish wasn't exactly proud of what he had to do, but he wanted out of New York and out of dealing drugs, and ten thousand dollars would be a good stake.

If he's rich, what's ten thousand, Irish thought and upped

151

the ante to fifteen, then twenty. Two hours later he walked out of the strip joint, holding his erection back through his pocket lining, half expecting, as he did wherever he went, a knife in his back. He stuck his hand in his other pocket and felt the surface of the small leather blackjack made of soft chamois leather and filled with shot and ball bearings. As he was in the country illegally, he'd never gotten into the habit of firearms. Being found with one meant instant deportation. But blackjacks were okay, lethal if you used them correctly.

He signaled the first taxi he saw and rode back to the park. It was nearly dark.

Irish had been drinking steadily for two hours and was mildly drunk when he saw the man walking across the park toward him. He had on the same raincoat and dark glasses. "Hello there, guv'."

The man sat down and swallowed nervously. "Where are we?"

"Fine, mate, we're fine," Joey Irish said. "It's settled. They bitched about the money and all, but I stood firm and held me ground and said this wasn't no bloody international assassination we was pulling, and to be happy with what you got."

"That's fine. Did they give you everything?"

"They did indeed. I promised them gratuities, governor. That's the only way to handle their lot."

"That was very smart."

"Yes," the Irishman nodded, realizing that it was, in theory. "Thank you."

"May I have it?"

"What, oh sure." He opened his coat and handed the man a paperback ledger of times, places, dates. "It's all there. I'm sorry I didn't get much on the veteran, but at least we know he was living at the rooming house in Tribeca for a while."

"Your job's finished for now," the sunglassed man said. He

152

flipped through the notebook, studied a page at random, and nodded satisfactorily. "I'd like to thank you. You're very reliable. I was worried you wouldn't be."

Irish touched his cap deferentially. "Cheers, mate, it was my pleasure at all times."

"You do understand my position and my need for complete privacy. If this got out. . . ." He tapped the ledger and looked frigidly at Irish.

Joey Irish smiled back. "You know me, guv'. People in my field have fuck all to go on but a reputation—Excuse me, guv'."

The man seemed unmoved. "Just give me your word as a gentleman that none of this will get out."

"I give you that word, mate," Joey Irish said piously.

"After tonight I don't want to see you again."

"I don't blame you, if this got out . . ."

The man stared at him thoughtfully. "Thank you. It makes things easier." He took his hand out of his pocket and Joey Irish watched it. He handed the Irishman a wallet. "That's a present from me. You don't realize how indispensable you've been. You'll find two thousand dollars in cash inside. Your tip." The Irishman flipped through it excitedly. His heart was thumping. "I trust they'll be no question of further compensation," the man said.

"No mate, not really."

"What—you qualified that."

Irish adjusted his cap. "Well, you see governor, it's like this . . . I got me another copy of that ledger at home and I'm, well, times is hard. . . ."

The man cut into Irish's sermon with an unsteady voice spoken in a half-tone. "You're blackmailing me."

"I don't like that word. It sounds cheap." Irish could see the man was taking it badly. A vein was swelling on the man's forehead at the hairline. Irish would have to get out of there to a public place for his own protection. In the park at dusk anything could happen. "Follow me, let's discuss it over a drink. Like gentlemen."

"Like what?"

"Just follow me, governor, and let me do the talking here on in." Irish thought he might have to tap him with the blackjack to calm him.

They rose, the man a little unsteady. They beheld each other silently and side-by-side sauntered into the ridge of trees at the periphery of the park. Small twigs snapped beneath their feet. The client had fallen back a step and Irish turned impatiently. "Come on, mate!"

"I hate to do this."

"What—" And as Joey Irish watched, horrified, his stricken feet frozen in the bracken, the sunglassed man withdrew a revolver from his raincoat pocket and fired it once, one unerring, unmuffled shot, into Joey Irish's sunken chest. Irish stayed perfectly erect, simply stepping back behind the impact. The man's sunglasses were askew and his strong face looked ruthless and wild. The sound of the shot hung in the air and in the trees like a ghost. Irish slumped to his knees in the soft earth, smiling crazily at the idea of his mortality. Then fell face forward, dead in the leaves.

The sunglassed man continued to stand there: the gun started shaking, violently, so he dropped it. He knelt and retrieved it. Looking over his shoulder, he paused, then flipped the warm body over and felt carefully for a pulse. The blood made a whittling sound as it drained from the body into the dry leaves.

He took his time and went through his victim's pockets. He emptied them. Inside was a wallet with two hundred and thirty dollars. He tore up the wallet and took the cash and the new billfold containing Irish's two-thousand-dollar tip. The camera was in the inside pocket of the tweed coat; he removed it and the blackjack and threw the blackjack into some weeds. Then he rolled the body into a thicket, dusted himself off, and left.

154

At the wall along Central Park West, he opened the camera and smashed the lens on the stone. The film came out in a long sheet of celluloid that he folded and put in his pocket. Next he stepped on the camera and dropped it in a trash bin near a construction site. There were no witnesses and he lowered his shoulders and crossed the street toward the anonymity of Broadway.

27

Cat and Mario spent three hours waiting in the West End Café near Columbia University. The third man, Hector, was outside in the patched-up Chevrolet alternately parking and moving the car each time the police cruised by. All three men were nervous and jittery and wondering where the fuck Joey Irish was. Cat had never known the "Irish" to be late. It wasn't his style, and besides, he knew what Cat and Mario were capable of if deprived of their dope.

To ward off the immediate need for a fix, Cat drank tequila and white wine and chain-smoked. He was perspiring and finding it increasingly harder to light his cigarettes. Mario came out of the bathroom, sniffing. He sat down in the crowded collegiate bar and drank half a glass of wine. "Home boy in there with some blow," he told Cat, speaking loudly above the music.

"Check 'em out," Cat said and got up and went into the men's room. A university guard had some cocaine and Cat nonchalantly asked him for a snort. The man complied; Cat walked out feeling a little better.

"Where the fuck is that son of a bitch?" Mario said tightly.

Cat looked at him: Mario's habit was nearly twice his own. He knew he could hold out until tomorrow if he had to. Looking at Mario and the wildness in his eyes, his taut movements, his sweat, he doubted his friend could last another hour.

He went outside and saw Hector pulling up in the Chevrolet. Cat went over and leaned in. "You see anything?" he asked.

"Hell no, he's playing us for fools, bro'."

"He'll come," Cat promised. "I known him seven years and he ain't let me down yet." Cat scanned the street in both directions, hoping for a miracle. His skin was beginning to crawl in spots and feel tight. "Fuck." He slapped the roof of the car. A young couple went by pushing a stroller and Cat glared at them and they hurried past.

Mario stood up anxiously when Cat returned to the bar. "What do we do man, I need something. A snort at least. Some kind of taste. I'm feeling the monkey." Mario's voice was unfamiliar.

Cat gave it a final thought. Joey Irish was three and a half hours late. What's more, Cat had told him the circumstances: all three of them were broke. By evening they'd definitely need a shot and Joey Irish had assured them he'd be there. He'd set the time and he'd even promised a cash bonus for doing so well with the job, and by the way, he'd said, the boys had steady work if they wanted it driving cigarettes up from Atlanta in a VW van.

He'd promised, Cat thought savagely, his fingers white on the bar.

"Another round?" the barman asked over a Rolling Stones song.

157

Cat nodded; he didn't intend to pay anyway. His back started to itch. He had a thought. To Mario he said, "Wait here."

The university guard was where Cat had left him in the stall of the men's room. Cat faked taking a leak at the urinal until a third man left. Swiftly he put the trash can in front of the door sash and jammed it there. He pulled his knife, the one Diaz had missed while frisking them. The blade clicked out. He kicked in the stall door; it fell off its hinges with a bang. Taking the terrified guard by storm, Cat held the blade under the line of his jawbone. "Give it up, motherfucker," he whispered—deadpan—no doubt about what he would do if the man refused.

"Sure man, be cool, all I gots is yours," the guard said, shaking. He handed over a dime bag of grass, a half-gram of drug-store–grade cocaine, and eighty-three dollars in cash. Cat stuck him and the man leapt back grabbing at the tiny wound on his neck.

"You ain't holdin' out, nigger?"

"No, I swear bro,' that's all there is, Jesus!"

The man was a Columbia campus guard, they didn't normally carry guns. Cat checked him anyway and found a razor and a roll of dimes. He flushed the razor down the toilet and pocketed the dimes. "Turn around, on your knees, motherfucker. Hands behind you." The man urinated uncontrollably in his trousers and slipped, trembling, to his knees. "Christ." Cat kicked him. Quickly he undid the man's belt and used it to tie his hands together. Then he tore the guard's pants down, revealing his ass. With the knife he slashed the soiled underwear. If the guard followed, he'd look ridiculous.

"You sit here for the count of one hundred or I'll slit your throat like a hog, motherfucker."

"Yes." The man spoke the word like a prayer.

Cat broke the lightbulb with a quick thrust of the stiletto point. The room blackened. He kicked the trash can free and passed calmly through the crowd; he nudged Mario. Outside, Hector was still there. They all three got in and drove to 116th Street and Lenox Avenue and spent the eighty-three dollars and traded the coke for a total of one hundred and thirty dollars worth of mediocre heroin.

They slept in the car in a vacant garage near 135th Street under the subway tracks. Normally they'd go to their respective old ladies' houses, but they'd committed a crime and chose to lay low. Cat was feeling no pain, so instead of dispatching Hector, he walked to a store and bought the *Daily News* and the racing form and some cigarettes. He was back in the car drinking coffee when he got to page eight and saw printed there the driver's license photo of Joey Irish. He scanned the article hungrily: Joseph Scott Mahoney was found shot to death in Central Park near 68th Street. One shot, a .38 caliber into the heart.

He skipped to the line that said the cops suspected murder by an acquaintance: the body was shot at close range; credit cards were left in the wallet and jewelry on the body, prompting police to speculate that "the attack was made to resemble a robbery."

He closed the paper and poured the rest of the coffee onto the street. Soon he would need another shot and now Joey Irish was dead. The idea alone made him scratchy. . . . His mind leapt around in the grip of panic . . . Who did it? Another junkie? Then he saw it clearly and it made sense.

Diaz did it.

Irish had been trailing him. Maybe Diaz turned the tables. The paper had said it was a .38 shell. Cops use .38s. Diaz was an ex-cop. Maybe Diaz killed him and stole his stash. Cat started the Chevrolet with tears in his eyes and drove to Diaz's apartment.

They were still high so they had very few reservations about going directly into the apartment building, up the stairs to Diaz's premises. The door was locked. Cat worked the lock with his stiletto; it wouldn't budge. Using the fire extinguisher they smashed the glass mesh door, only to find that it wasn't glass but the sort of plexi-glass from which they build basketball backboards. A door opened on the next floor. An elderly Spanish woman called out that she was phoning the police.

Furious, they retreated back to the car.

The doped consensus was to wait until Diaz got home, then jump him on the stairwell on his way up. Cat parked the car in an alley with a view of the building front. It dawned on him slowly as he sat at the wheel, drinking beer in quart bottles, that Diaz would still have the .38 on him if he killed Joey Irish—which he undoubtedly had. This bothered him. Neither he nor his two friends Mario or Hector packed heat. It seemed they were stopped so often by the cops, the risk would be too great. Packing a gun meant an automatic year in jail . . . without dope. His veins would dry out. He'd lose his woman and his little girl. Heroin was okay to have on you. So long as you weren't dealing it, the cops wouldn't give a damn. Guns were the things. Diaz had at least one. They didn't.

It took some time but the notion came to Cat within forty-five minutes of parking. They could get the girl! If Diaz was untouchable, they could get revenge with the girl, the one Diaz liked. Cat had seen them together holding hands. Cat thought: the next best thing. And all in the memory of Joey Irish. He looked at Mario. "You drive." The excitement was thick in his voice.

"What's up?"

"We get the girl." Cat shoved over and Mario took the wheel. Cat removed his stiletto. There was some dried blood on it from where he'd touched the nigger guard in the bathroom. He scraped this off with a dirty fingernail and practiced flipping the slender weapon as they drove off.

28

Diaz crossed the street. He could see her standing all alone in front of the St. Mark's cinema on 8th Street. The wind blew her black hair back and she reached for it calmly and tucked it behind her ears. She looked lovelier than he'd ever seen her, so lithe and feminine standing before the cinema door with practiced poise. Her chin was up and her hands in the pockets of her khaki coat. Instead of approaching directly, Diaz loitered on the sidewalk beside a hot dog kiosk, watching her. She reminded him of all the women he'd ever truly wanted, yet for one reason or another had never got to know.

A group of young people came out of the theater, arm in arm, smiling. Carmen very casually turned and watched them go, appraising them. And then it struck Diaz what had made him hesitate and study her as he had. All alone in front of the movie theater on a late October afternoon, she looked as if she had nowhere else to go, and he wondered if this was so. He felt a sudden deep closeness to her which transformed into a feeling of protectiveness. He stepped around the vendor's cart.

"Hello, Willy," she said.

She'd never used his Christian name before. "Have you been waiting long?" he asked.

"No, I just got here this minute."

"Oh." He stared at her, she looked uneasy.

"We'd better hurry. The movie starts at six."

They sat through two David Niven movies—Diaz's favorite actor—then ate dinner at a Mexican restaurant near Union Square. Throughout, she'd been pleasant but preoccupied as though some more important matter concerned her that made her anxious. Diaz asked her over drinks if there was anything wrong.

When she looked up her eyes were teary. She excused herself for the ladies room and when she came back he could see she'd been crying.

They took a cab to the West Side and Riverside Park and walked along the esplanade bordering the Hudson River. He tried holding her hand and twice she'd found ways of freeing herself. Her hands were cold. He felt his morale sinking; something in the back of his mind reminded him that all along this had been too good to be true. She couldn't care for him; he saw that now and walked beside her in sullen silence beneath the yellow lights of the esplanade.

Finally at the end of the path he stopped. "Look, Carmen, is there anything wrong? Would you rather I took you home?" The night wind had picked up and shook life into the trees along the path, rustling the autumn leaves.

She looked out over the river. The moonlight splashed across the tops of the swells. The water looked black and forbidding. "You wouldn't let me down, would you?"

The question stunned him. "What? No, never."

162

When she looked at him, her face was young and vulnerable. "I've always found it hard to trust people," she remarked softly. She crossed her arms. "I just need you to hold me, that's all."

Diaz frowned. Had he heard right? He felt his confidence rushing back. Perhaps it wasn't him. Perhaps she was troubled by another matter. Could it be that she felt equally as insecure? He stood behind her and wrapped his arms around her shoulders and chest. He kissed her neck and felt himself getting aroused by her scent.

"Sometimes, the nights scare me," Carmen said.

"Why?"

"I don't know. It reminds me of when I was a little girl and my father died. I remember feeling so terribly alone and so afraid that my mother would go too."

Diaz thought of Maria's children and the likelihood that these kids were having the same feelings. A question had been eating at him. It surfaced and he asked it. "Carmen, is there someone else?"

"No, Willy. There was, but that's over now."

Diaz turned her around and put his hands on her hips. They were firm and well shaped. He said, "The place on Park Avenue, all those odd hours . . . You didn't work there . . . Do you miss him?"

"No." She tried to twist back around, he held her firmly. Her glistening eyes crept up to him. "I missed you." She bit her lip and stared at his tie. "I'm beginning to think that all those times I visited his home, I was searching for something that wasn't there. I realize that now. And then you appeared investigating Maria's disappearance, and I got to know you. And now I think I might have found what I've wanted all along. I've been searching for you, Willy, for this."

She made perfect sense. All along through the years, he'd been searching for this. It seemed so natural. They'd fallen into it so swiftly that there was only one explanation: it was so right. He kissed her on the mouth and tasted her tears.

163

The feeling came alive in his heart and spread out like a fever into his limbs and in his groin. He touched her firm breasts and felt the nipples, pinching them lightly so she gasped and offered her tongue, and Diaz realized how long it had been since it had felt like this. This was love and there was no comparison.

He took her hand and walked her into the trees, oblivious to the elements and the night, and made love to her standing against a stone wall. She shuddered and clutched him and he came long and heavy, their faces wet with each other's mouth. Afterwards he remained inside her, numbed by the magnitude of his orgasm and by the passion that beat through them like a storm.

In the foyer to her building she stopped. Pressing both of her hands flat against his chest, she pushed him back against the wall. The look in her green eyes was coy and warm and girlish. It was remarkable, Diaz thought, how much more lovely she was without the anger. The hard edge had left her face. She moved gracefully and guilessly, like a child.

She produced from her purse a clipping torn from a magazine. Carefully, she unfolded it and when it was spread out, she presented it. He nearly laughed. The picture was of a cottage in the country somewhere with a picket fence and a yard and a brick walk lined with flowers. The paper was yellow and the creases were worn through. "It's very nice," he said, not sure how she wanted him to react.

She smiled and rubbed her head against his shoulder. "It's my house. I'm going to bring the children up in a house like this someday."

"That would be nice."

"It's all I want," she said. "It's all I've ever really wanted ever since I was a little girl, and I'll do whatever it takes to get it, even if I have to work two jobs and a hundred hours a week."

"And I'd come and visit you."

"Would you?"

"Sure, we could play with the snakes." Diaz grinned.

"Snakes? There are no snakes in New Jersey."

"Is that where it is?" he asked, careful not to press her for details that might destroy the fantasy.

"What? Yes, it's wherever I want it to be."

She folded the picture and put it away. He kissed her cheek. She checked the time and immediately remarked how tired she was and how she had to get up early the next morning. They made a date for the following evening.

"Thank you for dinner and David Niven and the walk in the park." She eyed him coquettishly. Then her expression sobered: "I've never trusted any one person entirely before—but there's something about you that makes me wonder . . . whether I shoud risk it."

"You should."

They kissed and said goodnight. Diaz waited until she went inside, then went out the front door and stood out of the light across the street.

It had been so long. In a sense tonight dated things. Not since Tina had it felt like this. He lit a filterless cigarette and smoked it leaning against an iron bannister. The air was cool and humid and carried the smoke away in dense cloudy patches. The street light overhead was dead and Diaz stared at her building and realized how far he'd drifted from what really mattered in life. Wasn't this it, he thought?

Then her door opened. Light from the foyer washed over the cement stairs. He smiled in anticipation as Carmen hurried down the steps. It occurred to him she hadn't seen him yet. It was dark out, her eyes were not yet used to it. He was about to run out and catch up to her, but the expression on her face disturbed him. She looked determined—as though the hard edge had crept back into her features. Her gait was measured but quick. Diaz followed her.

She hailed a taxi at the corner and again he felt like calling out. Instead he slipped into a cab and followed her to 89th

165

Street and Park Avenue. *His* building. She got out and went inside.

At first it seemed like a nightmare. He forced himself to think rationally. It might be nothing more than a monumental misunderstanding. Maybe she'd left something in there that she needed? Maybe she had a girlfriend in the same building? His mind searched for possibilities that would salvage things.

He sat back against the vinyl taxi upholstery and realized he was clutching at straws. The minutes ticked off and the driver pestered him and all Diaz could think of was Carmen inside with a man he'd never met and it made him want to vomit. He rolled down the window. The air chilled him; his senses were heightened as though he'd passed into some mild form of shock. He wanted a cigarette but couldn't remember which pocket they were in, and didn't want to waste energy searching.

Finally, after eighteen excruciating minutes he sat forward and touched the glass divider of the taxi. "Take me home please," he told the driver.

"Look pal, where's home supposed to be? There's seven million people in this town. How am I supposed to know 'em all?"

Diaz rubbed his temples. "Oh, One hundred and sixth and Second."

When the car reached its destination, the cabbie said, "I wasn't trying to be difficult back there, but I'm at the end of my shift and I ain't eaten in ten hours."

"I'm sorry," Diaz said, not thinking clearly.

"Don't apologize, pal."

He pulled himself out of the cab and closed the door quietly. The cab drew away; its tailights dazzled. Diaz bought a beer in a paper bag and walked with it, barely sipping it, for an hour. The beer was warm now from his hand. Across the street was his old haunt, the Pimlico Arms, where he'd gone to indulge his passions and get his mind off the

166

pain without the neighbors knowing. For twenty dollars he got a double room with a black-and-white television and a vibrating bed. He raised the phone and dialed the number from memory.

The madam answered. He placed his order, "Send someone attractive," gave his name and address, and hung up.

As he pondered it, her behavior began to make sense. He fit it into its own perspective and wondered how he could have been so stupid as to believe she cared for him. She'd had a fight with her sugar daddy. Diaz had simply been there at the right time and she'd used him as a buffer to occupy her emotions.

She had probably come home to find a phone message from him telling her all was forgiven, et cetera, and to please come back.

Diaz hated himself for being so naive. He was a man who prided himself on street *savoir faire*. Then why this? Carmen was after Park Avenue game; what could she possibly have seen in Diaz? Was he that fucking egotistical to think that a girl like that would want him?

He stopped thinking. The questions tore at him. He'd remained unattached for so long, why suddenly had he given in? Why, he wondered, had he opened himself up to the pain?

Then the truth fought its way free. Unlike all those before her, Carmen meant something to him.

But that was past. He was strong and he could bear it just as he'd borne other bouts with pain. Time would heal it.

He switched on the television set for company and pulled a flask filled with gin from his pocket and sat on yesterday's sheets, drinking it. Someone banged discreetly on his hotel door and he leapt up to let her in.

167

29

Hurrying out of her building, Carmen felt a brief swell of guilt. She pressed the beret flatter to her head and hastened down the steps to the corner. The guilty feeling reappeared and she smiled tentatively and dismissed it. There was no need to feel guilty tonight.

She stopped on the corner in the cold damp air watching for taxis. She thought of their coupling in the park. Her long legs were still slightly weak at the knees. There were brambles on her stockings. She hadn't planned for anything to happen, she was simply seeing him for a date. She enjoyed his company and found him physically attractive, and though she hoped eventually they would grow closer, nothing had been scheduled to happen tonight.

A car swerved past and she wondered if this was true. Hadn't she thought about Diaz during her times with David?

168

Hadn't she missed him? Hadn't the prospect of loving him made her ecstatic yet at the same time vulnerable and afraid? And now they had slept together. She smiled. Did you call it "sleeping together" even if you were in the woods, standing? A truck roared by, vibrating the sidewalk.

Carmen felt better. The idea of what she had to do tonight was not so unnerving. Diaz had given her the conviction she'd needed all along. He was the catalyst. He was flesh and blood and not just a figment of her wishful thinking, and in his presence, she liked herself.

A car started its engine further up the street and crept up the block with its lights off. She glanced at it: a blue Chevrolet wagon. Her father had driven a Chevrolet. Just then a taxi approached her from the opposite side of the street, crossing the lanes on an angle. It braked suddenly. To avoid a collision the Chevrolet spun away and accelerated into the traffic; its lights popped on. It merged with the traffic and disappeared. She gave the driver the address of David's building.

The doorman smiled and said hello. David wasn't there but was expected back by midnight. Relief washed through her. She thanked him. It was just eleven o'clock now. What she had to do would only take a minute. She climbed into the elevator.

She had her key still and used it to get into apartment 9A. The door opened easily. The front room smelled familiar, but somehow no longer seemed warm and private. The air was stale and smelled of disinfectant. Stepping inside she snapped on the light. The foyer walls loomed in around her. The silver striped wallpaper seemed tinny and cheap. Carmen crossed to the center of the living room where ritually they'd begun the charade. The room was spotless and by New York standards, huge. The ship painting, which had always seemed so bright and animated, looked dull. David had bought a new couch, this one with a seersucker pattern.

Her hand, she discovered, was poised at the cleft of her

169

throat. The memories crept up from every corner, suffocating her, making it impossible to realize that she had ever felt comfortable here. She tore the curtains aside and tried unlatching a window. It wouldn't budge. She located the switch to the air conditioning and pressed it. Cool air seeped into the room through vents in the floor.

Quickly she opened her coat—no wonder she was hot—and withdrew the thick gray bank envelope from her sweater. Unfolding the top, she thumbed through the money one last time: eight thousand dollars in fifties; all he'd given her plus interest. The thousand or so she'd earned typing manuscripts for David's friends she'd kept and had changed into a certified check that remained in her bag.

She set the envelope with the cash on the glass table against a scrimshaw carving of a whale's tooth. Then she buttoned her coat and padded back across the Persian carpet for the door. She remembered the lights and the air conditioning and went back to turn them off as his keys sounded in the door.

It opened and pale light shone in from the hall. David stood in dim relief in the doorway, tall, erect. He was wearing a fedora and clutching a valise. "Carmen."

She was standing in near darkness. Fright moved in her, a sense of panic threatened.

David switched the light on. He set his valise down and took the hat off. "What is it . . . were we meeting tonight? You know I completely forgot." He went over and kissed her: his lips were icy. When she made no move to return the kiss, he stared at her. Over her shoulder in the library he noticed the envelope on the coffee table. He looked at her again, then brushed by her and picked it up. The money fell out in a solid packet. David caught it, looked closely at it, then stared at her, perplexed. Recognition slowly lit up his face. "So . . . no note? Just goodbye, that's it? After five months, just this?" Angrily he threw the money at the couch. "Does that make it official, you're free of me now?"

His long face was flushed. A section of gray hair hung between his narrow eyes.

"David, I'm sorry."

"Christ."

"I thought it best . . ."

"Christ, is that really how you planned to do it? Don't I warrant more than that?" He was shouting now and his fists were clenched.

"I'm sorry if I've hurt you, but it wasn't right. I couldn't take your money because you'd been so kind to me. I wanted to remember us as friends, David. I couldn't think of any other way."

"Well, you didn't use much imagination, what am I some sugar daddy, some pimp to be bought off while you switch to a new stable? Is that how you view this?"

"Stop it." She found she was no longer so in awe of him. His distinctive face was contorted with anguish and in the back of her mind was the realization that she'd caused the anguish. She'd used him; whatever he did to her now, she deserved. His face blackened and he took a step toward her, raising his hand in frustration.

"David!" The word leapt from her throat.

Abruptly David stiffened. The raised arm sagged. He looked at the couch and the packet of fifty-dollar bills, then back to Carmen. Finally his stare fell to the floor. He covered his face with his hands and wept.

A sort of grief flooded through her; a grief for the living. Now she was in control. She advanced and guided him to the couch, then fixed him a brandy at the bar. She wrapped his long fingers around the glass. "Thank you." He sipped deeply from it.

"I lost my head. I don't know what came over me." He drank down the remainder of the brandy. "When I came in and found you . . . I actually thought you were here to surprise me. Things seemed to be going so well." He shook his head and pushed his hair back out of his eyes. "When I saw

171

the money and realized what it meant and that you were leaving me, I, for a second, I lost my head. I wanted to hurt you Carmen."

"I could tell."

He sat back and laboriously withdrew a needle-thin joint from his shirt pocket. He lit it and held a lung's worth, then exhaled. He passed it to Carmen and she refused. "Do you really think it's right to end like this, after all we've been through?"

"I do."

"I don't know, it just seems so dramatic." He hit on the joint. The red ember swelled.

"Splitting up is never easy." She realized then that it had been far easier than she'd ever suspected. She looked him up and down; his long, rather awkward figure seemed so alien. That she'd ever enjoyed making love to him was like a bad dream now.

"It wasn't necessary to return the money. That's yours to keep. You earned . . . it was a gift to a woman I thought I could love." He set down the joint and gripped his knees. "I've never had a really conventional relationship, you see."

"I have to go now." She stood. He caught her hand and kissed it.

"Take the money, Carmen, please, for me. We've spent five months of our lives together. That must count as something."

"No, David," she said firmly.

"Please." His tone was pleading.

"You heard me." Her beliefs gave her strength.

"Carmen, I want you to take the money . . ." He stood up. "Please come back here. It's my present, it's . . ." David was nearly crying again. He followed her into the hall, attempting to secure their bond with the money he worshipped. The closing elevator doors blocked off his supplications.

She signaled for a taxi then thought, happily: too expen-

172

sive, and crossed Park Avenue to Madison and rode the bus to 102nd Street.

For twenty minutes she stood on the stoop to the detective's tenement, her finger alternately depressing the small chipped button marked 2D. No reply. It was past midnight, where was he? She tried it once more, imploring him to answer. She needed him tonight. Finally she gave up and started home, buoyed by a kind of girlish enthusiasm, thinking of him.

Only when she reached her building did she admit to herself how exhausted she was. So much had happened today and all of it good. Leaning on the front door, searching in her purse for the keys, she realized that for the first time in her life she was thoroughly, unequivocally happy and giggled delightedly.

She glanced at the empty Chevrolet parked across the street and pushed into the building.

In the hallway she suddenly realized the TV wasn't going; it had been when she left. Popi usually watched it far into the morning. She shrugged, the sound must be down, and stepped inside. The smell of whiskey assailed her. Something fell and crashed. A voice whispered; someone laughed. Carmen turned, retracing her steps to the door . . . it's just a joke, it's Willy . . . feeling her way in the blackness for the light switch. A hand brushed by at her throat and she froze with the realization that it wasn't Diaz, and reached blindly and thought of the children.

30

The big man had been back at the house on Long Island for two days and nothing had changed. Things never changed, he thought, although secretly he saw this as a good thing. He had fixed the "bad" thing without altering the status quo—and now he was home again and nobody seemed to mind.

He'd been given an order. Very succinctly and without explanation he was ordered to take the dogs to the sea and shoot them and row their bodies out and dump them overboard. He wasn't told why, something about a newspaper article; but it was an order and who was he to disobey an order, particularly after what he'd done. Jesus, he was lucky just to be allowed home.

He carried the package of meat to the beach and dropped it unceremoniously on the pebbly sand. The meat was raw, a

174

rich blood color, and contained no bones: this was his own plan more or less and he wanted it to go perfectly.

Doberman Pinschers had always scared him. As a boy he had been bitten by one and he'd plotted all summer long to get his revenge. Finally he lured the beast to a corner of the garage where he'd been leaving steaks every day for a week. This time, however, the steaks were laid within a circle of hunting traps with serrated edges, and the beast stupidly fell for the bait. The traps snapped and broke two of the dog's legs. As it lay helpless, whimpering like a baby, he crushed its head with a mallet.

So the grim task that lay ahead this afternoon held a special memory for him. And as he led the four dumb, happy Dobermans from the kennel by the house to the meat on the beach, he was smiling secretly.

The dogs hustled down the slope and saw the meat. Their pointy ears pricked up. They turned to look at him and he said "Okay" enthusiastically. The animals pounced and tore into the steaks. He watched them for half a minute, then dug his boots into the sand and blew them out of the water with seven blasts from an automatic twelve-gauge shotgun.

He stopped, breathed deeply, and glanced through the falling darkness at the sea, then at the trees bordering the beach. The forest was thickest at this point: the beach led to the bracken and from there the tall shrubbery and then the pines. Kids sometimes fucked in there, he thought. The nearest pine swayed like a finger in the sea breeze.

His thoughts returned to the dogs. To get a better look at the damage he'd done, he knelt in the pebbly sand.

His heart leapt.

The largest and fiercest animal stood up. The man stared, struck dumb with the shock of seeing the dead come alive. The animal's thick coat—blood-flecked—shone in the partial moonlight and its mad eyes sparkled wetly; its teeth were showing. Expecting it to lunge, he instinctively put his hands to its throat. He hit its head with the barrel of the

175

shotgun. The weapon dropped. For a taut second he was the child about to be bitten by the Doberman at the rented house on Cape Cod. The only real fear he'd ever known returned to him.

Then the dog darted crazily up the beach and dipped into the blackness of the forest like a spirit, without a sound.

"Shit!"

By the time he'd draped the other animals in chains and rowed them out to sea, he'd nearly forgotten about the animal in the woods. It was bleeding and therefore wounded and would die eventually, he thought. Killing the dogs was his opportunity to prove himself and what was important was that the man in the house not find out about it. He didn't want the man to know he'd screwed up.

One hundred yards out in the rowboat he heaved the dogs into the sea one at a time. The boat rocked, bubbles foamed on the water and a black stain spread across its scalloped surface reminding him of the dead bartender and making him feel strangely repulsed. He rowed back to shore with the current, wondering if it was going to rain.

31

It was 3 A.M. and Diaz lay in bed staring at the white ceiling, ignoring the naked woman stretched out beside him. The night depressed him as it often did. Normally he thought of Tina: Tina whom he'd lost to a junkie in a supermarket where she'd gone to buy him ice cream. A bungled robbery attempt and an overzealous security guard . . . a wild shot . . . his wife was dead. He closed his eyes at the memory.

This time, however, this night was reserved for Carmen. He reasoned that the sooner he finished with the case, the sooner he could step back into the life he'd always lived; one without Carmen or the thought of Carmen or the awful vulnerability.

He tried concentrating on the events of the murder. Are there suspects? Then where are they? How would I do it?

Why would I kill a priest if I was kidnapping a girl? Where would I go afterward? He formed suspicions, wild ones with little merit, which did nothing to advance his cause. On the end table was the empty flask of gin. His stomach grumbled and he wondered if he was getting an ulcer.

Gingerly he removed the whore's leg from his groin. She made a catty noise and said something in her sleep. The room smelled of cheap cologne and beneath that the musky odor of sex and booze. That he could endure the whore's presence now, after the fact, he attributed to the gin and the feeling of utter loneliness the night had brought. He missed people: anyone whom he cared for and who cared for him; he missed Leary. He felt like a once optimistic man whose life had taken a turn for the worse: he could still picture what might have been, and it demoralized him. A distant yet potent fear gripped him that he might grow old alone. The whore placed her hands on her belly and rolled over. Diaz looked at her ass and felt little desire.

In the morning he got up slowly and stuck his head in the sink and turned on the cold water. He toweled his head. The whore muttered something unintelligible and turned over onto her back, spreading her legs. Her vagina glistened. Diaz could smell her. He said, "I'm not through with you. Wait for me."

He dressed and went to his office and started making phone calls. He discovered that Tim Deluca had been enrolled for a term at NYU before dropping out. He'd had two jobs: one as a waiter, the other as a messenger boy. Somehow he'd lost both and had been forced to live for a time on food stamps. His last known address in New York was the West Side YMCA at 63rd Street. There was an address for him in Maine. Diaz called information. That number was no longer in service. For ten dollars Diaz persuaded a clerk at the 'Y' to relinquish a file photo of young Deluca. The boy in the picture looked old for his years. He had a narrow head and a muscular neck. The eyes were weak and small like his father's. The kid looked like a loser.

Diaz thought: who am I to call anybody a loser?

In the lobby of the 'Y' he dialed the Madison Pub. A voice told him Mickey would be in to tend bar that night; a bright spot in an otherwise gray day.

The young future middleweight champion was at a table in Alphonse's Bar, drinking beer with a large Levantine man wearing the kind of pork-pie hat you rarely saw outside of the movies. The kid saw Diaz and indicated the back door with his thumb. "He's in," he said and turned back to the man at the table.

Alphonse was watching a game show in his underwear. The underwear was loose, the elastic was gone, and one of his nuts hung out. "Shit, don't you knock?" The fat man grabbed a towel off of the floor and hastily covered himself. "Jesus, Diaz—I'm busy. I got company, so whatever it is come back tomorrow."

A young Spanish girl came out of the bathroom wearing one of Alphonse's red brocade shirts. She had nothing on under it and her legs were golden.

"I didn't know you had a daughter."

"Shut up." Alphonse leaned forward and smacked the TV off. The towel dropped. The girl giggled. Alphonse fished for something in the cabinet beneath the portable television. He found a set of keys and threw them hard at Diaz. They missed and hit the wall. "There. Now go see that fucking car, my fucking car, and get the hell out of here."

"I don't want to see the car. I want you to sell it," Diaz said crisply.

"What—why?"

"Just sell it. Subtract my debt and any interest and give me the rest in cash." Diaz looked at the girl. She had a wide nose and no chin but her hair was long and black like Carmen's."

Alphonse sat back down and crossed his fat hairless legs. "Look, why don't you think this over. I'm one of the few people that knows what that car means to you, Puerto Rican. Why don't you go home and eat some beans and think it over.

179

Come back sober and then we'll talk." It was as close to compassion as Alphonse had ever come in Diaz's presence.

For a moment Diaz considered doing it. "No, I'm taking stock. I need the cash." He thought: to do what with, to go where with? Did he really want to leave? He did. Things had to change. "I'm leaving New York."

Alphonse was sitting up in the chair, the towel bunched over his groin, looking intrigued yet bewildered, like a priest in a locker room. "You're drunk."

"I'm not drunk; sell the car." Diaz picked the keys off the floor and went over and put them in Alphonse's jewelled hand.

"Diaz, I'm looking out for you."

"I'm all grown, fatso. Leave me alone."

Alphonse turned toward the girl. "Get in the bathroom, we gotta talk." The girl went, shaking her plump ass. Alphonse waited until she'd shut the door. They could hear her start to pee.

"The other night when things was heavy and I'm in here waiting for some gumbo SOB to show up at my door and blow my brains out, you came in. You listened."

Diaz wasn't sure of his point. "So?"

"That meant a lot at the time, listening to me. You're brave for a PR. I sort of owe you one."

"If you owe me one, then sell the goddamn car in a hurry."

Alphonse ignored him. "It turned out okay in the end. The prick I had beaten was in the hole to his family for six large which is why the wops was pissed off; they thought he wouldn't be no good for his payments. So me catching him before he leaves town saved the wops some dough too." He lit a cigar. "But thanks."

"For what?"

"For listening."

"I faked it."

"Fuck yourself." The girl came out of the bathroom, gig-

180

gling again. The shirt was open in front. The dark patch of hair at her pubis showed. Alphonse stared at her. "Slut."

"I'll be back next week," Diaz said.

"You're trusting me to sell the Jaguar and give you the difference?"

"I know what it's worth. I know where to find you."

"Big shit," Alphonse said and itched himself. "I know where Racquel Welch lives but that don't mean squat. And by the way, don't bother the kid on the way out. He's talking shop with a guy from the Garden. Some promoter is giving him a Friday night headliner, can you believe it? He's heading the card at the Garden at his age. Explain *that*, hotshot. That's more than you ever did in your whole career. Puerto Rican, they put you in for practice to make your competition look good. . . ."

Alphonse's mean streak was showing and Diaz looked at his wide ugly face and felt a little sorry for throwing his compassion back at him. He left.

"It kills you to admit that the kid is better than . . ."

Diaz wasn't thirsty. His stomach hurt him from too much gin and no food, but he sat at the bar and drank shots of Wild Turkey and wondered if Carmen had spent the night on Park Avenue.

Diaz lingered at the bar for twenty minutes before the promoter in the hat went in to talk to Alphonse. The kid came over and sat down beside him smoking a cigarette. Diaz waited until he set the cigarette in the ashtray, then picked it up and smoked it himself. The kid smiled. "Okay, daddy."

"The fat man says you're fighting at the Garden on the main card."

"Yeah, in two weeks." The kid ordered a beer from a middle-aged man with a Fu Manchu moustache. When it came he held it close and sipped it. "You were a fighter."

"You don't headline at the Garden that soon. What's the

181

catch?" The kid frowned and remembered to sip his beer. Diaz asked, "Who're you fighting?"

"Heraldo." The kid said toughly.

Now Diaz saw it; he'd suspected it as soon as Alphonse had mentioned Madison Square Garden. The kid was unknown. He had no backing, just guts and maybe raw talent. Heraldo was twenty-two and one and had an agent and management and a contract to sell razor blades on Puerto Rican television. The kid had made the grapevine via the amateurs and maybe some work in the ring at local gyms. The promoters had heard about him; they'd taken a look, watched him spar, saw something rough: he had enough talent.

They would give him an "opportunity," change his name, compile a phony stat sheet—maybe make him eight and two—and swear by it. The kid does okay for three rounds—the duration of all amateur matches. Heraldo knows this and paces himself. In the fourth round he moves in and confuses the kid, and, shifting tempos, cuts him. From there it might go another round, then the knockout. The kid gets three thousand dollars for losing and keeping his mouth shut, Alphonse gets fifteen thousand and an interview on local television.

The kid's become an "opponent" though. From then on all his fights are decided before he enters the ring. He might have the talent, but he's brought up all wrong, meeting the very best in his most fragile state. If he plays along he gets a reputation and fights other Heraldos; he eats well, maybe puts a down payment on a house. He gets hit a lot, starts thinking slow, ages quickly. If he doesn't play along, they dump him, maybe blackball him, but he needs the money so he takes on anything, until one night he gets caught good, gets fucked up, broken a little. Slips off the track and never quite gets back on.

Diaz looked into a last shot of bourbon. His stomach grumbled. "You know Heraldo's record. No matter what you've got, he's got experience. You're the opponent."

"I'll beat his ass."

"What record they giving you on the programs?"

"No record," the kid said, though in fact the programs would read six and two and say he fought out of Mexico City and had great promise.

Diaz thought of something. "How did you know I fought?"

"It shows."

"Not necessarily. I think Alphonse told you, and I think he told you how it went for me. How'd you do in the Golden Gloves?"

"I won in New York," the kid said proudly.

"So did I." Diaz rolled the shot glass on its base. "But they brought me up too fast. They needed something to fuel the Caucasian fires. Nowadays you need management from the word one."

"I got a wife and a son. I'm *their* management."

"So. You're working. You pick up some tips. It pays the rent."

"I got a second kid on the way. The wife ain't working." The kid's tone was softer, as if the subject of his family had revealed a tender side to him.

"How old are you, twenty-one?"

"Twenty."

Diaz gave him a thoughtful look. "And I guess you're happy."

"I ain't been this happy, ever."

"How much they paying you for fighting?"

"Two grand plus a percentage. A small one," the kid added to make sense.

"You can find a manager in a month. At least with management you got a chance. A manager checks you out, brings you up right, home boy, so you're not seeing Halley's Comet for the rest of your life and you remember your kids' names."

The kid looked intently at his hands on the bar. They were graceful hands, Diaz thought, and for some reason he remembered his mother when she used to wait for him in a field in the Bronx where, supervised by a priest from the parish, he'd boxed the other boys in a ring made of clothesline. "You just need time," Diaz said. At one point in his life, time was all he'd needed.

"Time ain't for free," the kid said.

"Alphonse and I were discussing you. He's keeping it secret, but he's giving you a bonus on account of how he believes in you and you've been doing a decent job around this dump. He's giving you a grand and some time off to get your act together. I've got some names of managers, regular guys looking for talent who won't B.S. you."

"Nobody ever gave me nothin'." He took a rumpled pack of cigarettes from his shirt and set them on the wooden bar.

"Don't mention it to the fat man because he hasn't decided to tell you yet. Just don't fight in two weeks and you get the money. That's the condition. No matter what anybody tells you, even Alphonse, you don't fight or the deal's off. Trust me."

Diaz stood up and left some money on the bar. The kid hesitated, then pushed it back. "Not tonight." The younger man looked embarrassed.

"Maybe I was wrong about you, and maybe you'll make something of yourself after all. You've got two kids and a wife's worth of incentive. Then again maybe you won't."

He waited until Diaz was at the door and blurted out, "Well, I ain't signed nothing yet." He bit his lip. "And God knows I don't want to end up like you, man."

Diaz tried his best to look indifferent and let the door swing shut.

32

She was there in the hotel room where he'd left her, looking
as if she hadn't moved. Her large breasts were spilled over
the sheet. The nipples were flat and there was a slick of
perspiration over her made-up face. She appeared to be
sleeping. Suddenly her heavily mascaraed eyes opened.
"You're back."

Diaz lit a cigarette and gave it to her. She edged up into a
sitting position and drew in a breath's worth. The smoke
poured out of her lungs as she talked. Her mouth was large
and sloppy and slightly turned down at the corners. Her hair
was kinky and braided into cornrows in back. "I ain't been
paid, yet," she said over the cigarette. Diaz almost laughed.
"I need that first," she said.

He took two crisp twenty dollar bills from his pocket and
set them on the sheet. Her small hand jumped for the

money. There were only two bills, forty dollars, ten more than he needed to give her, but she had to count it. Staring at him she said softly, "Thanks." She stretched for the floor and stubbed the cigarette dead on a faded square of carpet. Then she tucked the bills into the toe of a high-heel shoe. The sheet slid down; her hips were fleshy and broad. She had hair around her navel.

Diaz undressed and lay beside her and snaked his hand across the plumpness of her ass to the warm, soft cleft between her legs. Her vagina was hot and perpetually moist with anticipation. She had the musky smell young girls get when they've just reached puberty and are innocently unaware of themselves. He rolled her over and ate her. "Daddy—"

At 10:00 P.M. he answered the door. He'd lain in bed half conscious, listening to the persistent pounding against the thin walls of his mind, eyes half cracked, wondering, floating. He pondered his health, then his ambitions, his sanity. What do you think Carmen's doing right this second? Who is she doing it with? Would he be rich? Was she really like that? In his sleep he had a painful thought that maybe he'd judged wrong and that she hadn't gone back to Park Avenue to be with her lover, whoever he was. The pounding wouldn't stop and it struck him how loud it really was, a sharp resounding sound. Then he understood: the door.

"Where you going?" the whore mumbled.

Diaz ignored her. His knees buckled as he stood and he was forced to sit back on the bed. His mouth tasted of gin and whiskey. He walked to the sink; the water was tepid. He splashed some onto his face and stepped into his pants. He threw the door open and the noise immediately stopped. Silence followed. The kid from Alphonse's was standing anxiously on the threshold. He had on a raincoat one size too small for him.

"Oh hello, kid," Diaz said calmly, as if the kid showing up at his secret hotel room at the Pimlico Arms was the most natural thing in the world.

186

The young man's mouth twisted into a knot. His voice was quick and winded. "There's been trouble. The woman you know, she got attacked. I heard it and thought you'd like to know."

His first reaction was to wonder why the kid had on a raincoat when it hadn't been raining out. Then it hit him. The woman he knew had been attacked. Which woman? Carmen?

Incongruously he thought of Carmen's boyfriend on Park Avenue and the hatred burned like a knife in his stomach. Diaz would kill him. He gripped the door frame for balance. Slowly his senses returned. An unnatural stillness followed. Do Park Avenue lovers beat their women, he wondered?

"Who did it?"

"They don't know."

"Who's they?" He realized he was asking the wrong question. "How is she?"

"Okay now, I think. I don't know the details. They beat her up in her apartment." The kid left out the rape part.

Diaz realized that it couldn't have been the sugar daddy. Why would he go there? And why was Carmen back at her apartment? Hadn't she spent the night on Park Avenue?

The whore was whining for attention. Diaz said, "Quiet!" He took the kid's wrist. "Where is she?"

"St. Luke's Hospital, but she's okay now."

"Wait for me." Diaz dressed hastily, throwing on his shirt and coat. He put his shoes on without socks and stuffed the tie in his pocket. Without glancing at the bewildered prostitute, he fastened the buckle of his belt and led the kid into the hallway. Their feet padded across the cheap, all-purpose carpet as the door eased closed.

33

Leary was in the waiting room at St. Luke's dressed in his street clothes with a raincoat draped over his wrist. His red hair was mussed and he needed a shave. They met at the water cooler near the nurse's station. "I was looking all over for you." He gave his cigarette to Diaz. "She's fine, Willy. She's upset, of course, but she'll come through fine. She's a strong girl."

"When did it happen?"

"Last night. I heard the report through the night sergeant at the Twenty-Sixth precinct. He knew the girl and he knew you. I came over as soon as I heard."

"Thanks," Diaz whispered. His throat felt parched. He took a drink from the water cooler. Leary was studying him and for an instant an intense fear flickered inside him. "You said she was okay?"

188

"She'll be fine."

"I want to know what happened before I see her."

"You can't see her; she's sedated. She'll be out until to-morrow afternoon."

Diaz sensed something. He knew Leary too well. "Why are you staring at me? Level with me, how is she?"

A pained, almost embarrassed expression crept up through Leary's bloated Irish features. "All right. You should know, she was raped. There were three of them and they took turns with her, then they beat her. They were high when they broke in. They overpowered the family, tied them up, and waited for her to come home."

The color drained from Diaz's face. They'd raped Carmen. She hadn't stayed on Park Avenue after all. She'd returned home.

"The rest of the family is fine. The older man took a beating, but he's a tough old bird. He went with his wife to a retirement home for the next few days. The kids were shaken up, but they're safe."

"Where are they?"

"At my place. Nilsa wouldn't let a welfare guardian have them—so we took them in." Leary crossed his arms. "They were junkies and they were bad for a fix, otherwise Carmen thinks they never would have left. They took pictures, Diaz. It seemed . . . for some reason they wanted to get to you."

A whimper of crazy anger escaped him. He shut his eyes and wracked his brain for an answer. Who, for Christ's sake? Who would know he even knew Carmen? "Who were they?"

"We don't know for sure."

"Bullshit." Diaz spat the word out.

"Not for sure we don't. You know the kind of trash that walks these streets."

Diaz was about to demand an answer when the obvious truth sprang into his head: the junkies in the Chevrolet. They knew where she lived and that Diaz was dating her. And what's more Diaz had angered them. He'd shot up the

189

engine to their car and thrown their weapons in the river. Diaz thought: they hang out in the Bronx. He remembered the neighborhood.

"We've got their descriptions and I've got my men on it plus the detectives from the Two-six. We'll pick them up. There are only so many places a junkie can hide."

"Fuck your men. Your men were on her sister for eight months and look where it got them."

Leary pulled a full pack of Camels from his raincoat and steadily tore the cellophane off. He lit one and stretched his bull neck.

Diaz unbuttoned his coat and looked down the antiseptic corridors of the hospital. An intern went by wheeling a man in a body cast. Diaz said, "I'm sorry I said that. I'd like to see her."

Leary shrugged his heavy shoulders. His tattersall suit crumpled beneath the arms. "She's out like a light."

"That doesn't matter."

Leary led Diaz to her room along the hall. The big cop paused. "I told you, they beat her." His words held a cautionary edge. "It was a junkie thing—they went crazy, like animals."

"I'm okay," Diaz said.

In the mountain of blankets and pillows that swelled up around her, she resembled a child. Her slender frame was curled up fetally, her long arms quietly at her sides. Diaz shuddered when he saw her face. Her cheeks were puffy and swollen blue and her nose was bandaged with a strip of surgical tape across the bridge. The skin around both of her eyes was blackening. The right side of her jaw, the side he could see, bore the knuckly imprint of a fist; four contusions, evenly placed, testified to a particularly savage punch. Her lips were split vertically in places.

He stood beside the bed, not quite knowing what to do with his hands. He had an urge to lie down next to her, to hold her and tell her softly that it was all better now. She

190

was safe because he was there and no one would ever hurt her again. A vision of Carmen's house in the country came to him and he saw himself there, playing with the children, and he felt a little stab of longing and loss in his heart. Looking at her still noble features, he thought selfishly: I'm vulnerable.

He tried to imagine what she'd been through and wished he could take her pain away by touching her and feeling it himself. Leary had said the junkies were out for him. Then why hadn't they attacked him? Why her? A deep palpable sadness mingled with feelings of terrible guilt and frustration.

Diaz knelt and kissed the unbruised portion of her cheek. The muscles of her face shivered. A tear formed in the corner of her eye and got caught in her eyelash. "I'm sorry," he said and kissed her again.

On the bureau in the room was a bunch of flowers arranged in a ceramic vase. He asked Leary who had sent them.

"Nilsa."

The initial shock of hearing the news in the hotel corridor had sobered him, lifted him out of the reaches of total drunkenness. He felt now as though he hadn't even had a drink.

Now he'd seen her and he knew the facts. The junkies had been out to get him through her. He'd hassled them and they'd reciprocated by raping his woman. Junkie rationale, he thought disgustedly. Yet, his knowledge of the culprits burned through the shock like a hot sun through the fog. Bolstered by the sweet tension of revenge, his senses were clear and alert. He felt hungry.

At home he put on a black leather jacket, dark pants, and cowboy boots. There was eighteen hundred dollars left of the original money in the bag under the tub drain. He folded the bills and stuffed the wad into his pants pocket. His service revolver had a 3-inch barrel; he'd sawed off the excess inches when he'd quit the force. He broke the cylinder open, jammed in six cartridges, flicked it closed, spun it. It whirred with a smooth clicking like the noise of a roulette wheel. Without its extra inches of barrel, the gun fit his pocket.

He stuffed a handful of cartridges into his coat, then removed them. He opened his palm and the bullets bounced on the desk like dice, clacking: click-clack. The gun was loaded; if he needed more than six shots, he needed more than a gun.

It took his two hours but he found their car in front of the Top Hat Lounge near the South Bronx neighborhood where he'd traced the garage. Diaz recognized the Chevrolet. Stooping, he sunk an ice pick into the front left tire. When he tore it free, the air hissed out.

It was cold and the streets were empty. He didn't know what time it was, it didn't matter. His breath frosted like smoke. He turned the corner into a narrow, gravel-strewn alley. Fifty yards into brick-walled alley a rusted wire fence twelve feet tall created a cul-de-sac. There were two street lights here in a cluster, the bulbs suspended like tiny suns. Only one bulb functioned, and this on half power which radiated a tired glow making Diaz's skin look ashen. He turned and measured the distance to the street.

He chose a spot midway down the alley where the lamplight bleached the pale surface of the brick. His spindly shadow danced across the wall. Kneeling, he cleared a shallow space in the dirt with his hands, ripped some weeds, withdrew the revolver, and lay it flat in the grave. He replaced the weeds so you couldn't see there was a gun there unless you knew. With a piece of sidewalk flint he chalked a circle on the wall four feet above the weapon. He blew on his hands and warmed them. His heart was hammering and there was sweat on his back beneath the leather jacket. Pausing at the entrance to the alley, he considered the odds that he could lead them here tonight and take care of it. He thought: they can't hide.

A tall Puerto Rican in a black suit with high-heel shoes intercepted him at the door to the Top Hat. The man's ears were cauliflowered and he had on a signet ring. "What it be like?" the bouncer asked.

Diaz tried passing him but the man stopped him with a broad hand and said pleasantly. "Gots to check you out, bro'." He frisked Diaz carelessly. "You're okay."

Diaz staggered an uneven path into the noisy crowd. He did a conspicuous circuit of the bar, stepping drunkenly, casually screening the room. So far nothing. They must be at a table, he decided. His beer came, he spilled it, offered to mop it up. Went in to the bathroom. There was a danger he would find them in here, in which case he would decide at the moment whether he would try to take them en masse, unarmed but for the ice pick in his boot, or retreat and stick to his plan. They weren't there. A man offered to sell him crack. A younger man with an afro offered to blow him. Diaz walked out. The smoke and the noise sickened him. The crowd was pressed together like subway passengers at rush hour. Most of the patrons wore denim or leather clothing and imitation gold or platinum jewelry. A fat lady smiled seductively at him. He acknowledged her drunkenly and slipped by her as she tried to rub her breasts on his arm.

Then he spotted them in a booth by the dance floor. The disco light sparkled and for a clean white instant, their stares met. Diaz pretended he hadn't seen them.

It all came down to now, he told himself. Eventually they would learn of the cops' determination to catch them and they would flee the city. Unless he could make them believe he was drunk and get them to follow, he might lose them for good and he couldn't let that happen.

Diaz turned and purposely slipped on a spilled drink. He fell and banged his knees hard on the floor. He picked himself up, thinking: that had to look real. He continued playing drunk as he shoved through the crowd toward the bar. A couple passed him clutching mugs of beer. Diaz bumped the woman, pushing her aside with his chest, appearing to be off balance. Her boyfriend caught Diaz by the elbow. The girl tripped, both beers spilled. "You son of a bitch," the boyfriend shouted. Diaz apologized, smiling, and the irate man reached for him.

Diaz let the boyfriend grab hold of his coat then pinioned the man's wrists in a vice-like grip. They struggled for a bit like Sumo wrestlers, Diaz guiding them as they waltzed through the crowd, disrupting others. Suddenly the bouncer appeared and Diaz gathered momentum and swung the boyfriend into the bouncer so that the bigger man was forced to catch him. The bouncer grabbed the smaller man in a headlock. The girlfriend opened her mouth to scream above the music.

Diaz slipped outside. The cold air was a crisp tonic on his skin. He rested against a parked car, observing the entrance to the Top Hat. The dark-skinned junkie was watching him from the door to the club. He resumed his drunken charade for the length of the block, walking slowly. Then paused to urinate against a fire hydrant. Smiling still, he surveyed the sidewalks, his expression unfocused and seemingly aloof. The bouncer appeared at the entrance to the club and threw the boyfriend onto the sidewalk. The girlfriend materialized at his side, hollering, and helped her man to his feet. Cat appeared amid the crowd at the door and Diaz looked casually away, glancing back long enough to see Cat talking to the bouncer. Cat would be asking the bouncer about the obligatory frisk at the door and whether Diaz, the man who'd started the fight, had carried a weapon.

This was the pause that preceded the choreographed attack. Diaz walked in an uneven line as far as the corner. He turned and hustled across the street along the opposite block to the alley. At the mouth of the alley he leaned against a building and retched and waited and retched again until he heard them scuffling across the pavement. He dipped into the alley.

Their footsteps grew louder; by his reckoning they would be turning the corner of the alley in seconds. He zipped his leather coat up to his neck. Moving fluently, discarding any pretense of drunkeness, he reached for the ice pick in his boot and gripped it tightly and knelt in the darkness, waiting. Then he stood and stepped into partial view in the middle of the alley.

"All right," he said tonelessly in a phrase lost in the cold scutter of feet on gravel.

For an instant he remembered what they'd done to Carmen in her house because of him, in front of the children and the grandparents. He clenched the ice pick tighter and hovered on the weak periphery of light with murder in his heart.

Cat raced in as Diaz expected, a little blindly. In the short sprint across the alley he was winded and his breath was ragged. Cat reached into his shirt for something and Diaz ran at him and struck furiously with his fist on the bridge of the nose. The bone snapped and blood spurted. Cat sidestepped, reaching for balance. Diaz stuck him in the shoulder with the ice pick; he screamed. Diaz hit him again in the throat using all of his strength—*there, motherfucker*—and kicked him as he fell gasping for breath.

Mario had paused in the alley for a weapon. He found a piece of brick, and while Diaz was finishing with Cat, caught the detective on the cheek in a wild brick sucker punch. Diaz lurched back in the instant before impact, avoiding the brunt of the blow. The brick dropped, Mario retrieved it; Diaz kicked him in the head on the temple with his boot. Mario released the brick and walked stupidly, taking crazy bow-legged strides. Diaz struck him viciously on the side of the neck. He slid down the wall, unleashing a deep moan.

There was a sound as the third man emerged from the darkest part of the alley holding a two-by-four. Diaz turned away from Mario, who was no longer a threat—the kick to the head might have killed him—and faced the third man, Hector, who was coming at him with the section of wood held high over his head. Diaz shifted to the right so that the blow missed his head and grazed his left arm and bounced off his calf. The wood vibrated against the hard earth. Diaz punched him once in the face. His head lurched back but he stayed on his feet. He retreated a step, swinging the board. His grip slipped and the two-by-four went flying. Unleashing a wild drug-induced shout, he charged Diaz from a karate stance. The detective crouched. Hector kicked and Diaz— the boxer—timed it and blocked it and stabbed the ice pick deep into the exposed thigh. The man screamed. The ice pick stayed lodged in the leg, stuck into the bone.

Hector crumpled, whimpering, on the gravel and Diaz pounced on him, burying his fingers in the exposed throat. The young face changed color in the dark, the eyes widened and popped. The head thrust forward in a desperate effort and Diaz slammed it back; it twisted and he dug deeper, and in an alley filled with stillness and the drumming of his own ragged breath, he watched the life drain reluctantly out of the junkie in slow, painful increments and he thought of Carmen: Carmen would forgive these people; she would punish but forgive.

The thought lingered; he tried to dismiss it but it stayed with him. Carmen would forgive them.

Then why am I killing this one? Carmen's likeness gradually faded and the corpse in his grip sank back into focus. The man looked so young now. His black hair was curly like a girl's. His chin was unshaven, yet practically hairless, and Diaz thought it over, finally saying to the man: you didn't know what you were doing. Hector's body twitched. Diaz released his clutch.

His hands were numb. Slowly color seeped back into the white cleated finger marks in the soft flesh of the neck. Diaz yanked the pick out of the unconscious body and threw it. The man still wasn't breathing.

He *had* killed him.

Diaz shifted and blew air into the man's mouth, filling the lungs. He sat back: nothing. He tried again, this time pressing down on the chest cavity to empty the lungs; then he refilled them. A gasp—the head shook. Diaz slapped him in the face. The blank eyes flickered and closed and the lungs began to draw breath independently.

Diaz crawled to the mark on the wall. Glass in the gravel cut his palms. He realized the feeling was returning to his hands. He slumped against the wall beneath the chalk mark where the revolver lay, thankful that he hadn't had to use it. He would call Leary and tell him he'd made the collar. They had a good case: there were enough witnesses to the rape.

He noticed his cheek was bleeding and the blood had traced a path to his chin and mouth. He felt lightheaded. He reasoned he could call Leary from a pay phone or a bar or he could find a patrol car.

Cat picked himself up slowly from the ground. His face was mangled and swollen. The slender nose was crushed flat to his face; there was blood in his eyes. He was trying his best to smile. "Fuck you. You killed Irish," he blurted out. "Now we pay you back . . . I get you . . . You're owed it."

Diaz thought: there's absolutely no fear in his voice. No fear but no control; the junkie's dilemma. He's got nothing to lose. It's that simple.

Cat reached into his shirt for his stiletto. He got it out and looked at it as if he was looking at a friend in need. The blade snapped out with a whine and six inches of steel glistened dully, reflecting the lone lamp light.

Unluckily Diaz had stabbed Cat's right shoulder and, as he saw now, Cat was left-handed. Cat screwed his face up and Diaz felt his insides racing against the awful debilitating fatigue; he just wanted to sleep. His fingers tingled and felt sore.

Diaz said, "Put the knife down."

"You killed Irish . . ."

197

"Put it down."

Cat staggered and found his step. His eyes narrowed.

"Put it down."

His sneakered feet brushed against the gravel. The thin knife was poised on a straight angle for stabbing. His fist had blood on it.

"Put it down." Diaz reached into the earth behind him. "Why did you kill him?"

Diaz hadn't killed anyone. "Put it down!"

"No!" a shout. Cat leapt.

Diaz fired twice at the springing figure, catching it high up in the pectorals, severing an artery. The body collapsed grotesquely backward and landed with a thud, one sneaker twitching. Diaz reached over and held the foot still. He felt the muscles and the nerves protesting death. The foot steadied. He slumped back, staying very still, listening to the concussive echo of the revolver, still clenching it, remembering rather than feeling it in his grip. He let it drop with an open hand, distastefully.

Mario was moving. The third man, Hector, started to talk aloud, asking the kind of irrational, somnambulant questions you hear in a hospital at night.

Diaz got up and dragged Cat so that his broad back leaned against the brick, inadvertently below the chalk spot where the gun, the instrument of his demise, had lain hidden. He pried the scarred fingers from the handle of the stiletto. It closed silently and he pocketed it.

Cat's eyes were open and his face seemed less severe in its relaxed state. The eyes were no longer slits peering through a cloud of dope, but rounded and clean like a boy's.

Leary had said they'd taken pictures of her. He patted the body's pockets and removed the roll of exposed film they'd shot of Carmen naked.

He touched the man's forehead, tracing a scar with his fingertips, and combed a wild tuft of hair back on the head. Tears puddled in his eyes as the blood puddled in the dead man's lungs. "I'm sorry," he said and taking the revolver again, opened it and let the bullets fall out into the dirt. He no longer felt any compulsion to call Leary.

Diaz put the gun in his coat and shuffled out of the alley feeling dirty and remote like a notch on a gun.

The subway smells sickened him. He had money for a taxi but he wasn't thinking. His head hurt and his cheek stung from where the brick had smacked him. Gingerly he felt for the wound with dirty fingers and probed the rough edges of the divot of flesh. It was nothing, just a scrape. Then why was he nauseous? He almost lost his balance and staggered out of the way of a garbage can.

The cold air soothed the flushed surface of his face. He wondered if he was getting a fever. He'd killed someone tonight but tried not to remember. He'd killed others; it was never easy though it was sometimes worse. His mouth was sour and he felt like vomiting, but opted for feeling the nausea rather than submitting to it.

He went dizzy on the stairs to the subway platform. The dark, fetid air swelled up at him. It was like breathing car exhaust. The blackness before him sparkled and made him think of sleep. He shook his head violently, side to side, and his headache worsened. Sweat broke out on the backs of his hands. Then the noxious feeling passed. He thanked God and stumbled down the last few stairs thinking of Leary. Leary would appreciate the tip: an alley full of casualties. Three "have-nots" down, one deceased. One spic detective and borderline "have" still up and determined. It came to him again that they'd raped Carmen in her apartment and he remembered that she hadn't spent the night on Park Avenue and this rallied him for a few steps.

A dark-complected man in an overcoat moved out from behind a steel pillar. In his hands he held a violin case tucked halfway under his arm. The leather case was scarred and faded and the overcoat was frayed. He looked hungry

199

and unpredictable and there was a fringe of beard on his tiny recessed jaw.

As the man opened the violin case to reveal the rifle or the machine gun, Diaz pulled the revolver and trained it on the man's chest at the breastbone: it had stopped Cat. He felt drunk.

The street musician removed his bow and violin and with practiced calm pretended not to see the bloodied man with the handgun. The streets were full of them at this hour, this far north. He raised the instrument and started playing and the sweet sounds rang across the tiled corridor, down the tunnel and Diaz thought—remarkably, because he hadn't thought of her since—of the fat woman from the bakery who wore no underwear and used to let him look under her dress when he was five.

The music took him on a short tour of his past, through some good times when he'd felt clean and wore new shoes to church . . . Had he made his bed? Why was Papa mad? . . . After a while his mind cleared. The musician stopped and began again, a racier tune. Diaz fished a bill from his pocket and laid it in the open case on the floor. He backed up and waited for the train.

Twenty minutes later he got off in Manhattan and made his way to the Madison Pub. He stood outside in the blackness and waited with his collar up. It started to rain: thick, cold drops of city water that made a sifting sound on the sidewalks.

Mickey came out after everyone else had left and loitered in his leather overcoat while he fiddled with the lock. Diaz had forgotten how big he really was.

The detective moved and pressed the revolver deep into the cheek above the beard line on the lantern-like jaw. "I'm going to kill you if you don't cooperate. I won't if you do."

Mickey said nothing. His gray eyes whitened and he looked directly ahead. His mouth opened reflexively and he closed it. "What?"

"I just want the truth," Diaz said quickly. He glanced at Mickey's eyes, saw they were steady, checked the rain. It was late; at this hour, in this weather, Madison Avenue would be empty.

He collared Mickey and led him further back into the alcove between the buildings and out of the rain. He spread him against the wall, legs out, arms stretched. "Look at me, slowly." It seemed easier than explaining from scratch. "Do you remember now?"

Mickey arched his heavy neck. "Christ." He looked at Diaz and recognition glinted in his face. His thick animal brow tightened with anger. "You . . . where's my brother?" The words fell out, dry and lifeless like pieces of chalk.

"I don't know your brother."

"Where's Otis?"—the voice more determined, rising an octave.

"I don't know."

"Where?"—One word, fast and desperate, like a lamb's bleat, but rougher.

Diaz sensed it before Mickey even moved. Somehow he knew the barman would try it: boxer's instinct. And he shifted away as the man erupted off the wall, pivoting, eyes bright, large arms swinging. Mickey tried lunging but missed.

Diaz held the revolver on its side and smacked him once on the temple. It nicked him and red showed. Mickey grunted and felt for the source of the pain as if he hadn't expected it. The wild spark died in his eyes. He kept his trembling hand on his temple and sat down on the cold wet ground in the alcove. "I'm hurt," he said evenly. "That hurt."

Diaz thought: *you pussy.* He closed his eyes and counted to two and put the revolver back against Mickey's forehead thinking: I have to do this. The gun's muzzle pressed into the skin on the sloping forehead, making a mark. Some blood seeped out of the mark on his temple.

201

"I'm sick," Mickey said, and rocked over on his side and hawked. The puke rained onto the concrete and the pungent odor of vomit spread across the alcove. "You don't know Otis, honest?"

"No, we've never met."

Mickey looked as if he believed him.

"I won't shoot you if you cooperate," Diaz said.

"I heard you."

"You believe me, don't you? I can see it on your face that you trust me 'cause you know otherwise I'll make this bark and you believe I'll do that." He stopped and collected his emotions. He wasn't here to berate.

Mickey nodded into the revolver. His eyes darted up as a taxi cruised by. Its tires sputtered in the rain.

"Don't look outside, look at me."

Mickey nodded again and shrugged his large shoulders into the leather overcoat. He looked at his vomit and dry heaved once.

Diaz slid two fingers into his shirt and removed the picture of Maria. "You remember her now, don't you, Mickey?"

"Yeah."

"I thought so. Last time I might have believed you and forgotten your bad manners and left you alone, but you gave the game away. You made a crack and called her "Charo." Charo's a blond singer—a bleached blonde."

"I remember. So?"

"Look close. Do you see her hair in the picture? I can't. She's wearing a scarf." Diaz showed him. "Always tell the truth and you never have to remember anything."

Mickey saw his mistake and grimaced.

"You don't lie well. When you were interviewed on the news, all of New York could tell you were bullshitting. Tell me about Maria."

Mickey's expression changed into a sort of what-the-fuck look. "I don't give a shit about the guy. That's why I'm talking," he said prefacing it.

"Okay."

"You said the girl was in some trouble?"

"She still is. We can't find her."

The bartender's eyes skipped to the gun at his head. For a moment he was crosseyed. Diaz kept it there. "They came in twice a week for cocktails. That was a year ago and I ain't seen either of them in months."

"How many months?"

"At least six, maybe more. She would have dinner sometimes, and he would drink vodka and talk to her. They talked quietly like they were girlfriend and boyfriend or something. Usually they sat in the booth in the back. At first I thought she was a prostitute he'd picked up on Eighty-sixth Street, but the more I saw of them and how he treated her and all, I figured it was his mistress." He had trouble with the word; he lisped it.

"Who was the man?"

"I dunno, he was pretty normal looking. He looked rich. He had nice clothes. Sometimes he'd drive up in a limousine and she'd either be here already in the booth, drinking, or she'd come in soon after he arrived."

"Describe him to me."

"Average, sort of old. Handsome still, I guess."

"What was his name?"

"I didn't ask."

"Didn't she use it? You must've heard."

"Yeah, she used it, but I didn't listen. A bartender has to know when not to listen." Mickey said this piously, like a Freemason discussing his code. "He never volunteered it to me."

"Did he ever come in with anyone else?"

"Never, just them two. Nobody else."

"That's not enough." In a moment of frustration Diaz drove the gun barrel further into the forehead, forcing it back so the neck muscles bulged.

"That's all, honest!"

"Where did he live? What did he do? Give me details."

"Jesus, I don't know. I swear."

"Did he pay cash or use a charge? Maybe you've got receipts."

"Cash, always cash. He never signed nothing."

"Who drove the limo?"

"I don't know."

Diaz turned the information over in his mind. He breathed cold air through his teeth, ignoring the rotten vomit smell.

"I think he was from the Island," Mickey suddenly added. "I just remembered."

"Where?"

"I don't know exactly, but I remember one time he was late by an hour and that wasn't like him and the girl got uptight. I had the Knick's game on and they had a report about a pile-up on the Long Island Expressway, and I remember thinking that that's where he came from. It figured, so I mentioned it to the guy when he comes in finally and he looked at me funny and ignored the question."

"That's all you can remember?"

"Yeah."

Diaz believed him. Mickey had lost the dignity required to lie. "Thank you."

"You ain't seen my brother, Otis?"

"No, I haven't."

"I wonder where he went, it ain't like him to stray. He's like a kid really and wouldn't leave town without telling Mom." Mickey's eyes wandered as he groped for an answer.

Diaz stood up. Most of the hate was gone and with it the adrenaline. He lacked even the energy to stretch his limbs. Distractedly he lowered his revolver and waited for the tendrils of defeat to embrace him. They started faintly on his spine. He could feel his cuts and bruised knuckles and his ribs were sore. "I'm sorry if I scared you, but I had to know."

204

"Whatever," the bartender said without interest. "Hey!" he called and Diaz stopped. The revolver was still entwined in his cut hand. Mickey raised his head slightly. "You wouldn't have shot me over this, would you?"

Diaz paused and considered it. "No," he said, raising the gun to the dark sky and squeezing it twice. Two dry, ratcheted sounds followed. "It wasn't loaded."

"—The fuck."

Diaz put his collar back up around his throat and disappeared into the persistent freezing rain.

34

Diaz went home and didn't have a drink, washed, showered, and shaved. There was aspirin in the medicine cabinet: he swallowed four of them. He put petroleum jelly on the cuts on his face and hands and slept on his back. In the morning he called a nurse he knew at St. Luke's. She put on her coat and went out in the rain. Diaz paid her thirty dollars and she stitched up his cheek and knuckle in the light of the bathroom. She put butterfly tape on his forehead and wrapped gauze around his hand. She was going to be a doctor someday and claimed Diaz inspired her. She handed him a phial of antibiotics and gave him a neck rub. Her breasts were barely contained in her thin cotton uniform and she'd left the top two buttons undone. Diaz's face felt tight from the Novocain. He stared purposefully away from her and she said she had to be getting back. They shook hands.

The color was returning to his cheeks and he wasn't sure if this was a sign of health or the flush of fever. His brown eyes looked clean in the mirror when he rolled them. He shaved his moustache off. For two hours he sat at his desk with the radio on, making lists and thinking out loud. The street sounds reflected the stages of the morning. Two men were having an argument about a parking place. A mother was scolding her child for tearing his raincoat. It was close to lunch time. More quarrels occurred before lunch, he reasoned.

His mind was alert. It allowed him to reassess things with insight and pinpoint where he'd gone wrong.

He had to stop thinking about Carmen.

He felt the skin where his moustache had been. He thought: *I'm really very adaptable*. Things rarely defeated him entirely. His resolve for handling problems and searching for solutions was indefatigable. Then why had this case exhausted him?

He called the hospital to check on Carmen's condition. She was still sedated.

On the blotter he'd scribbled incomplete sentences, words, scraps of thoughts pertaining to the case. His eyes picked up the words "Otis and Mickey." Both men were bartenders at the Madison. Mickey's brother was missing. Coincidence? For a minute his mind fogged. A question surfaced. Why would the junkies be following Maria's sister? What conceivable link could Carmen have to any of it? Unless she was involved as unknowingly as Otis, the absent bartender. Another coincidence? No.

There was a missing thread. His mind reached for it blindly. Whoever was behind the attack on Carmen—and had perhaps kidnapped the bartender—was acting calculatedly, deliberately trying to erase any clues that could lead to the killer, if there was a killer. And if they'd truly wanted to silence her, wouldn't they simply kill her?

He paused and drank a beer on an empty stomach. The

207

cold malty liquid felt good going down. It struck him that he was building his case on a weak foundation. He had few facts, only suppositions. Unless he got some assistance in the form of confirmation, he wasn't sure how long he could continue. How long can a man beat a dead horse?

Inadvertently he scribbled the word "dead" beneath "Mickey and Otis."

An idea like a charge swept through him. He dialed Leary. A subordinate got on and said, "Lieutenant Leary is presently vacant from his station." Why is police talk so turgid? "Would you care to leave a message?" He would. "Tell Leary our killer is on the loose and he just murdered a bartender from the Madison Pub."

The adjutant's indifferent tone immediately perked up. "Who is this?"

"Diaz." Diaz put the phone down, changed into his old torn blue suit, and went out.

He bought a paper. There was no mention of the man he'd slain in the alley. Diaz hadn't expected it; junkie casualties rarely made the papers, even the tabloids. The violent death of a junkie was deemed by most cops as "natural causes." The other two junkies had probably recovered and dragged the punctured body to the river, prayed over it, removed all valuables and dumped it in.

Diaz had no set route so he decided to visit the scene of the crime in the hope that this would jar something loose from the granite slab of thought in his mind. The door to Carmen's apartment was unlocked. This surprised him. Nothing was disturbed, although Diaz noticed the furniture in the middle room had been swept carelessly to one side. There was a spot of blood on one wall and powder where they'd dusted for fingerprints on the door frames.

Without thinking he opened a beer in the kitchen. It tasted flat. He poured it into the sink and ran the cold water. Then he walked through each room of the apartment. The air still smelled of children, but children long gone. The heat

208

was on, but the rooms had a clammy chill. The apartment was too quiet, like a room in a motel where nobody stays. He locked the door.

On the way back to the subway a limousine was slowing down at the corner, making way for a black family in church clothes. Diaz passed by the newsstand at the subway entrance.—"Where you been?"

He looked up, realizing then that he'd been walking in a daze like a sleepwalker. He recognized the half-Chinese newspaper man. "Palm Beach. I go there to avoid the damp." He noticed it was raining again. The cold light rain sprinkled the back of his neck.

"What, don't they like Puerto Ricans in Palm Beach?" the newspaper man asked, regarding the cuts on Diaz's face and hand.

"Not particularly, no."

"Should have gone to Miami, bro'. You shaved off your moustache."

"Yes." Diaz turned for the subway, bored by the repartee.

"Wait." Diaz stepped back a foot. The man's expression was suddenly more serious. "Remember that girl you wanted, the one from the neighborhood? I saw somebody else looking for her too."

At first the revelation was wasted on him. He'd so nearly come to accept defeat on the case, that the idea of a lead confused him. "Who?"

"I don't know who, I didn't ask. Some big ugly white guy who looked like he was playing Marine."

"What?" Now the man had thoroughly confused him.

"Well, he looked like a Marine only he acted a little retarded. Of course that doesn't mean shit either because half of the freakin' military is retarded."

Diaz thought: some big ex-Marine type is casing the neighborhood in daylight looking for Maria. He saw it: the man in the alley . . . the priest killer in the combat boots.

Who else could it be? "What did he say, exactly?" Diaz stepped up and grabbed the newspaper man's arm.

The man edged back away from him. "Jesus, I don't know. He just asked if I'd seen her recently."

But didn't he have Maria, hadn't he kidnapped her? Why would he be looking for her? "Was it this exact picture?" He flushed the faded picture of Maria.

"One like it."

The intentions of the ex-Marine type became clear to Diaz; he felt physically sick. The fever seemed to blossom in the very tissues of his brain. The big man wouldn't be looking for Maria—of course not. Maria and Carmen looked alike. The man who'd murdered the priest and maybe killed the bartender was after Carmen. "What did you tell him?" Diaz snapped the question.

Now the Chinaman looked outright scared. "You know me, home boy, I didn't tell him dick."

"Where's a phone?"

The newspaper man pointed.

Diaz rushed over to a pay phone. The cord was cut. "Damn." He remembered where there was a functioning phone and started back in a jog toward Carmen's apartment. The streets were slick with the rain. He passed a church in the middle of the block. A limousine was outside and rice from a wedding was scattered across the pavement. His foot slid and he nearly slipped.

The door to her apartment was locked. He'd locked it. He withdrew the dead junkies' stiletto and stabbed the lock mechanism. The door opened easily. He stood, breathing. Nobody home, nothing had changed. The telephone was on the dining table. The cord was wrapped around a table leg and he untangled it and sat down on the edge of a chair. Looking over his shoulder he saw he'd trailed rice into the house on his boots. He slammed the phone down and raced outside, down the short flight of stairs, and broke into a sprint.

His heart hammered in his head, irritating the fever. Slowly his legs and arms stopped pumping. The limousine was gone from in front of the church.

Although Diaz saw no point in it, he made an obligatory walk up the block. The idea had come to him when he'd seen the rice on the carpet. It was swollen and pasty from a wedding many hours before. The party was over but the limousine was still waiting. For what?

Maria's date had used a limousine. Mickey the bartender had said so.

Diaz returned to her apartment and locked the door from the inside. Salsa music came blaring down from the floor above. His legs and arms were shivering from the fever and the sudden exertion. He concentrated: first the Marine, now the car. A pack of cigarettes was lying on the table. He drew one out, pinched the filter, lit it. A great lungful of smoke relaxed him. He coughed up some mucus. Leary had returned to the precinct and came to the phone.

Diaz spoke quickly. "I'm at her apartment. There was a car outside a minute ago that I think belonged to Maria's boyfriend, an eighty-six black Lincoln Continental."

"What's the license, I'll track it down."

"I didn't get it, it happened too fast. By the time I'd made sense of it, he'd gone. It was him though. The bartender said he drove a limo."

Leary hesitated. "Diaz, every reefer dealer in Harlem drives a limousine."

Diaz's throat burned from the cigarette. He stubbed it out on a plate. His nose tickled from the smoke. "Listen there was a man in this neighborhood this morning flashing a picture of Maria, asking questions. He was big like the man who killed the priest and he dressed like a Marine."

"You saw him?"

"He was seen. It all figures, the limousine from the bar and the giant from the alley who wore combat boots." Mickey had confessed seeing the boyfriend and Maria to-

211

gether: that man had been of medium build. "It's the boy-friend's chauffeur, the priest killer."

"Why would he come back?" Leary asked bluntly.

Diaz thought, how the hell should I know. But he spoke and the answer was there: "He wants Carmen. He thinks she knows something; she doesn't, but he thinks she does. Just like he thought the bartender knew something."

"But if that's true, Diaz, he got the wrong man. I'm checking your lead at the bar. The bartender who's missing only worked part-time and mostly during the day."

Diaz shot back, "He fucked up. There were two brothers tending bar at different times, maybe they looked alike. Check the morgue, would you, for an Otis Sweeny. If he's been murdered it would mean that Otis was mistaken for Mickey by the killer."

"I'm checking and I'll get back to you. Give me an hour."

Diaz's thoughts rushed back to Carmen. The killer was on the loose, looking for her. Diaz had roughly eighteen hundred dollars left of the money. "He wants her, Leary, just like he wanted the priest and the bartender. Can you get her protection at the hospital? I'll pay for it."

"Forget about it, she's a taxpayer. Let Koch and the city take care of it. I'll put a man on around the clock if it'll make you feel better. But do you think he'd go there?" Leary asked.

"If he can figure it out. Nothing stopped him from killing a priest in Spanish Harlem or visiting his victim's apartment in broad daylight." He remembered something. "Did your men lock the door when they left Carmen's building?"

"They weren't my men, Diaz, but what do you think? Does leaving a door unlocked on One hundred and twenty-first Street in that neighborhood sound like something a cop would do?"

"I don't know. Her door was open."

The two cigarettes smoked back to back had made Diaz slightly dizzy again. With the back of his hand he touched

212

his forehead. His skin was boiling. Something startled him and he stood up. The chair toppled, he reached for it and dragged the phone from the table. The crash was deafening. His hand went to his waist; he'd neglected to pack the service revolver.

A kid went by outside dragging a rusty wagon with a rope.

Diaz sat down and picked up the phone. The noise subsided.

"Jesus, what was that?" Leary shouted.

"A chair dropped."

"It sounded like the fucking roof caved in."

The wagon reminded him of Maria's children. "How are the kids?"

"They're okay. Actually they're cute kids. Nilsa's teaching them how to draw."

"He might have found something in the apartment to lead him to the hospital."

"All right, Diaz, hold on. I'll put two cops on it round the clock." The lieutenant's voice was gruff though sympathetic. It dropped an octave. "He's got you worrying, kid."

"I'm the worrying kind," Diaz replied.

"No, you're not." The line died.

In the kitchen he found an economy-size bottle of generic aspirin tablets. He crushed five in a coffee cup using a spoon. He added water and swallowed the bromide.

Before leaving he took a last look around the apartment and wondered in which room they'd raped her.

35

He realized the fever was worsening if that was possible. His flesh around the stitches was hot and throbbing and he felt exhausted. As he left her apartment he felt hungry and saw this as a good sign. At a corner restaurant he ordered a hamburger and a carton of fries and a milk. He sat on a bench on Third Avenue and ate. The food had no flavor. Two minutes later he threw half of the burger and all of the French fries in a trash can and walked at a brisk pace to St. Luke's Hospital on 114th Street, where he sat in the lobby for two hours. Twice he went up to check Carmen's room. Both times he noted two leather-coated policemen standing an alert vigil at her door. In the hospital shop he bought a bouquet of roses and paid a boy two dollars to deliver them. He borrowed a pen and scrawled "From Willy with affection." He sealed the card and after he'd given it to the kid with the flowers to deliver, felt a little stupid about what he'd written.

The chills started in earnest on his walk home. Diaz tried ignoring them and found that if he thought of Carmen, he could suspend some of the pain and feel a different kind of hurt. Then a sort of belated guilt caught up to him and he began to feel worse. In essence she was in there because of something he'd done. He was convinced that the incident with the junkies had nothing to do with Maria.

Despite his physical condition, he had an urge to keep moving. The case had been resuscitated. The main suspect had been casing the streets for Carmen. With luck he would return. Then there was the chance they could tie him into the disappearance and possible murder of Mickey's brother. This might produce something. Another thread maybe, he thought. Give a man enough thread and he'd hang himself. In a slim, remote way, Diaz's faith had been restored. Despite Deluca's despairing attitude, Diaz had hope again and this encouraged him to go forward.

Back at his office he took two antibiotic pills. His legs felt weak so he sat on the couch and thought of Carmen and making it with her in the park. His memory drifted. The shivering started and he lay sideways on the couch and pulled a blanket over his legs.

Something jarred him out of sleep. He sat up and kicked the blanket off. His body was perspiring, although the office air felt cool. His skin smelled oily and his mouth was bitter. Eventually he stood up long enough to find the phone. The ringing stopped and his head rushed. "Yes."

"Diaz, what's the problem there, have you been drinking?"

He recognized Leary. "No, nothing."

The lieutenant said suddenly, "I've got two things to tell you. First, Otis Sweeny, brother of Mickey, your bartender, turned up floating in the East River with a head wound. Somebody had given him both barrels of a twelve-gauge. A tugboat captain spotted him. The lab matched the teeth, then the brother came down and identified the body."

Diaz grunted something in response and rested his jaw in his hand and pictured Mickey on his knees outside of the bar.

Leary hawked into the phone. Each cough was like an ice pick thrusting into Diaz's brain. Diaz said, "Hold on," and discarded the phone on the couch.

From the refrigerator he took a quart bottle of orange juice and drank deeply from it. He rinsed his teeth and spat into the sink in the bathroom.

"I'm back."

"Goddamnit, are you okay?"

"Yes, I've got a cold. What's the second thing you wanted to tell me?"

"I think we have a lead with the Dobermans," Leary said, purposely suppressing his excitement. "We received a call this morning from the Great Neck Police Department. Doberman Pinscher parts, more than one dog, washed up on the beach where some family was picnicking. They were dog lovers and the guy was with his family so he called the local cops. The Long Island boys tied it in with our story about the priest and Maria Juarez."

"What happened to the dog?"

"Dogs. They'd been shot with a twelve-gauge. One of them was bitten by a shark."

Mickey's brother had been shot with a twelve-gauge.

There was a metropolitan tri-state map in his drawer. Diaz shuffled over, stretching the phone. He found the map and thumbed through it until he found Long Island. "Great Neck has beaches along its north shore for seven miles."

"The cop said it was in the easternmost section."

Diaz fingered the area. "No one lives there. It's a picnic area."

"They found them there, now shut up a minute. I've got a question for you and we both know you owe me. Did anything lead you to believe the killer lives on the Island? I have to know this."

"I need some time to answer that," Diaz said.

"You just did."

"Can I have the time? If the Long Island cops found out they'd be all over the place."

"So?"

"They'd fuck up. I don't want to lose this."

"Nope."

"Goodbye."

"Wait!"

"Six hours."

"No, Diaz."

"Twelve. I don't even know where on Long Island to look."

"Six," Leary said reluctantly.

"Thank you."

"Don't thank me, Diaz. It's not for you."

"Either way."

"It's for her kids. And by the way, save yourself the trouble and stop spying around the hospital corridors like some washed-up cop."

Diaz hung up on him.

He smoothed down the worn surface of the map and studied it. The boundary of the eastern shore ran for two miles around a wooded peninsula in either direction. If the dogs were shot and dumped there, it would mean whoever did it would have to drive through the picnic grounds or the forest. Diaz knew the area from a time he'd visited Great Neck with a police buddy. But did anyone live there? He recalled the vegetation being thick and the ground impenetrable. He moved his finger west on the map. That would mean the dogs were dumped at the picnic grounds, a conspicuous move from someone trying to hide them. He scratched the little green-and-brown area indicating the spot.

When Diaz had been there, it'd been cold and the sandwiches soggy and the wind had blown away the beach umbrella. But there were no houses. To confirm this, he called the Great Neck tourist information bureau. A senior citizen answered on the first ring.

Diaz asked him for a list of recent tides, wind directions, currents. The older man couldn't help but suggested the Coast Guard and provided the number. Diaz called them and jotted down the information as they relinquished it, working it out speedily in his mind. The wind had been from the east-southeast for a week. The water was calm but the winds were strong and the currents were dictated by their direction. He gave them a hypothetical problem about a lost suitcase: "My son was fishing and it fell overboard. I found one of the shoes on the picnic grounds."

They speculated: "Given the currents the suitcase or its contents might wash up on the eastern beach—the picnic grounds—if it originated anywhere within a ten-mile radius of the same beach. That is, if it just didn't sink to the bottom."

Brilliant.

Diaz thanked them and hung up. Using a pencil he figured the radius on the map. The easternmost section was too densely residential and could therefore be eliminated. You couldn't shoot Dobermans and throw them in the water without being seen. Similarly he eliminated the western section, which was unreachable and uninhabited. The dogs had been dead only a few days, "no more than two." They couldn't have drifted far. He eliminated all the options and through a series of calculated guesses figured on a small pebbly beach four miles east of the picnic grounds.

The map said Beesley Bay. Diaz looked it up in the index: "An exclusive section of privately owned homes dating back to the original settlers of the northern Long Island shore . . ."

Limousine land. He sat down with his hands on his knees, his head swirling.

For a silent, insightful minute he envisioned the beaches and the residents of a place like Beesley Bay and suddenly needed a drink. He downed four shots of whiskey and felt better. Next he showered, put on clean underwear, a fresh shirt, and the ancient blue suit. From the drawer he grabbed his revolver and a full box of cartridges and all of the money. In his pocket was the pearl-handled stiletto he'd taken from Cat. Using a single strand of cello tape, he secured the knife to his ankle under his sock.

In the corner photography store he bought a Polaroid camera and a pack of film. Then he rode the IRT south to Spring Street in Soho and walked to Prince Street.

The gallery's heavy wooden door chimed. Before the gallery owners could stop him, Diaz snapped photos of six different paintings in quick succession and caught each picture as it was ejected from the camera.

At the corner of West Broadway and Canal he gave the camera to a bag lady who snatched it suspiciously, then hobbled off into a doorway. A girl walked by in a tweed overcoat too big for her. She smiled at him. A bird was singing somewhere, a throaty salute to Soho. Two art students traipsed by, arguing. He peeled the film apart, waved each shot in the slight breeze, and pocketed the pictures.

By now he was sweating again and the pins of his legs felt tired. Walking was drudgery. He was hungry but he knew he probably couldn't hold food down. A taxi took him to Alphonse's Bar and he walked around the back way to the garage. The kid was in the dirt yard on his knees playing with a skeletal Alsatian. They both turned at the sound of someone opening the fence. The kid stood up and nodded and put his hands in his pockets. The dog growled and the kid nudged it with his knee and it shut up.

Diaz ignored them both and yanked the garage door open. He took two keys from his pocket; one was covered in nylon tape. He peeled this off and used the tape to attach his IOU to the garage wall. The Jaguar started with a roar. He throttled it hard and the engine calmed. It shifted easily into first and he set out for Long Island.

36

The coastal road along the North Shore of Long Island leading to Beesley Bay was narrow and winding; a road, Diaz
thought, more appropriate for northern California country. It
had taken him an hour in the Jaguar averaging 75 miles per
hour on the Long Island Expressway. At the Great Neck exit
he pulled off and drove east another eleven miles until a sign
indicated he had entered Beesley Bay.

He followed the road on its course along the coastal
boundary. On the higher ground to his right the vast houses
of the landowners peered down at the forest and the white-
capped sea. Through breaks in the autumn foliage it was
possible to see the pebbly shoreline. The Jaguar took the
five-mile ribbon of road smoothly, hugging the curves, accel-
erating on the inclines. Diaz doubled back and drove the
road again in a lower gear. He counted eight estates perched

above the road. Of the eight houses four appeared shut down for the season; four were probably year-round residences.

Diaz eliminated the seemingly abandoned properties and made his first stop at a large Georgian house with a gravel drive. He backed in to within twenty-five yards of the building and took off his dark glasses. Some sweat from his forehead trickled into his eyes; he blotted it on his shirt sleeve. The air was brisk and the sun was diminished by the afternoon clouds that drifted languorously before an early moon. His fever had leveled off, leaving him drained and his limbs sore and aching. When he removed his jacket to fold it, his shirt was sweat-soaked.

A light went on in the house and a small dog barked. He removed the Polaroids of the gallery paintings from his pocket and with an artist's eye compared them to his view of the landscape and the Long Island shore: there was no comparison. Undaunted, he drove out and tried the property at the extreme east of the Beesley Bay Road. Again there were no pictures that bore a close likeness to the panorama. Momentary doubt assailed him. The pictures were all similar, but none matched. Could they have been of any shoreline? He made two more anxious circuits of the road until he realized his mistake.

The property he sought, obscured at a dip in the landscape, ran below the road, on the side nearer the ocean. Because of the awkward angle of the road at this particular point, his eyes had been poised for oncoming vehicles and he'd missed the driveway completely. Now he saw it, and he idled the engine and coasted into it for fifty uneven yards. The road flattened into a white cement lane lined on each side with Belgian block. A regiment of tall oak trees bordered the driveway.

Diaz looked at the large brick house standing at the end of the lane forty yards away. It was compact: as tall as it was wide. The whitewashed brick was smothered halfway with

222

ivy. Lights were on in the third floor in each of the far windows. From a distance the ivy gave its plain face shading, like the shading of cheekbones, and the large black door stood like a mouth in its very center. The lighted windows were eyes. Diaz felt the sea breeze and put his coat back on.

The lawn and hedges preceding the house were overgrown and showed signs of neglect; pieces of dead tree limbs were strewn on the lane and had been dragged to one side so as not to impede traffic. He parked behind a phalanx of shoulder-high rhododendrons, got out of the car, removed the revolver from his pocket, and put it in his coat. Removing the Polaroids from his pocket, he jogged away from the house toward the crashing of the sea. He still wasn't sure.

He went as far as the bluff where the terrain sharpened: fifty yards behind him sat the house. Fifty yards hence the Long Island Sound slapped incessantly against the shoreline. The small waves surged, then withdrew, rattling the pebbly beach as if an uncertain traveler was striding across it. A solid wall of pines started at the beach to his right. They swayed, echoing the cold sea breeze. The air smelled of salt. He looked at the horizon.

The wind blew the curls of his hair, cooling his fever. He held the pictures up for the hell of it, because he already knew, and a new sort of fear started in him.

On his way back to the car he spotted the dog kennels at the rear of the house. They would be empty now. Diaz's eyes skirted. A small hunched figure appeared in the southernmost window of the nineteenth-century building, pausing for a fraction of a second. Diaz lay flat at the base of a shrub, watching. He thought, he's home now. After five minutes he got up and walked back to the car. It was five o'clock and the light was beginning to wane. Leary had promised him six hours and he'd used up two and a half. He smoked cigarettes and waited for the cover of darkness and the courage to attack.

The night had advanced until the house was only a shape on the horizon. It was dark enough. Diaz took a last series of deep breaths: his throat felt raw from the cigarettes. The fever was still with him, giving him alternating sensations of hot and cold. Sweat had sopped through his clothes. His teeth chattered and twice he had to look out over the starry horizon to keep from vomiting. Occasionally his eyes went out of focus.

He walked toward the house, using the cover of a row of hedges to shield himself from view. When he reached the side of the house by the dog kennels, his heart was beating loudly in his temples.

Eventually the throbbing yielded to the noises of the sea. Several yards below, the waves broke implacably on the rocks and Diaz wondered through the sense of fear and the physical pain why he was there. The final irony, he thought: he would earn his bonus after all.

The kennels were built of chain-link fencing with a wooden frame for a roof. The entire structure led to a small brick wing attached to the house itself. The surface of the cement slabs outside was clean. The dogs had been gone for at least two days and the kennel had been hosed down. He felt for the latch in the fence, slid it, crossed the concrete walkway to the door beyond the kennel, and was inside.

The brick room was musty and smelled of old dog chow and leather. A shelf full of dog gear, brushes, leashes, mace, ran along one wall. Beyond this was a door leading directly into the house. Suddenly a strip of light flared beneath the inside door. Diaz expected it to open and hurriedly ripped the gun from his coat, his heart skipping, feet flat, thoughts wavering between what lay on the other side of the door and the image of the man beyond it.

Some cutlery rattled. The light died. Footsteps sounded across a tile floor.

He thought, the kitchen. The gun sagged some and suddenly he was struck by the feeling of opportunity lost. His prey had been alone in the kitchen, unaware. Diaz could have confronted whoever it was and overpowered him. He told himself to relax; there was no point in rushing it.

After a cautionary minute he slipped inside. The large modern room smelled of cinnamon. It was the kitchen.

Whoever had been in here moments before had moved on. He glanced behind him and started for the next room.

The house talked to him. The wind rocked the furthest corners of the roof, making the woodwork groan like a man in pain. Inside it was damp and cold, cooler even than outside. He crossed light-footed through these rooms, aiming the gun at the floor. Whole rooms were apparently closed off in the house. The furniture in them was naturally arranged but cloaked in gray sheeting. A certain deathly stillness prevailed, and as Diaz stood in the midst of it, watching, his muscles exhausted and tensed, he imagined a crypt where time stands still and the dead come alive after-hours. And he thought of the dead, like the dead priest and the bartender and the junkie he'd killed, and the fever gradually faded, changing into a sheet of ice that gripped him. The revolver dropped with a bang and slid along the hardwood floor. For an instant he no longer cared—the fatigue was that bad. He gripped a covered chair for balance and the sheet slid off. The chill passed. He knelt and picked up the gun. With his return to consciousness, the fear returned. It angered him that he'd dropped his guard.

The first floor was empty. He climbed the giant stairway at the front of the house, treading on the furthest edges of each step to quell the squeaking of the wood. He smelled something as he came to the head of the stairs. The silence screamed at him above the sullen creak of ancient timbers. Distantly he could hear the cold sea.

Something stank.

To his left a series of gilt sconces lit the carpeted corridor. He walked toward the light, leveling the gun before him.

The smell faded; Diaz backtracked until he picked it up again and took the alternate route to his right. The corridor was black and he moved more cautiously, half-expecting the killer to lunge, screaming from the darkness. At the end of the hall he could make out the face of a door, partially open. Light from somewhere shone lifelessly on the door's cut-glass knob. Diaz touched it. The door swung in with the whine of a stiff hand raked over slate.

The smell came from in here.

Despite the absence of electric light, he could see. The room fronted the ocean and the moon and the stars illuminated the bedroom in silhouette, giving dimension to her figure and mercifully, he thought, hiding the ravages of time. He felt the ice again. The muscles of his stomach fluttered and he wanted to gag. He fought the feeling.

The horror seemed to draw him in, much as a child is drawn curiously to the unknown, or an adult inexplicably to danger. He heard his breathing, slow and hoarse, the calm breath of fear. The gun was growing heavy. He ignored it as he removed a pack of matches from his pocket. Laboriously, with an unsteady hand, he tore a match free from the folder and struck it.

The match sizzled. She smiled crazily. Diaz jerked back, horrified. The flame died and he dropped the match book.

He breathed shallowly from the top of his lungs, through his teeth, and felt for the matchbook on the floor, found it, and lit another.

That she'd been dead the entire time, there was no question. Her hair, though neatly combed, was stringy and brittle. Her once beautiful features were fantastically wizened and drawn. Lines ran deep in her hardened flesh from cheek to chin. Her slender mouth was forced open through dehydration and the teeth were bucked and yellow: the death smile. Her nose was narrow and dark at the tip and her hands were fixed nonchalantly at her sides, clutching silverware. Her nails were long and only half polished. Beside her head on the pillow was a small golden locket, heart shaped, and bearing the inscription "Maria" in thin Gothic print. She'd been coated with something, a fine powder, which had helped to preserve the eyes. And she stared up at him with the dull, dumb look of the dead and he sighed.

The match expired, he lit another.

Patches of mummified skin had begun to mottle and fall off her neck. Her legs and body were covered with the same gray sheets as the unused furniture downstairs. Diaz saw through the sheerness the sunken definition of a once generous bosom and below, the receding curve of a ruined pregnancy.

He suppressed an urge to vomit. Crossing the room quickly, he unlatched the glass doors to the terrace outside. The sea breeze bore back against the house into the open doors, disturbing the deathly calm and upsetting the curtains. He stood in it and filled his lungs.

Feeling flushed, he walked back inside. There was a tray covered with fruit and a plate of eggs on the table by her bed. He stared at it incredulously, put his hand in his pocket to touch the gun, and went out into the hall.

Diaz found him on the third floor, propped up behind the desk in his study. His middle-aged features had sagged. The last vestiges of a fading youth, the image Diaz had come to remember him by, had faded completely. He was an old man facing real desperation for the first time. There was no life in his face, only death, and the kind of utter hopelessness one expects to find at a funeral, which this was in a way, Diaz thought.

"Hello, Deluca."

"Diaz . . . you knew."

Diaz paused before answering. He thought, I didn't know anything. "Maria was pregnant. That figured from the very beginning—the priest, her attitude toward children; one of the books she'd borrowed from the library was on prenatal care. Whoever kidnapped and killed Maria didn't want that baby born."

"And you thought it was Timmy?"

"For a while. I checked with the medical examiner. Tim was over the limit when he ran his motorcycle into the truck. He was drunk. It appeared, it could appear, he was upset over the loss of Maria. Then it turned out Maria liked men and, according to the bartender, had an older boyfriend, a wealthy one. Then my leads started disappearing. Someone began tailing Carmen, Maria's sister. It was all too neat. The fuck-ups went hand in hand with the leads. Someone, an insider, was privy to the information. The dead Dobermans and the bartender indicated the kidnapper was from Long Island. You said you lived in Maine, yet your phone was disconnected there, leading me to think your residence was only a rental. You were a banker. Wouldn't a banker own property? Maybe not. Then the dogs washed up on shore. A shore not unlike that in your pictures. You gave me that."

"Not intentionally."

"You were Maria's older man. When your son found out, he couldn't stand the pain of betrayal. That's what gave him the urge to play tag with a truck."

"No, it's not like that!"

"Yes it is, I'm afraid. You caused Tim's death, Deluca. You with the manners and the morals."

"Don't please."

"You killed Maria and the priest in the alley because they knew too much and Maria was determined to have your child. You had Carmen followed and the bartender killed."

Deluca buried his face in his hands. "I . . . I'm sorry. It happened so suddenly. There weren't supposed to be any deaths, but there was no way I could handle it . . . I never meant for it to end like this." Deluca looked up, his face tired and gaunt. "What would you do? After Timmy died, I lost myself."

228

"Tim didn't die until after Maria disappeared."

"Yes, but she was threatening to tell. She would've told Tim. She wanted to marry me. I had to do it. . . ."

"Maybe, but you didn't kill her. You had no part in that."

"I did, I had to. So much was at stake."

"You came to me genuinely concerned for this woman. You wanted her found."

Deluca pressed forward. "I was covering myself."

"You wanted her found. Then at the end, you changed your mind and told me to forget it."

"I was lying."

Diaz said, "You're lying now."

"No, honestly, I was cornered. I had no way out . . ."

"Shut up."

Deluca looked stunned. He stared down at his empty brandy glass, sipped it without realizing it was empty. His hands moved aimlessly, fluttering upon the surface of the desk. He pushed his lank gray hair around with sweaty palms.

"Who killed Maria?" Diaz asked.

"I . . ."

"No you didn't. Aside from it not being your nature, you don't weigh enough. The priest's neck was cut clean through with a sharp wire. You don't have the sort of strength for that. The bartender who was killed was the brother of the full-time barman, the one who'd seen you. If you'd been behind that killing, you'd have killed the right man and not his brother. It doesn't add up, none of it. Something happened three days ago that shocked you into trying to stop me investigating. That something was Maria. Someone brought Maria's body back to this house. The killer brought her here. Who is her killer to you, Deluca?"

Deluca swallowed. "Listen, that bag on the floor, I was going to use it to go away. There's two hundred thousand dollars in cash in the bag. It's yours. Take it and leave. Forget this ever happened."

Diaz stared at the black satchel. "The police know," he said flatly. "It's too late for that."

Then the giant man stepped into the room and Deluca uttered, "Oh, no."

Diaz froze and withdrew the gun.

Deluca stood up and wavered. He gripped the edge of the desk. The large towheaded man stood poised in the doorway, fists clenched. He looked nervous, Diaz thought, like a little boy who's been caught shoplifting and is about to be scolded, and not at all like a man who could kill three people in cold blood.

A gentle note infused Deluca's voice as he said, "Nicholas, please leave us now, we're talking." Nicholas had on combat boots. His face was broad and flat like a boxer's. His eyes glistened.

"Is he the police?" Nicholas asked.

"No."

"Is he trying to take me away?"

"No, Nicholas. Please go away now. Go to your room. I have to talk to this man alone."

"But he's upsetting you, Dad. And you've been drinking."

"Leave us, please."

Diaz recognized a genuine affection in the older man's tone. He glanced at the satchel and the money and thought, it's too late.

The murderer, Nicholas, turned wearily and disappeared from the doorway. His footfalls creaked along the corridor.

"You can put your gun away. You're perfectly safe," Deluca said.

Diaz kept it out. His mind strained to complete the puzzle. "You had two sons." He let the gun hang at his side.

"No, three," Deluca said slowly. "One died in a boating accident many summers ago. Then there was Timmy. Nicholas is the only one left."

"Nicholas killed the priest and the bartender and Maria."

"Yes."

"You didn't hire me to find Maria. You hired me to find Nicholas. If I found Maria, I found him."

"Until three days ago I had no idea where either one was. Then Nicholas brought her back to the house. He'd accidentally killed her while attempting to kidnap her. In the end, he brought her home." Deluca pressed forward. "In fact, she was home all along. Nicholas had been storing her body in a utility shed on the edge of the property."

"What did Nicholas have against the priest and Maria?"

Deluca looked away nervously. He stared apprehensively into his brandy glass. "I'd like to refill my drink if I may." Diaz nodded and the tall man crossed the room to the bar. The brandy bottle in the cabinet was empty. Without hesitating, Deluca poured the glass to the top with gin. He returned to his desk and sat down.

"Nicholas is a good boy. Since childhood he's had a learning problem. He wants so much to please me. After Vietnam, he returned to America and things went badly for him; he couldn't keep a job, he experienced moments of severe depression. Occasionally he required psychiatric counseling. Throughout it all, he loved me, though. And he loved his brother Tim. There was no rivalry between them. How could there be: Timmy was an overachiever, a truly smart kid. And Nicholas was . . ." The glass came up and he drank from it. His mouth puckered.

"All my life I've kept a diary, Mr. Diaz. It was something my father did and his father. A diary is my way of talking over life's more exacting problems . . . I have nobody else to talk to. Somehow Nicholas discovered this document. I believe in being totally honest in what I write . . . I wrote the truth: Maria's pregnancy, our affair. Maria's priest had continuously advised her against an abortion. I noted this and allowed myself to write freely my opinion of this man of God." He drained the drink, then rose suddenly and staggered to the bar for the bottle. Holding it, he leaned back

231

against the bookshelf; his breathing was labored and his eyes wet.

For a moment Diaz thought he was having a heart attack.

Diaz went over and took the bottle out of his hands. He found mineral water at the bar and poured a glassful for Deluca, who accepted it gratefully. He returned to the desk and fell into the chair.

Diaz asked, "And Nicholas read the diary?"

"Yes, he did. He saw what pain the woman had put me through. He overreacted and thought he was helping me."

"How did Tim find out?"

"That was my second mistake. After Nicholas and Maria disappeared and the police had been harrassing Tim, I felt I had to tell him. I had to let him know what had become of his older brother. This was some months after the priest's murder. That same night Tim drove his motorcycle . . ." A sob caught in Deluca's throat. "I'd like to think it was an accident."

"Then you hired me?"

"No, then I collapsed. I panicked. Everything that meant anything to me had been destroyed in a matter of months. Eventually I came to you because the police had recommended you. If you could find Maria, I knew I'd find my other boy."

Diaz thought of the junkies in the car and Carmen's rape. "You hired someone to follow me and Maria's sister. Why?"

"Panic, pure unwarranted panic. I needed you watched to ensure that if you found Nicholas, I would know it immediately. You knew the circumstances of the girl's disappearance. You might have gone to the police first. If I had you followed and you found Nicholas, I could approach my son on my own. He would listen to me. The men who followed you knew nothing of Maria or the priest or any of it. . . . You see I couldn't risk losing Nicholas."

It still didn't figure. Diaz said disgustedly, "The men you hired were dope addicts. They raped Maria's sister. Was that part of your plan?"

"No, I didn't . . . they had their own methods, my mistake was in not monitoring them more closely. Their leader tried to blackmail me. He said he would tell everything and threatened to go to you and the police with the documents he'd kept at my request. I couldn't take that risk. I was too deeply involved."

"You killed him?"

"I shot him once. He died." Deluca's voice was tremulous.

Diaz understood. The junkies' supplier had been killed and the junkies assumed Diaz had done it. That's why they'd raped Carmen. That's why they'd followed him into the alley, blinded by hate. "Nicholas killed the bartender?"

"Yes," Deluca said, "He's always had a great faculty for remembering. Something must have jarred his memory and he realized that the bartender was a threat to me."

Diaz had succeeded in getting the bartender on the local news stations. Nicholas had seen him on television.

"It's over now, isn't it?" Deluca asked. His hands slipped below the desk.

"Yes, it is," Diaz said.

Deluca's pale eyes were wet and in their depth Diaz recognized the look of idiocy he'd seen before in desperate men, men who for one reason or another had been drawn over the edge into the void beyond rational thinking, where nothing mattered.

Deluca leaned marginally forward. "They'll take Nicholas away. What will they do to him?"

"I don't know. He's sick."

"Do they sentence sick men to death?"

"Yes," Diaz said. It was an honest statement. Most murderers were certifiably mentally unstable.

"Do you think I'm sick, Diaz? Did that occur to you at any point? Did you wonder about me ever?"

He seemed to want an honest answer. Diaz took a moment to consider it. "No, you've been pushed too far."

Shock spread across Deluca's face. "But I've killed a man," he said meekly.

"I've killed men," Diaz said.

"Yes, but that's your privilege."

Tears came into Deluca's eyes. His lips were trembling in a form of mild shock, but he was not so far gone as to be immune from the pain.

"Moses killed a man," Diaz said.

Deluca said as if to himself, "You know it's not the pain that makes men fear life; it's the idea of pain."

"That's true," Diaz said and watched Deluca casually raise a large brown revolver from below the desk. The barrel pointed lazily at Diaz then continued upward in a pronounced arc. Diaz felt his stomach tighten, bracing against the noise.

"Stop!" He took a giant step.

There was a bang, an instant of recoil. Then a thud as Deluca's body flopped violently onto the desk. From a nickel-sized hole in the side of his head a geyser of blood escaped. It pumped and then stopped, and then pumped. The pressure ebbed as the life drained out of him. His thin frame shook convulsively. Then it was over.

"Dad!" A terrible animal sob. Nicholas lumbered into the room, his boots clattering, his large face contorted in shock. He reached his father and cradled the lifeless head in his huge arms, squeezing it: more blood spouted out of the wound. "God, Dad, don't leave me now, don't go . . ." His voice choked off into a cry from within, a whistling noise full of sorrow and despair.

Diaz was six feet away holding the service revolver at his side. He contemplated shooting Nicholas, taking away the benefit of the doubt from a man who'd killed three people.

Nicholas started sobbing and shook his father's head. The mouth opened stupidly and blood ran out onto the shiny surface of the desk. Then he paused, spying Diaz through his tears. "You did this." His father's body slid slowly across the desk top.

"No, Nicholas, he shot himself."

"He was happy before. Then you came here. You knew the girl, Maria, who started all the bad shit in the first place." His voice rang with hatred. Despite his limited comprehension, he'd pieced some of the events together.

"Your father hired me to . . ."

Nicholas hesitated, a sudden charge of anger pulsed through him. He tore the gun from his father's hand. The arm flapped out, mimicking life. The corpse shifted. "Dad!" Nicholas lifted the head again and rechecked it. More blood poured out of the wound. Deluca's eyes were swimming in their sockets. The lids blinked open, lifelessly.

Diaz raised his gun and shot out a window in the room. The glass crashed. "Drop the gun, Nicholas!"

Nicholas was blubbering now, crying like a baby. His large face was red with anguish and he looked childlike and pathetic and insane. Diaz looked at the pair, the father and the son, and saw the large weapon in Nicholas's two hands as it began to move. He had to get the crazy man's attention and had a sudden grim thought. "Drop it, Nicholas, or I'll shoot your father!"

Nicholas shook his large head violently, still protesting. He steadied his father's gun.

Diaz aimed and fired. The corpse jumped. The terrible thought struck Diaz that Deluca was not yet dead. He weighed the chances: no one could survive a head wound like that.

"You're killing him!" Nicholas screamed.

"Then stay still. Drop the goddamned gun."

"You killed Daddy!" The big man surged forward. "Stop!" Diaz fired again. Deluca took the second bullet in the ribs and simply edged back along the polished desk top with the momentum of the slug.

"You stop!" Nicholas yelled and charged and Diaz thought of the priest and turned the gun on Nicholas and shot him once in the shoulder, breaking his arm.

The bullet stood him up, staggered him, while he fumbled

235

to point his father's ancient weapon. He fell sideways, the revolver dropped and skidded under the desk.

Nicholas picked himself up, screaming wildly, and charged in deadly earnest, head down, bloodied shoulder hunched.

"No!" Diaz aimed at his heart and squeezed the trigger. Nicholas dodged and the bullet nicked his arm and splintered a hole in the paneling behind him. He pitched forward, spinning with the momentum. Diaz braced and fired again, this time missing his target completely as Nicholas stumbled. A collision was imminent and Diaz leapt back to avoid it. With a terrific shout Nicholas threw himself into his fall.

It happened in an instant. In his attempt to jump clear Diaz slipped on the Persian carpet. He crashed back, off balance, as Nicholas dove for him, reaching out wildly with his unbroken arm. Somthing caught Diaz's right hand and held on for a split second with the force of steel, wrenching the hand savagely. Diaz's gun went flying and a moment of crippling pain was followed by a tear and then a snapping sound. The pain subsided somewhat.

Nicholas lost his grip on Diaz and completed his fall, slamming into the bookcase against the wall. Books showered down on his momentarily inert form.

Diaz endured the pain of his broken hand and managed to stand. The room was spinning. He willed his head to clear and his senses to return. Slowly Nicholas picked himself up from against the bookcase. He steadied himself on one knee. Diaz drew his leg back and kicked Nicholas as hard as he could in the kidney. The big man screamed in agony and crumpled as Diaz fled the room.

In a sprint Diaz reached the staircase and vaulted down it, tripping over the last ten steps and falling on his broken hand. The pain was unbearable but he had to continue. With monumental effort he righted himself, glanced behind him, saw the front door, and ran for it.

He thought of the car. If he could get to it he could drive

away and come back with reinforcements. What other choice did he have?

Night had fallen. He ran blindly across the lawns to where the Jaguar was hidden. His breathing was stilted; if he got out of here he would stop smoking and exercise more and eat properly. The Jaguar was there behind the rhododendrons, mercifully, where he'd left it. With his left hand he extracted his car keys from his right pocket.

He would go for help and come back to get Nicholas. The door opened. He slipped inside; the soft leather upholstery was like sitting on a cloud.

Then all at once he saw it. His eyes had grown accustomed to the night. *The fucking steering wheel was gone!*

"Shit!"

He hauled himself out, legs first, threw open the hood, studying it. The engine was stripped. Wires had been severed and the carburetor smashed in.

He thought, I'm wasting time.

Summoning his reserves of energy, he jogged back across the lawns to the garage, his eyes peeled for Nicholas. His ankle was swelling and, overwhelmed by fatigue, he knew he wouldn't get far on foot. Although he'd shot Nicholas, there was no telling how badly he was hurt. Diaz would hotwire a car and get out of there this way.

The wooden door to the garage rose on a rusted track: Diaz held it up, supporting it with his shoulder as he gazed inside at the two Mercedes and the limousine.

"I got you."

Diaz froze. A chill started in his stomach. He thought: he has got me.

Nicholas stepped out of the shadows of the garage, a huge mass of muscle and bone. He'd recovered and anticipated the detective's next move and here he was inside, waiting for him, like fate, and Diaz saw no way out. Moonlight spilled through a window highlighting the blunt contours of the madman's face. His white shirt was dark with blood about

237

his right shoulder and arm. He raised the revolver in his left hand.

Diaz let go of the door. It fell. The gun went off and the garage throbbed with a hard white light. The falling door caught the bullet meant for Diaz's chin. The wood of the door made a terrific crack as it split apart.

Diaz ran.

Where? His mind was doing tricks.

The water! He could run along the beach to the next estate, if there was one; Jesus, let there be.

He heard the surf slap against the pebbly shore as he conquered the lawn for the beach. He could swim it if he had to. He could swim; he'd often swum as a boy in the pool on 110th Street. With his broken right hand it was impossible to find his stride. His legs were like jelly and he could no longer feel his feet.

At the crest of the hill Diaz turned. Nicholas was charging across the lawn, waving the gun, and Diaz remembered being a child and the terrible fear of being chased by an enemy you knew would get you. If only he had his gun.

They hit the beach thirty yards apart, Diaz could hear the punch of sneakers in the sand behind him and the uneven breathing as Nicholas closed the gap, eating up the distance between them with his enormous strides. The ground softened where the sea met the sand, making it even harder to run.

The night air throbbed with the explosion of the gun and Diaz lost his footing, sprawling crazy-legged into the sea. His head went under and the sudden freezing silence made him think that drowning wouldn't be so bad. He broke the surface gasping for air. The icy water seemed to freeze his lungs, choking him suddenly. The cold took away most of the pain; his broken hand no longer hurt. A wave hit him and slapped sense into him. He spat water. The ground stopped spinning. Nicholas was at the water line, bent with fatigue, his shirt black with blood and his eyes wild.

Diaz sat up in the water to his stomach. Nicholas was shouting at him, the huge childlike man who'd killed the priest and killed Maria was in the surf to his ankles waiting to finish it. And Diaz decided then that he'd reached the limit of his endurance, there was only so much a man could take. He was only human after all, and he'd tried his damnedest, but he just couldn't pull it off.

It was no good, he was going to die, he realized philosophically, and he imagined himself face-down in the water, and out of this imagery he formed a final strategy. Taking an enormous breath, he dipped forward onto his stomach and face in a floating position, his feet dancing across the sand.

The peacefulness of the frozen sea made it easier and from the peace he extracted a sort of courage, *things could only get so bad*. He reached almost casually for his sock and tore the small pearl-handled stiletto free from the single band of tape securing it. He floated, his body reflecting the gentle roll of the swells, feeling the rush of the waves agitating the pebbly beach and the suck of the tides as each wave withdrew, marveling at the strength of the sea, anesthetized by the cold. He'd let his breath out entirely and his lungs were bursting and for a tortured minute he wanted to come up and sacrifice everything for a breath of cold delicious air, and then Carmen appeared and then Maria accompanied by the priest . . . forgive me, Father . . . and last, Deluca was there in the swirling blackness, condoning Diaz's final initiative with an imperceptible nod of his slender head as Diaz began to fade.

He bobbed into a trough between waves and heard the splashing sounds and the activity in the water as something displaced the pebbles and walked across the sand.

Nicholas grabbed him by the arm and rolled him belly up and Diaz spun with the motion, depressing the stiletto as he rolled, coming alive again for the second it took to complete the arc of his turn. Nicholas hadn't a clue, and Diaz thrust the knife to the hilt and on an angle into the big man's heart.

239

He felt the instant of shock as Nicholas realized his error, and then the initial spasms as the life shuddered out of him. Diaz held on long enough to yank the knife out again, using his weight and the strength in his frozen fingers. Almost as an afterthought, he breathed.

Diaz went under again and surfaced in chest-deep water further from shore. Nicholas had dragged himself to the edge of the beach and was sitting in the tiny waves, his powerful hands clutching the spot above his torn heart, the blood pumping out of the hole in his chest, his face whitening. Looking at him, Diaz felt a form of sympathy. It was almost as if Nicholas hadn't known any better than to do what he'd done.

The strong currents threatened to draw Diaz deeper into the blackness toward the twilight away from the shore. He let himself drift, but when he was no longer able to touch the bottom, he thought of Carmen and began the endless swim to land. He was shivering when he reached the beach and his teeth were chattering and his legs were numb. He shuffled to where the big man lay dying, stretched out now in the surf.

Incredibly Nicholas was still alive. His eyes were open and each small onslaught of waves washed up to cover his face and make him blink. The eyes were soft and dark and the look of madness had left them. For a moment he resembled his father. His mouth opened and the whites of his eyes shifted and his pale lips moved as he tried to speak. Diaz listened for the death throes that never came. The sea washed through Nicholas's crew cut and the dark eyes became opaque and Diaz watched him die. "Have mercy on him," he said finally in a voice swept up in the mournful requiem of the wind and carried out to sea.

He walked back up the sandy hill to the house. Something in him, his cynical side, prompted him to return to Deluca's office. He checked the body and lay it out flat on the carpet. With his fingers he closed the thin white lids of the eyes.

Deluca's face was passive and the hair mussed, and Diaz found it hard to imagine this face ever being alive at all. It had the pallor that deprives the dead of any sense of reality.

This was, thought Diaz, part of the mystery of life. Once gone, life could never be restored; it could be perpetuated, but never created and never revived.

Which made tonight all that much more of a tragedy, he thought.

In the black bag beside the desk was the money Deluca had used to bribe him with, stacked up neatly and squarely in bundles of hundreds. Diaz hesitated and left it alone and went downstairs and hotwired a Mercedes. At the end of the driveway he braked and reversed as far as the house. He went back in and returned with the bag and set the money on the passenger seat. Then he drove to Manhattan with his broken hand.

37

For a week he lay in bed in his suite at the Carlyle, re-
cuperating. He kept the lights off and lived for three days on
pain-killers and the occasional plate of eggs from room service. He read magazines and for most of the time the television was on. Leary visited him twice.

Four bones had been broken in his right hand. The doctor
who set the cast advised him with a grin that he'd soon be
able to play the piano again and Diaz asked him why and
the doctor finished and went away. That same night he'd
checked into the Carlyle. He'd remembered the name of the
hotel; Deluca had stayed here and something about Deluca
Diaz admired although he would never admit it to anyone.

On the fourth day he drew the curtains and turned the
television up louder. He ordered sandwiches from room service and orange juice and a plate of fruit. Once he left his

room to drink a ginger ale in Bemmelman's Bar downstairs. That night there was no blood in his urine and he slept for twelve hours.

He repeated the regimen, eating healthily, sleeping regularly, so that by the seventh day he felt truly rested.

From a box under the king-sized bed he removed the aluminum suitcase and opened it on the mattress. It took him just under an hour with his cast on to cut and stack the money. He divided it two to one in her favor. It was blood money and she'd earned it. A paper shopping bag was in the closet, Diaz used it to wrap her share. Inside the suitcase he piled all of his clothes and a hotel towel. He showered and dressed in the navy blue suit and blue-and-white checked shirt he'd ordered by phone from Brooks Brothers, a store recommended by the hotel valet. The material smelled fresh. He left the hotel and got a haircut on Madison Avenue. For the first time in weeks he felt clean.

Diaz stood in front of her apartment and held a finger over the tiny chipped buzzer. Carmen came to the door, her left arm in a sling. Her skin was marked beneath one eye and her bottom lip was bluish. But all of the swelling had subsided and she looked beautiful again. Diaz felt a tiny surge of emotion.

"Oh, hello."

For a heartbeat they stared at each other. He thought she was going to cry, but she battled the tears back and kept a straight face.

"Lieutenant Leary told me you broke your hand," she said. "I want to thank you for finding Maria's killer. It's easier to know for certain. Now we can start our lives again and the children won't be kept waiting."

"That's true."

"Where are you going?" Carmen looked at the aluminum suitcase.

"Puerto Rico," he said, though he had no real plans. "I'd like to get away from the city for a while."

"That would be nice." An almost inaudible sigh issued from her parted lips.

"Here." Diaz removed the folded shopping bag from under his arm. "This is yours. It should help," he said, and thought of what Carmen had been put through on his behalf. A part of him wanted to say, "I killed that man. None of his junkie friends will ever bother you again." He felt a chokiness about his throat as though his voice might break if he tried to talk.

"I left messages at your hotel," Carmen said. "Didn't you get them?"

As a precaution against her not leaving messages, he'd instructed the management to relay only those calls from the Police Department.

"I've got to run," he said turning away from her, feeling the pain of guilt and beneath it a sort of shame and a sort of self-hatred.

He drove in a rented car to a Spanish-owned travel bureau on 125th Street and bought his ticket. The flat-chested travel agent flirted with him and he looked at her steadily, thinking, what do you see in me, baby?

"What happened to you, William?" she asked, getting his name from the ticket voucher.

Without thinking he replied, "I lost my wife."

The girl looked pained. "Oh, my, I'm so sorry." After a pause when she tried to read his face, she reached out and touched his good hand and caressed the long fingers until he regarded her. "You were in some kind of accident?"

"No, it wasn't an accident really."

She ignored the remark. "You're going to Puerto Rico all alone to get over it."

"Yes, only I don't think I'll ever get over it. I don't think I deserve to."

The woman frowned and her fingers moved to his wrist.

"It's been six years, you see, and no one could ever take her place and I was stupid to think someone could," he said.

The woman removed her hand and Diaz added, "There's so much sadness in the world. Did you ever think of that? It sometimes makes you wonder why we bother struggling."

The woman bristled. Empathy had been replaced by a veiled contempt for Diaz and his self-indulgence. "It's a free country. You don't have to stick around."

"That's a good way of putting it," Diaz said.

He got back in the rented car and drove and when the gas gauge started blinking, he pulled over and filled the tank. A sign on the shoulder of the road indicated that he was in Connecticut in the midst of the state near a quarry and a forest and the million-dollar homes like the ones he'd read about that Paul Newman inhabited. He got out and breathed the crisp country air, leaning on a picket fence that someone had constructed, incongruously, in the middle of nowhere. The paint was blistered and chipping off in sections.

He let his thoughts drift from the present to the past events of his life that meant something. And it occurred to Diaz that any memory he harbored was of the sad sort, born of tragedy or trauma or pain. All of them, without exception, saddened him.

As he so often did at times like this, he started to rid his mind of the memories. But a part of him he was only beginning to know prevented him from erasing the thoughts this time. It was, he concluded, a time for reflection and unless he confronted the pain, it would never leave him. It had never left him, he knew, but then he had never consciously faced it before.

He wiped his eyes clean on the sleeve of his new suit, thankful that he was in the wilds of Connecticut where no one could see him cry.

Three and a half hours later he was back in his apartment. He packed a small bag with tee shirts, two pairs of khaki trousers, and the sort of red, white, and blue bathing suit that nobody wore anymore. A tattered Panama hat was hanging from a hook in the closet. He put it on and left the apartment without appraising himself in the mirror.

He would drive the car to the airport and drop it off at the rental agency. Which he did. In the departure lounge he sipped seltzer water and did the *Daily News* crossword puzzle. His flight was announced and the fat pasty-faced man beside him wished him a happy landing. Diaz thanked him and started for the prescribed gate. He'd elected to carry his small valise on board and had it now at his side.

The flight attendant took his voucher and Diaz asked for it back.

"Is something the matter, sir?"

He pocketed his ticket without answering them and walked back into the departure lounge where he found a pay phone. He fed his quarters in and dialed her number. He made a mistake, hung up, got a dial tone, deposited his change, and tried again.

When she answered, he said, "Carmen, would you come to Puerto Rico with me?"

"Diaz, I missed you."